"WHY DID YOU DO IT?"

The wall-clock at the White Cottage struck its three soft notes. Then, into the quiet, there came footsteps. They had come down from Melling House as Rietta herself had come an hour and a half ago. They were in the passage now, and the door opened. Carr came in and said,

"He's dead."

Rietta stood looking at him. When she said nothing, Carr raised his voice to her as if she were deaf. He said,

"Do you hear?—James Lessiter is dead."

His next words cut across the numb surface of her mind like a knife.

"Why did you do it?"

Bantam Books offers the finest in classic and modern English murder mysteries. Ask your bookseller for the books you have missed.

Agatha Christie

DEATH ON THE NILE
A HOLIDAY FOR MURDER
THE MOUSETRAP AND OTHER
  PLAYS
THE MYSTERIOUS AFFAIR AT
  STYLES
POIROT INVESTIGATES
POSTERN OF FATE
THE SECRET ADVERSARY
THE SEVEN DIALS MYSTERY
SLEEPING MURDER

Patricia Wentworth

THE FINGERPRINT
THE LISTENING EYE
MISS SILVER COMES TO STAY
SHE CAME BACK
POISON IN THE PEN

Margery Allingham

BLACK PLUMES
DANCERS IN MOURNING
DEADLY DUO
DEATH OF A GHOST
THE FASHION IN SHROUDS
FLOWERS FOR THE JUDGE
TETHER'S END
THE TIGER IN THE SMOKE

Dorothy Simpson

CLOSE HER EYES
THE NIGHT SHE DIED
PUPPET FOR A CORPSE
SIX FEET UNDER

Catherine Aird

HARM'S WAY
HENRIETTA WHO?
HIS BURIAL TOO
LAST RESPECTS
A LATE PHOENIX
A MOST CONTAGIOUS GAME
PARTING BREATH
THE RELIGIOUS BODY
SLIGHT MOURNING
SOME DIE ELOQUENT

Elizabeth Daly

AND DANGEROUS TO KNOW
THE BOOK OF THE LION
HOUSE WITHOUT THE DOOR
NOTHING CAN RESCUE ME
SOMEWHERE IN THE HOUSE
UNEXPECTED NIGHT

John Penn

AN AD FOR MURDER
STAG DINNER DEATH

Miss Silver Comes to Stay

Patricia Wentworth

BANTAM BOOKS
TORONTO • NEW YORK • LONDON • SYDNEY • AUCKLAND

*This low-priced Bantam Book
has been completely reset in a type face
designed for easy reading, and was printed
from new plates. It contains the complete
text of the original hard-cover edition.*
NOT ONE WORD HAS BEEN OMITTED.

MISS SILVER COMES TO STAY

*A Bantam Book / published by arrangement with
Harper & Row, Publishers, Inc.*

PRINTING HISTORY

J. P. Lippincott edition published in 1948

Bantam edition / March 1983
2nd printing . . . . January 1986

ISBN 0-553-25362-X

Published simultaneously in the United States and Canada

---

*Bantam Books are published by Bantam Books, Inc. Its trademark,
consisting of the words "Bantam Books" and the portrayal of a
rooster, is Registered in U.S. Patent and Trademark Office and in
other countries. Marca Registrada. Bantam Books, Inc., 666 Fifth
Avenue, New York, New York 10103.*

PRINTED IN THE UNITED STATES OF AMERICA

O   11   10 9   8   7   6   5   4   3   2

Chapter One

MARY STUART WROTE, "My end is in my beginning." It is easier to agree with her than to decide what is the beginning, and what the end. When Miss Silver came down to Melling on a visit to an old school friend she became involved in a story which had begun a long time before, and whose end may yet be quite unknown, since what happened yesterday must needs affect today and set out a pattern for tomorrow. It is not, of course, necessary to follow the pattern, but is sometimes easier, and ease is always tempting.

Just where does the story begin—twenty-five years before when two young girls went to a dance and met the same young man? A fair girl who was Catherine Lee, and a dark girl who was Henrietta Cray—Catherine and Rietta, distant cousins, schoolfellows, and bosom friends, eighteen years of age, and James Theodulph Lessiter just turned twenty-one. Perhaps it begins there, or perhaps still farther back when three generations of Lessiters took whatever they wanted from the world and paid out of a steadily dwindling capital till in the end there wasn't much for the last of them except an impoverished estate, a shabby old house, and an inherited conviction that the world was his oyster.

The story might begin there, or a little later when what James Lessiter wanted most out of all the world was Rietta Cray. He told her so in the orchard of Melling House under a May moon when she was nineteen and he was twenty-two. She told Catherine, and Catherine condoled. "You know, darling, there really isn't any money at all, and Aunt Mildred will be furious." On the strength of long association and distant kinship, Mrs. Lessiter was Aunt Mildred to both the girls. None of which would have made either of them anything but a most unwelcome daughter-in-law, and what little money there was remained quite firmly in Mildred Lessiter's hands. James couldn't lay a finger on it. He went out into the world to make

1

his fortune with large expectations and a conquering air. At twenty-three Catherine had married Edward Welby and was gone from Melling, and Rietta was settling down to nurse an invalid mother and bring up her sister's boy, Carr Robertson, because Margaret and her husband were in India. Margaret died there, and after a decent interval Major Robertson married again. He sent money for Carr's education, but he did not come home, and by and by he practically ceased to write. He died when Carr was fifteen.

Perhaps the story begins there with Carr's grudge against a world which would have got along very well without him. Or perhaps it begins with Catherine Welby's return as a childless widow. Mildred Lessiter was still alive. Catherine went to see her, cried a good deal, and was offered the Gate House at a nominal rent. "Really quite sweet, you know, Rietta—those dear little crinkly roses all over it. And being in the grounds of Melling House—well, it's rather nice, don't you think? And Aunt Mildred says Alexander can keep up the garden for me whilst he's doing all the rest. It's too, too sweet of her, and I shall be able to live on practically nothing at all, which is just as well, because that's about as much as I shall have when everything is settled. It's a very great shock to me Edward's affairs being in such a state, and you know, when you've been accustomed to having everything it isn't at all easy to come down to thinking about every halfpenny—is it?"

Rietta gave her an odd fleeting smile.

"I don't know, Cathy, but then, you see, I've never had—" she paused deliberately, and then added, "everything."

It was fifteen years after this that Miss Silver came down to visit her old friend Mrs. Voycey.

Chapter Two

As THE TRAIN came to a standstill in Lenton station, Miss Maud Silver closed a capacious handbag upon her knitting and the purse from which she had just extracted her railway ticket, and descending a rather inconveniently high step, stood looking about her for a porter and for Mrs. Voycey. The question of whether she would recognize her after a lapse of years which might very easily have obliterated any likeness to the girl whom she remembered was naturally in the forefront of her mind. Cissy Christopher had become Cecilia Voycey, and the friends who had started as schoolgirls were elderly women.

Miss Silver did not consider that she herself had changed very much. Looking pensively that very morning at a photograph taken when she was leaving school to enter upon her first engagement as a governess, she reflected that even after all this time it was not at all a bad likeness. There was now some grey in her hair, but a good deal of its original mousy brown persisted, and probably would persist to the end. She still did it in just the same way, with an Alexandra fringe very firmly controlled under a net. Her neat features had not altered. Her pale, smooth skin had become older without losing its pallor or its smoothness. As for her clothes, they were not the same, but they were in the same manner—the black coat in its fifth year of faithful service, the little fur tie older, thinner, paler than it had been ten years ago, but still so cosy, so comfortable. Even in the summer she went nowhere without it, much experience having warned her how extremely cold and draughty a village can become overnight. Her hat almost perfectly resembled the hat in the photograph, having a great many bows of ribbon at the back and a bunch of forget-me-nots and pansies on the left-hand side. This continuity of what she felt to be quiet good taste should make the task of recognition easier for her friend. But Cissy Christopher —well, candidly, almost anything might have happened to Cissy Christopher. The picture of a large raw-boned girl with a poking head, a rattling tongue, and quite enormous feet came back from the past.

Looking along the platform, Miss Silver shook her head and dismissed the vision, for there, advancing to meet her, was a massive figure in thick checked tweeds and a rather battered hat on the back of her head. Not Cissy Christopher, who had been dead and gone for many a year, but quite undoubtedly Cecilia Voycey, flushed, bustling, hearty, and full of the kindest welcome.

Before she knew what was going to happen Miss Silver was being kissed.

"Maud! I'd have known you anywhere! Well, of course we're both a few years older—we won't say how many. Not that I mind. I always say being elderly is the best part of one's life. You've got over all the tiresome things like being in love, and wondering what's going to happen to you—you've made your friends, and you've made your life, and you go along very pleasantly. Hawkins—here!" She reached out sideways and grabbed a passing porter by the arm. "This lady has got some luggage. Tell him what it is, Maud, and he'll bring it out to the car."

As they drove away from the station yard in the small car which appeared to be a very tight fit for its owner, Mrs. Voycey was loud in her pleasure at this eagerly awaited reunion.

"I've been counting the days—just like we used to when it was getting on for the end of term. Funny we should have lost sight of each other for all these years, but you know how it is —you swear eternal friendship, and at first you write reams, and then you don't write so much, and then you don't write at all. Everything's new, and you meet a lot of different people. And then, of course, I went out to India and married, and I wasn't very happy, though I dare say it was a good deal my own fault, and if I had my time over again, which I wouldn't for the world, I'd probably manage much better. But anyhow it's all over now. Poor John died getting on for twenty years ago, and we'd been separated for some time before that. I came in for some money from an uncle, so I was able to leave him, and I've been living at Melling ever since. My father was the parson there, you remember, so it's always felt like home. He only lived a year after I came back, but I built myself a house and I'm very comfortable. Now, what about you? You started off as a governess—what on earth made you take up detecting? You know, when I met Alvina Grey—she's a sort of distant cousin—and she told me all about you and that frightful murder case—the woman with the eternity earrings—well, first of all I thought it couldn't be you, and then she described you, and I thought perhaps it was, and then I wrote to you and —here we are. But you haven't told me what made you take it up—detecting, I mean."

Whatever else the long years had changed, Cecilia Voycey still had Cissy Christopher's rattling tongue. Miss Silver gave her slight prim cough.

"It is rather difficult to say—a combination of circumstances —I believe I was guided. My scholastic experience has been extremely valuable."

"You must tell me all about everything!" said Mrs. Voycey with enthusiasm.

She had at this point to draw in very close to the side of the lane in order to avoid two young people standing under the opposite hedge. Miss Silver, observing them with interest, saw a girl in scarlet and a tall young man in grey flannel slacks and a loose tweed jacket. The girl was excessively pretty —really quite unnecessarily so. A singular figure for a country lane on an autumn day, with her flaring clothes, her pale gold hair, her careful complexion. The young man had a dark, tormented look.

Mrs. Voycey waved a hand out of the window, squeezed past them, and explained.

"Carr Robertson. He's down here on a visit to his aunt, Rietta Cray who brought him up. The girl's staying there too. He brought her—just like that, you know, without a with your leave or by your leave—at least that's what Catherine Welby says and she always seems to know all Rietta's affairs. Manners of the present day! I wonder what my father would have said if one of my brothers had just walked in and said, 'This Fancy Bell.'"

"Fancy?"

"That's what he calls her—I believe her name is Frances. And I suppose we shall hear that they are engaged—or married!" She gave a hearty laugh. "Or perhaps not—you never can tell, can you? You'd have thought once bitten, twice shy. Carr's been married already—another of these flighty blonde girls. She ran off with someone, and died. It's only about two years ago, and you'd have thought it would have made him more careful!"

"She is very pretty," said Miss Silver mildly.

Mrs. Voycey snorted in the manner for which she had so often been reproved at school.

"Men haven't a particle of sense," she declared.

They came out of the lane upon a typically rural scene—a village green complete with pond and ducks; the church with its old graveyard; the Vicarage; the village inn with its swinging sign depicting a wheatsheaf whose original gold was now almost indistinguishable from a faded background; the entrance pillars and lodge of a big house; a row of cottages, their gardens still bright with sunflower, phlox, and michaelmas daisy.

"I'm just on the other side of the Green," said Mrs. Voycey. She took a hand off the wheel to point. "That's the Vicarage next the church—much too big for Mr. Ainger. He's a bachelor, but his sister keeps house for him. I don't like her—I never did—though I don't say she doesn't make herself useful in the village, because she does. He'd like to marry Rietta Cray, but she won't have him—I don't know why, because he's a very charming person. Anyhow, that's Rietta's house, the little white one with the hedge. Her father was our doctor —very much respected. And the drive going up between those pillars takes you to Melling House. It belongs to the Lessiters, but old Mrs. Lessiter died a few years ago, and the son hasn't been near the place for more than twenty years, not even to his mother's funeral, because it was in the war and I believe he was out of England. He was engaged to Rietta, you know, but it didn't come off—no money, though he's made a lot since—just one of those boy and girl affairs. But neither of them has married anyone else, and now we're all quite terribly interested because he has just come back. After all these years! Not of course that anything is likely to come of it, but in a village you might as well be dead as not take an interest in your neighbours."

At this point Miss Silver was understood to say that people were always interesting.

Mrs. Voycey slowed down to avoid a dog.

"Shoosh, Rover—you can't scratch in the middle of the road!" She turned back to Miss Silver. "Somebody's bound to run over him some day, but I hope it won't be me." She pointed again. "Catherine Welby lives in the lodge of Melling House—there, just inside the pillars. They call it the Gate House, but it's really just a rather better sort of lodge. She is some sort of connection of the Lessiters—very convenient for her, because she gets the house for practically nothing, and all the fruit and vegetables she wants into the bargain. So I hope James Lessiter won't turn her out, for I'm sure I don't know what she would do if he did."

Miss Silver coughed.

"Her means are narrow?"

Mrs. Voycey nodded with emphasis.

"Practically non-existent, I should say, though you'd never think so to look at her. I'll ask her to tea, and then you'll see for yourself. She's still very pretty, though I always preferred Rietta's looks myself. They're the same age, forty-three, but no one makes anything of that nowadays. Creams, powders, washes, lipstick, and permanent waving—really, as long as you keep your figure there's no need to look any age at all.

Catherine might be no more than thirty. Of course if you put on weight like I have you're out of it, and anyhow I don't suppose I could have been bothered—fiddle-faddles aren't in my line. Ah now—here we are!"

As she spoke she turned in at the miniature drive of a miniature villa. Beds of scarlet geranium and bright blue lobelia bloomed on either side of the front door. They were hardly less brilliant than the red brick of the walls. After twenty years' exposure to the elements Staplehurst Lodge looked as if it had just come from the builder's hands, with its emerald paint, its shining door-knocker, and its generally spick-and-span appearance. It stood out from the village background like a patch of pink flannelette on some old soft brocade. This, however, was not a simile which would have occurred to Miss Silver, who had no affection for domestic architecture of the early English type—"so dark, so inconvenient, and often so sadly insanitary." She considered Staplehurst Lodge a very comfortable residence, and was both touched and pleased when her old friend slipped a hand inside her arm, squeezed it affectionately, and said,

"Well, this is my little place, and I hope you'll have a happy visit here."

Chapter Three

CATHERINE WELBY CAME out of the Gate House, passed between the pillars which marked the entrance to Melling House, and walked along the footpath to the White Cottage. The grass verges on either side were still green although it was late September. A single glance at them showed what kind of summer it had been, but this afternoon it was fine, and so warm that Catherine was even a little too warm in the pale grey flannel coat and skirt which threw up the fairness of her skin and the bright red gold of her hair. She was, as Mrs. Voycey said, a very pretty woman, her figure still slender and her eyes as deep a blue as they had been when she was eighteen. But over and above her prettiness she had something which is far more uncommon. Whatever she wore appeared to be just right both for herself and for the occasion.

Her hair was always in the same becoming waves, never too formal, never untidy.

She went in through a small white gate and up a flagged path, pushed open Miss Cray's front door, and called,

"Rietta!"

In the sitting-room Rietta Cray gave a quick frown which brought out the likeness to her nephew and called back,

"I'm here. Come in!"

If there was one person she didn't want to see at this moment it was Catherine Welby. She did not as a matter of fact wish to see anyone at all, but if you live in a village, it's no good not wanting to see people, because you have to. She was perfectly well aware that James Lessiter's return had set everyone remembering that they had once been engaged, and wondering how they would feel and look, and what they would say when they met. Twenty years is a long time, but not long enough to let a village forget.

She did not get up when Catherine came in, but continued to bend forward over the table at which she was cutting a child's frock out of an odd length of material. She had known Catherine for too many years to disturb herself, and if she were to take the hint and think her too busy to be disturbed, there would be no harm done. Her scissors snipped through the end of the stuff before she looked up to see Catherine lighting a cigarette.

"You look very busy, Rietta. Garments for the poor?"

The quick frown appeared again. In some curious way it gave a young, impulsive look to the dark, straight features. No one had ever called Rietta pretty—her cast of looks was too severe for that. "Pallas Athene, with a touch of the Gorgon's head," as a friend of James Lessiter's had once said after being snubbed. But she had her moments of beauty—fleeting, stormy moments for the most part. As to the rest, her hair was dark, her eyes grey and finely lashed, her figure in the Greek tradition, and her manner a little on the abrupt side. She looked up now and said,

"What is it?"

Catherine had made herself very comfortable on the window seat.

"Well, really, Rietta! You know, sewing isn't your line—it always puts you in a bad temper. You ought to be thankful to me for coming round and interrupting you."

"Well, I'm not. I want to get this done."

Catherine waved her cigarette.

"I'm not stopping you, darling—you go on pinning the thing together. I just thought I'd come around and ask you whether you've seen James yet."

This time Rietta didn't let herself frown. She had a moment of black rage, because of course this was what everyone in Melling was wanting to know. Then she said in the expressionless voice which goes with being angry,

"No. Why should I?"

"I don't know—you might have. As a matter of fact I haven't either, but of course he only came last night. I wonder what he's like, and whether he's worn as well as we have. You know, Rietta, if you took the least trouble, you could look—well, thirty-four."

"I don't in the least want to look thirty-four."

Catherine's dark blue eyes opened widely.

"What's the good of saying a silly thing like that? What you need is colour—you always did—and a softer expression. You ought to practise in front of the glass."

Rietta's lip twitched. Her anger was gone. She could enjoy Catherine. A picture of herself practising soft expressions at a looking-glass assuaged her a good deal.

"We might practise them together," she said.

Catherine blew out a light cloud of smoke.

"Now you're laughing at me. I thought you were going to bite my head off when I came in. I do wonder if James has got fat. Such a pity if he has—he was so nicelooking. You did make a most awfully handsome couple—only of course he ought to have fallen in love with somebody fair like me. You know, it was very nice of me not to try and take him away from you."

Rietta Cray lifted those fine grey eyes of hers and allowed them to dwell for a moment upon Catherine. Since it was perfectly well known between them that Catherine had tried and failed, there appeared to be no need to say anything more about it. Rietta therefore said nothing. After a moment she went on pinning the small pink frock.

Catherine laughed amiably and returned to James Lessiter.

"I don't know whether it's worse to get stout or scraggy. James must be forty-five." She drew at her cigarette and added, "He's coming in to have coffee with me tonight. You'd better come too."

"No, thank you."

"You'd better. You'll have to meet him some time. Get it

over in a sensible friendly way when you can be looking your best, instead of bumping into him anywhere by chance when your hair is coming down in the rain, or half the village is lined up watching to see how you take it."

For a brief moment a bright touch of scarlet gave Rietta Cray the colour she lacked. A dangerous anger had set it glowing. It was instantly controlled. She said,

"We're not schoolgirls. There is nothing to take. If James is going to be here, naturally we shall meet. But I shall be very much surprised if he stays for long. He will find Melling very dull."

"He has made a lot of money," said Catherine in a pensive voice. "Look here, Rietta, do come off your high horse! It's going to make a lot of difference to have Melling open again, and after all, you and I are James's oldest friends. It can't be very cheerful for him coming back to an empty house. I do think we must give him a bit of a welcome. Come along in to coffee this evening!"

Rietta gave her a straight look. It would have been so much more natural for Catherine to want to have—and keep—James Lessiter to herself. She was up to something, and presently, no doubt, the cat would slip out of the bag. Or most likely not a cat at all, but one of Catherine's sleek, silky kittens, with innocent eyes and whiskers dripping with cream. Only you don't get cream in bags, or anywhere else in this post-war world. She said nothing, only looked and allowed herself to smile just enough to let Catherine see that she hadn't got away with it.

Did a little natural colour deepen the very careful tinting behind the thin haze of cigarette smoke? Catherine Welby got up gracefully and without haste.

"Well, come if you can," she said. Then, turning before she reached the door, "Carr out?"

"He and Fancy have gone in to Lenton."

Catherine Welby laughed.

"Is he going to marry her?"

"I shouldn't advise you to ask him. I haven't."

"He'll be damned silly if he does. She's too like Marjory. It'll be the same story all over again."

"You haven't any right to say that."

Catherine blew her a kiss.

"Waste of time trying to high-hat me—you ought to know that after all these years. I'm just using my common sense, and

you'd better use yours and choke him off if you don't want
another crash—I should think it would just about finish him.
Did he ever find out who Marjory went off with?"

"No."

"Well, she saved everyone a lot of trouble by not surviving.
I mean, after she'd come back down and out and he'd taken
her in and nursed her, he couldn't very well have got a
divorce, could he? Solitary instance of tact on her part, but
rather wasted if he's going to do the same thing all over again.
Well, I'll be seeing you."

Chapter Four

FANCY BELL LOOKED sideways under her long lashes and
observed her companion's gloom. With a faint sigh she turned
to the much more agreeable spectacle of her own enchanting
face and figure reflected in the looking-glass at the back of a
milliner's window. A bit daring that scarlet—hit or miss, as
you might say—but to judge from the way in which practically
every man they passed had looked and looked again, it was a
hit all right. A lovely contrast they made, her and Carr. Very
goodlooking he was—nobody could say anything different.
And of course nothing like that dark, gloomy type for making a
fair girl look even fairer than she was. And he was ever so nice
really, only it would make things a lot easier if he would smile
a bit and look as if he was enjoying her company. But of course
you couldn't have everything.

There was a hard core of common sense behind that very
decorative façade. You couldn't have everything, so you had to
make up your mind just what you wanted most. Young men
with plenty of money asked you to go away for weekends.
Well, she wasn't that sort of girl and she let them know it—no
offence meant and none taken, but they didn't generally try it
on a second time. The show-girl business was all very well
while it lasted, but it didn't last for ever. The sensible person
who was Frances expected Fancy to get her a chance of
settling in life, and she knew just what she wanted—a lift in
the world, but not such a big one that your in-laws were going
to look down on you—enough money to have a nice little home
and, say, three children—and someone to do all the rough

work, because you don't want to let yourself go, and she'd always kept her hands nice. Of course she'd have to do a good bit, especially after the babies came. She wouldn't mind that. Frances had it all planned out. She was considering whether Carr Robertson would do for the lead in this private play of hers. He had a job and he had a little money of his own, and Fancy would find it quite easy to be in love with him, but Frances wasn't going to let her do anything silly.

She put up a hand and pulled at his sleeve.

"Here's the place Mrs. Welby said, where she has her hair done. I'll be an hour, if you can put in the time. Sure you can?"

He said, "Oh, yes," in an indifferent tone.

"All right. And then we'll have tea. So long."

He watched her go with a curious feeling of relief. There was going to be a whole hour in which nothing would be expected of him. He needn't talk, make love, or abstain from making love. His feeling was very much like that with which one sometimes sees one's guests depart. Their presence may have been welcome, their company enjoyed, but there is something about having your house to yourself again. Only when he did have it to himself there was always the possibility that the welcome solitude would be invaded by an unlaid ghost —Marjory's step on the stair . . . her laughter, and her tears . . . her failing voice: "No—no—I'll never tell you his name. I don't want you to kill him. No, Carr—no!"

A real voice broke in upon his mood. He glanced up with the quick nervous frown so like Rietta's and saw Mr. Holderness looking benevolent. One of his earliest recollections was the benevolence of Mr. Holderness accompanied by a half-crown tip. As far as Carr could see, he hadn't changed a bit —dignified presence, florid complexion, kindly gaze, and rich rolling voice—general slight flavour of the eighteenth century from which his office with its Georgian panelling had never emerged. The firm had ranked as old-fashioned county solicitors then, and the tradition had been maintained ever since. He clapped Carr on the shoulder and enquired whether he was down for long.

"Rietta will be glad to have you. How is she? Not working too hard, I hope. Last time I saw her I thought she was looking as if she had been overdoing it, and she told me she couldn't get any help in the garden."

"No, she's had to give up the vegetables. She hasn't much

help in the house either—only Mrs. Fallow for a couple of hours twice a week. I think she does do too much."

"Take care of her, my boy, take care of her. Good people are scarce, and she won't look after herself—women never will. Between ourselves, they've every virtue except common sense. But don't say I said so. No witnesses, you know, and I shall deny it—I shall deny it!" He let out a fine reverberant laugh. "Well, well, I mustn't stay gossiping. I've been in court all day, and I must get on to the office. By the way, I hear James Lessiter is back. Have you seen him at all?"

Carr's lips twitched into a smile as quick and nervous as his frown.

"I've never seen him in my life. He was off the map before I fetched up in Melling."

"Yes, yes—of course—so he was. And now he's come back a rich man. Pleasant to come across a success story once in a way —very pleasant indeed. You haven't seen him since he got back?"

"I don't think anyone has. As a matter of fact I believe he only arrived last night. Mrs. Fallow has been up there helping the Mayhews."

"Ah, yes—Mrs. Lessiter's cook and butler—very worthy people. Mayhew calls in at the office every week for their wages. That is how I knew that James was expected. He'll be ringing me up, I expect. It's made a lot of work, his being out of the country when his mother died. Well, goodbye, my boy. I'm glad to have seen you."

He passed on. Carr watched him go, and felt his mood changed by the encounter. There had been a time before the world was shattered. Old Holderness belonged to that time, he might even be said to typify it. Life was secure, its circumstances stable. You had the friends you had grown up with, the friends you made at school and college. Term followed term throughout the year, with bright intervals of vacation. Half-crown tips mounted to ten shillings, to a pound. Henry Ainger had given him a fiver on his eighteenth birthday. Elizabeth Moore had given him an odd old picture of a ship. He had felt romantic about it from the first moment he saw it hanging in a dark corner of her uncle's antique shop. Odd how a little paint and canvas can become a magic casement. He had seen himself sailing out into life on an enchanted tide—

On a sudden impulse he walked down the street, turned to

the left, and stood looking in at Jonathan Moore's shop window. There was a fine set of red and white ivory chessmen in Manchu and Chinese dress—war formalized into a game. He watched the pieces, admiring the exquisite precision of the carving, angry underneath. Then all at once he straightened up, pushed open the door, and went in. A bell tinkled, Elizabeth came to meet him. The anger dropped out of him and was gone.

She said, "Carr!" and they stood looking at one another.

It was only for a moment that he was able to look at her as if she were a stranger, because though it was nearly five years since they had met, he had known her all his life. But for just that one moment he did see her as if it was the first time—the tall light figure, the clear windblown look she had, brown hair ruffled back from the forehead, bright eager eyes, and a quick tremulous smile. He got the impression of something startled into joy, ready to take flight, to escape, to become unobtainable—the whole thing much too fleeting to pass into conscious thought. She spoke first, in the voice which he had always liked—a pretty, clear voice full of gravity and sweetness.

"Carr—how nice! It's been such a long time, hasn't it?"

He said, "A million years," and then wondered why he had said it. Only it didn't matter what you said to Elizabeth—it never had.

She put out a hand, but not to touch him. It was an old remembered gesture.

"As long as that? My poor dear! Come along through and let's talk. Uncle Jonathan is out at a sale."

He followed her into the little sitting-room behind the shop —shabby comfortable chairs, old-fashioned plush curtains, Jonathan Moore's untidy desk. Elizabeth shut the door. They might have been back in the past before the deluge. She opened a cupboard, rummaged, and produced a bag of caramels.

"Do you still like them? I think you do. If you really like something you go on liking it, don't you think?"

"I don't know about that."

"I do—I'm quite sure." She laughed a little. "Whatever happens or doesn't happen, I shall always have a passion for caramels. I've never stopped being thankful that I can eat them without putting on an ounce. Look here, there's the bag between us, and we can both dip in like we used to."

He laughed too, all the tension in him relaxed. To come

back to Elizabeth was to slip into a place so accustomed, so comfortable, that you didn't even have to think about it. An old coat, old shoes, an old friend—unromantic, undemanding, utterly restful.

She said, "Is it too early for tea? I'll make some—" and saw him frown again.

"No. I've got Fancy with me—Frances Bell. We're staying with Rietta. She's gone in to Hardy's to have her hair done, and she will want tea when she comes out."

Elizabeth's very clear eyes dwelt on him consideringly.

"You wouldn't like to bring her in here? I've got quite a new cake."

He said, "Yes, I would."

Elizabeth nodded.

"That's lovely. Then we can just sit and talk. Tell me about her. Is she a friend of yours?"

"No."

He didn't know he was going to say it, but it was no sooner said than he thought, "My God—that's true!" What sort of a mess had he got himself into, and how far in had he got? It was like walking in your sleep and waking up to find yourself with one foot over a killing drop.

"Tell me about her, Carr. What is she like?"

The tormented look was back again. He turned it on her.

"She's like Marjory."

"I only saw her once. She was very pretty." It was said without rancour, yet they both remembered that one meeting, because it was after it that Elizabeth had said, "Are you in love with her, Carr?" They were here alone together in this very room, and when he looked away and couldn't meet her eyes she had taken off her engagement ring and laid it down on the arm of the chair between them, and when he still had nothing to say she had gone out through the far door and up the old stair to her own room overhead. And he had let her go.

Five years ago, but it came back like yesterday. He said, "Why did you let me go?"

"How could I keep you?"

"You didn't try."

"No—I didn't try. I didn't want to keep you if you wanted to go."

He was silent, because he couldn't say, "I didn't want to go." He had known Elizabeth all his life, and Marjory for three short weeks. At twenty-three it is the new, the unexpected, the unknown, which evokes romance. If the enchanted distance turns upon nearer view into a desert, you have only yourself to thank. Marjory hadn't changed—he had always had to remind himself of that.

He found himself leaning forward, his hands between his knees, words coming at first jerkily and then with a rush.

"It wasn't her fault, you know. I was damnable to live with —and the baby died—she hadn't got anything. Money was tight. She'd been used to having a good time—lots of people to go about with. I couldn't give her anything to make up for it. The flat was so cramped—she hated it. I was always away, and there wasn't any money, and when I was there I was in a filthy temper. You can't blame her."

"What happened, Carr?"

"I was sent to Germany. I didn't get demobbed till the end of that year. She never wrote much, and then she didn't write at all. I got leave, and came home to find strangers in the flat. She'd let it. No one knew where she was. When I got home for good I tried to trace her. I took on the flat again, because I had to live somewhere and I'd got this job in a literary agency. A friend of mine started it—Jack Smithers. You remember, he was up at Oxford with me. He was crocked in the war, and got away with this business before the ugly rush."

Elizabeth said, "Yes?"

He looked up at her for a moment.

"I had a sort of idea perhaps she would come back. Well, she did. It was a bitter cold January night. I got in just short of midnight, and there she was, huddled up on the divan. She must have been pretty well frozen, because she hadn't any coat, only a thin suit. She'd got the eiderdown from the bedroom and put the electric fire on, and by the time I got in she was in a burning fever. I got a doctor, but she never had a chance. The swine she'd gone off with had left her penniless in France. She'd sold everything she had to get home. She told me that, but she wouldn't tell me his name. She said she didn't want me to kill him. After all he'd done to her—she talked when she was delirious, so I know—after all that she was mad about him still!"

Elizabeth's voice came into the silence.

"She might have been thinking about you."

He laughed angrily.

"Then she wasn't! She kept his photograph—that's how I know, and that's how I'll find him some day. It was in the back of her compact under the bit of gauze that's supposed to keep the powder in. I expect she thought nobody would find it there, but of course she didn't know she was going to die." His voice went harsh. "She wouldn't have believed it if anyone had told her."

Elizabeth said, "Poor Marjory!"

He nodded.

"I've kept that photograph—I'll find him some time. It was just the head and shoulders cut out and the cardboard scraped down at the back to make it fit, so there's no photographer's name, but I'll know him if I meet him."

"People don't go unpunished, Carr. Don't try and play hangman. It's not your line."

"Isn't it? I don't know—"

There was a silence. Elizabeth let it gather round them. She was leaning back now, watching him between her dark lashes, her long thin hands resting quietly on the green stuff of her skirt. The cream sweater she wore with it came up high about her long throat. There was a small pearl in the lobe of either ear.

Presently Carr began to speak again.

"Fancy's rather like her, you know. She's been a manne-quin. At the moment she's a show-girl—out of a job. She's worked very hard and she wants to get on. She hopes for a part in what she calls a regular play. I shouldn't think there's a chance in a million that she can act. She has to be rather careful about her vowels, because they pronounce them differently in Stepney where she grew up. I believe Mum and Dad still live there, and she wouldn't dream of cutting loose, because she's a nice girl and very fond of her family."

"And just where do you come in?" said Elizabeth.

He looked up with a flash of rather bitter humour.

"She wants to get on, and she's considering me as a stepping-stone."

"Are you engaged?"

"I believe not."

"Have you asked her to marry you?"

"I don't know."

"Carr, you must know!"

"Well, I don't, and that's a fact."

She sat up suddenly, her eyes wide open, her hands clasped.

"You've been letting yourself drift and you don't know where you've got to."

"That's about the size of it."

"Carr, it's suicidal! You don't have to marry a girl you don't care about."

He said, "No." And then, "It's quite easy to drift that way when you don't really care what happens. One gets lonely."

Elizabeth said very quick and low, "It's better to be lonely by yourself than to be lonely with somebody else."

The pain in his eyes shocked her.

"Damnably true. I've tried it both ways, so I ought to know. But you see, that once-bitten-twice-shy business doesn't work —you always think it's going to be different next time."

Elizabeth said with energy, "Carr, I could shake you! You're talking nonsense and you know it. You did go honestly off the deep end about Marjory, but this time you don't even pretend you care a snap of your fingers about this wretched girl."

His old provoking smile flashed out.

"Darling, she isn't a wretched girl. On the contrary, she's a very nice girl, a perfectly good girl, and a devastatingly pretty one—platinum hair, sapphire eyes, lashes about half a yard long, and the traditional rose-leaf complexion. Wait till you see her!"

Chapter Five

THE TEA-PARTY WENT off as well as could be expected. Fancy had kicked a little.

"But who is this Elizabeth Moore? I'm sure I've never heard you speak about her. Does she keep a shop?"

"Her uncle does. He's rather well known as a matter of fact. The Moores used to have a big country house out beyond Melling. Three of them were killed in the first world war, and the three lots of death duties smashed them. Jonathan was the fourth. When it came to everything being sold up, he said he'd have a shop and sell the things himself—that's how he started. Elizabeth's father and mother are dead, so she lives with him."

"How old is she?"

"She's three years younger than I am."

"But I don't know how old you are."

"I'm twenty-eight."

"Then—she's twenty-five?"

He burst out laughing.

"Bright girl! How do you do it? Come along—she's got the kettle on."

Mollified by the discovery that Elizabeth was well advanced towards middle age, Fancy followed him. She was ready for a cup of tea all right. Having your head in one of those drying machines made you ever so thirsty. She was still farther reassured at the sight of Elizabeth and the friendly shabby room. Miss Moore might be an old friend and all that, but no one could call her a beauty, and she wasn't a bit smart. That skirt she had on—well, it wasn't this year's cut, nor last year's neither. And the jumper, right high up to the neck and down to the wrists—not a bit smart. Yet almost at once she began to have a feeling that her own scarlet suit was a bit too daring. The feeling went on getting stronger until she could have burst into tears. She couldn't say Miss Moore wasn't pleasant, or that she and Carr did anything to make her feel like a stranger, but there it was, that's what she felt like. They weren't her sort. That was nonsense—she was as good as anyone, and much prettier and smarter than Elizabeth Moore. Silly to feel the way she did. Mum would say not to go fancying things. And then all of a sudden the feeling went and she was talking to Elizabeth about Mum and Dad, and how she'd got her first job—all that sort of thing, quite nice and comfortable.

When Elizabeth took her upstairs before she left, Fancy stood in front of the fine Queen Anne mirror and said,

"This is an old house, isn't it?"

She could see Elizabeth reflected in the mirror—too tall, too thin, but something elegant about her, something that fitted in with the house and the furniture.

Elizabeth said, "Yes, it's very old—seventeenth century. The bathroom used to be a powder-cabinet. All horribly inconvenient of course, but quite good for business."

Fancy took out her powder-puff and began to touch up a flawless complexion.

"I like new things," she said. "I don't know why people bother about old ones. I'd like to have a silver bed, and a suite of that grey furniture, and everything else blue."

Elizabeth smiled.

"It would be just right for you, wouldn't it?"

Fancy pursed up her mouth and applied lipstick with an expert touch. She said, "M——" Then, without turning round, "You've known Carr a long time, haven't you?"

"Oh, yes."

"Do you think he'd be difficult to live with? I mean, he gets these moods, doesn't he? Did he always use to get them?"

She could see in the glass that Elizabeth had moved. She couldn't see her face any longer. Her voice came a little slower.

"I haven't seen him for a long time. He's been away, you know."

"Did you know the girl he married?"

"I saw her once. She was very pretty."

"I'm like her, aren't I? I didn't exactly know her, but——"

"You are a little like her."

"Same type."

"Yes."

Fancy put away her powder-puff and lipstick, pulled at the zipper of her scarlet bag. She said in an odd tone,

"I suppose that's why——" She turned abruptly. "A girl wouldn't want to be just a stand-in for somebody else—would she?"

"No."

"I mean, I wouldn't want to be jealous about her, or anything like that. I knew a girl that married a widower, and she wouldn't set foot in the house till he'd cleared out all the pictures of his first wife, and I didn't think that was right, not with her children there. I told Mum about it, and she said, 'A man that would forget his first wife would forget you—don't you make any mistake about that.' That's what Mum said, and I wouldn't be like that, but I wouldn't want to marry a man if I was going to *be* the photograph, if you see what I mean."

"I see exactly what you mean."

Fancy heaved a sigh.

"He's ever so goodlooking, isn't he? But when it comes to living with someone—well, it might be a case of handsome is as handsome does. I mean, you've got to think before you go into anything, don't you?" She gave a little quick laugh. "I don't know what you'll think of me, talking like this. You're sort of easy to talk to, I don't know why. Well, I suppose we'd better be going."

On the way home she said,

"She isn't a bit like I thought she was going to be. She's sort of nice."

Carr's mouth twisted.

"Yes—she's sort of nice."

He said it as if he was laughing at her, but there wasn't anything to laugh at. Carr was funny that way. You did your best to brighten him up and make a joke or two, and you might as well have done it to a brick wall. And then all of a sudden he'd laugh when there wasn't anything to laugh at. However, so long as he did laugh—

She pursued the theme of Elizabeth Moore.

"Pity she hasn't got married, isn't it? I'd hate not to be married by the time I was twenty-five."

He laughed outright this time—and what was there funny about that?

"Well, my sweet, you've got quite a long way to go, haven't you? What is it—another five years?"

"Six. And I don't know what there is to laugh about! A girl oughtn't to leave it too late—Mum says so. She says you get set in your ways, and it's no good when you're married, because the man'll want things his way. I don't mean to say she'd think he ought to be given in to all along the line, but where there are two, it stands to reason there's got to be a bit of give and take, and when the children come along—well, there's a good deal more giving than taking, if you know what I mean. That's what Mum says, and she brought up six of us, so she ought to know."

Carr had stopped laughing. He had never felt less in love with Fancy, and he had never liked her so well. He said,

"Your mother's a very sensible woman—I'd like to meet her. And I shouldn't wonder if you didn't make someone quite a good wife some day, my sweet."

"But not you?"

She didn't know what took the words off the tip of her tongue, but there they were—she'd said them right out. And he was looking at her with a funny little smile in his eyes and saying,

"No, I don't think so."

Her lovely rose tints deepened. The big blue eyes looked honestly back at him.

"I know what you mean. We both thought perhaps it would do, but it won't. I knew that as soon as I saw you with that Elizabeth girl. You've been fond of her—haven't you?"

His look went bleak.

"A long time ago."

"I'd say you'd been very fond of her—I'd say you were pretty fond of her still. You seem to sort of fit in together, if you know what I mean. Were you engaged?"

He used the same words again.

"A long time ago."

They walked on in silence. Fancy thought, "We can't go the best part of two and a half miles and never talk. I should scream, and he'd think I'd gone batty. It's so quiet in these country lanes—you can pretty well hear yourself think." She spoke to break the silence.

"She's fond of you too—I could tell that."

He was frowning, but he wasn't angry, because he put his hand on her shoulder and patted it.

"You can always start a marriage agency, if you don't get off yourself. And now we'll stop talking about me, and you can tell me all about Mum and the other five of you."

Chapter Six

CATHERINE WELBY LOOKED round at her sitting-room and thought how pretty it was. Some of the things were shabby, but they were all good, because they had come from Melling House. The little Queen Anne writing-table would fetch a couple of hundred pounds any time she liked to ask for it. Like the Persian rugs it had been a present from Mrs. Lessiter—or so nearly a present that no one was likely to dispute it. Mrs. Mayhew would remember hearing Mrs. Lessiter say, "I'm letting Mrs. Welby have those rugs and the little desk out of the Blue Room." She had added, "They might as well be used." But there would be no need for Mrs. Mayhew to remember that, nor would she do so unless encouraged, and it wasn't Catherine Welby who would encourage her. Nearly all the furniture in the Gate House had come to her on the same slightly debatable tenure. She meant to make no bones about it with James Lessiter. It was, in fact, one of the reasons why she was now expecting him to coffee. The contents of the Gate House were to be exhibited to him in the guise of his mother's gifts.

She looked round her with gratitude and appreciation. Aunt Mildred had certainly meant her to have the things. Why, the curtains had been cut down from an old put-away pair dating from goodness knows when—faded, but what a heavenly brocade, with its dim rose background and formal wreaths just touched with blue and green. There had been enough of it to cover chairs and sofa, and the cushions repeated the colouring of the wreaths.

Catherine dressed to the room. A mirror over the high mantelshelf reflected her dull blue house-gown, her pretty hair, the turn of her head. All at once she heard the step she was waiting for. She went out into the narrow space at the stair foot and threw open the front door.

"James—come in! How nice! Do let me look at you! We mustn't say how many years it is, must we?"

He was bare-headed, in a dark suit without coat or scarf. As she went before him into the lighted room, he laughed and said,

"It mightn't be any years at all so far as you are concerned. You haven't changed."

She had a radiant smile for that.

"Haven't I?"

"You're prettier, but I expect you know that without my telling you. What about me—do I get anything?"

She looked at him with genuine amazement. He had been a goodlooking boy. At forty-six he was a much handsomer man than anyone could have expected. The photograph Aunt Mildred had been so proud of really hadn't lied. She went on smiling and said,

"I expect you'll do very well without any more conceit than you've got." Then, with a ripple of laughter, "Oh, James, it is nice to see you! Just wait one moment and I'll fetch the coffee. I only have a morning girl, you know."

He looked about while she was out of the room. Very familiar stuff, all this furniture—some of it good. He supposed his mother had put it in for her. He'd have to see Holderness and find out where he stood from the legal point of view. If he was going to sell the place, the Gate House would go with it, and he would have to give vacant possession. But if Catherine had it unfurnished and paid rent for it, it might not be possible to turn her out. The bother was, there was probably no set agreement, and nothing to show whether the presence of the Melling House furniture constituted a furnished let. If it did, he could give Catherine notice, but if his mother had given her the furniture, he probably couldn't. Pretty woman Catherine—prettier than she had been twenty-five years ago—a little too plump in those days. He wondered about Rietta. Just on the cards she might have put on weight—those statuesque girls did sometimes. She must be forty-three.

Catherine came back into the room with the coffee-tray and the name on her lips.

"Have you seen Rietta?"

"No—not yet."

She put the tray down on a little table with a pie-crust edge. A valuable piece—he remembered it. He thought Catherine had done herself pretty well, and a little more than that.

"It would be fun if we could get her to come over, wouldn't it? I think I'll try. There's one thing, she won't be out."

"Why?"

Catherine laughed.

"My dear James, you must have forgotten what Melling is like. It hasn't changed."

She was lifting the receiver as she spoke. He came across and stood by her side, heard the click as the receiver was taken off, heard Rietta's voice—like Melling, quite unchanged.

"Yes?"

"It's Catherine. Listen, Rietta—James is here. . . . Yes, right beside me. And we both want you to come over—and if you're going to make Carr and that girl of his an excuse, I shall know exactly what to think, and so will James."

Rietta again, quietly.

"I shall be very pleased to see James again. Don't keep any coffee for me—I've had mine."

Catherine rang off and turned a laughing face.

"I thought that would fetch her! She wouldn't want you to think she minded meeting you."

"Why should she?"

"No reason in the world. It's funny neither of you has married, isn't it?"

He said rather abruptly, "I've had neither the time nor the inclination. One travels much faster alone."

"You've travelled fast?"

"Tolerably."

"Got where you wanted?"

"More or less. There are always new horizons."

She gave him his coffee with a sigh.

"You must have had wonderful times. Do tell me about them."

Rietta Cray came into the little square space at the foot of the stair and laid her coat across the newel. She was angry because Catherine had trapped her into coming. She had said "No," and she had meant "No," but to say it again with James Lessiter listening was just one of the things she couldn't do. It must be as plain to him as to everyone in Melling that she met him with friendly indifference. She glanced at her reflection in the old wall mirror. Anger had brought the colour to her cheeks quick and bright. She had come over just as she was, in the old red dress she wore at home. The shade was becoming, the long classic folds suited her. She opened the sitting-room door to hear Catherine say,

"How marvellous!"

James Lessiter got up and came to meet her. He said, "Well, Rietta?"

Their hands touched. She felt nothing. The anger went out of her, the tightness relaxed. Because this wasn't a ghost come back out of the past to trouble her—it was a stranger—a handsome, personable, middle-aged stranger.

He and Catherine had been sitting one on either side of the hearth. She took the chair between them and sat down, an alien figure in Catherine's pastel room. All at once it had a crowded look—too many small things lying about, too many pale, delicate colours. She said,

"I've only just come over to say how do you do. I mustn't stop. I have Carr and a friend of his staying with me."

"Carr?" He picked up the name as any stranger might.

"Margaret's boy. You remember she married Jock Robertson. They left Carr with me when they went out East, and they never came back, so I brought him up."

"Carr Robertson—" It was said as you might say any name. "I'm sorry to hear about Margaret. How old is the boy?"

"Beyond being called one. He's twenty-eight."

"Married?"

"He was. She died two years ago."

"Bad luck. I seem to be asking all the wrong questions."

She said, "These things happen."

Catherine leaned sideways to put down her coffee-cup.

"You needn't mind, James. None of us really knew Marjory —she wasn't interested in Melling. I don't suppose Rietta saw her a dozen times. And as for Carr, I think we may say he is in process of being consoled. The friend whom he has brought to stay is a particularly dazzling blonde."

Rietta said, "That's cheap, Catherine."

Her old downright voice, her old downright anger. Pallas Athene disdaining a mortal. A handsome creature Rietta, probably not too comfortable to live with. He began to ask about people in the village.

Some twenty minutes later when she got up to go he said, "I'll walk round with you."

"There's no need, James."

"Pleasant things are not always necessary. I'll come back if you'll let me, Catherine, so I won't say goodnight."

It was dark outside—no moon, but no cloud, the stars a little veiled by what might be a mist before the September sun came up again, the air mild and moist, with a faint smell of wood smoke and rotting leaves.

They had gone about a third of the short distance before he said,

"I really wanted to speak to you, Rietta. I don't quite know what arrangements my mother made with Catherine about the Gate House. I wonder if you can help me."

She slowed her step to his.

"I don't know that I can. Why don't you ask her?"

He sounded amused.

"Do you really think that would be the best way to find out? I was thinking of something a little more impartial."

"Then you had better ask Mr. Holderness."

"I'm going to. But I've an idea that he mayn't know very much about it. You know what my mother was—she had her own ways of doing things—very much the autocrat, very much the *grande dame*." He gave a short laugh. "It might never have occurred to her to mention a private transaction between herself and Catherine. What I should like to know is whether she ever mentioned it to you. Here, let's turn and walk back again. Did she?"

"Yes, when Catherine came back here after her husband died she said, 'Aunt Mildred's letting me have the Gate House at a nominal rent.' And next time I saw your mother she told me, 'I'm letting Catherine have the Gate House. Edward Welby seems to have left her with about twopence-halfpenny a year.'"

"Nothing about rent?"

"No."

"Anything about furniture?"

"Yes, your mother said, 'I've told her she can have the two groundfloor rooms knocked into one, and I suppose I shall have to let her have some furniture.'"

"That might mean anything. What I want to know is, was the furniture given or lent."

"I don't know."

"Some of it's valuable."

"I suppose it is. The Mayhews might know."

"They don't. There seems to have been a sort of drift going on for years. Every now and then my mother would say, 'I'm letting Mrs. Welby have this or that, or the other,' or Catherine would say, 'Mrs. Lessiter says I can have so-and-so,' and off it would go down to the lodge—absolutely nothing to show whether the thing was being given or lent. And mind you, I don't believe my mother would have given her some of the things she's got down there."

"She might have. I suppose the only person who can say whether she did or not is Catherine herself."

He laughed.

"My dear Rietta!"

There was so much sarcasm in both voice and laugh that it really was not necessary to add anything to those three words.

They reached the lodge gate and turned again. Back out of the past came the memory of the many, many times they had walked like this—under the moon, under the stars, under the shadowing dusk, too much in love to be able to say goodnight and go in. The love was gone with their youth and those faraway hours. What was left as far as Rietta Cray was concerned was an odd haunting sense of familiarity. In Catherine's room James Lessiter had seemed like a stranger. Here in the darkness she recaptured, not the old love, not any emotional feeling, but the old sense of a familiar presence. It prompted her into hurried speech.

"James, couldn't you—just let it go?"

He laughed again.

"Let her get away with it?"

"Why not? You've done without the things all this time. You've made a lot of money, haven't you? And no one can really be sure what your mother meant. Catherine will be —dreadfully upset—if there's a row."

"I dare say." He sounded amused. "But you see, it isn't so easy as you seem to think. I've had a very good offer for

Melling House, and I'll have to give vacant possession. That
goes for the Gate House too. If it was let to Catherine as a
furnished house, that's all right—I can give her notice and
she'll have to go. But an unfurnished let would be quite a
different pair of shoes. Well, here we are at your gate again.
I'll have to go back and see what I can get out of Catherine,
but unless she's changed a great deal more than I think she
has, it's not likely to be anywhere within a street or two of the
truth."

"James!"

He gave another laugh.

"You haven't changed much either. You're still a good
friend, and I'm still a bad enemy. You don't owe Catherine
much, you know. She did her level best to queer your pitch."

"That's all past and gone."

"And you don't want me to be hard on her now. Well, well!
It doesn't pay to be made your way, Rietta, but I quite see you
can't help it. You don't try, do you, any more than I have any
intention of trying to alter my own way? It's served me quite
well, you know. If there's an uttermost farthing due, I'm out to
get it."

"I don't know what you mean."

"Don't you? Well, I'm just wondering whether Catherine's
acquisitiveness has stopped short at a mere transfer of furniture. I've an idea it may have carried her well over on to the
wrong side of the law."

"James!"

"I've an extremely good memory, and it seems to me that
there are quite a lot of things missing of the small, expensive
kind which would be rather easily turned into cash. Let me
open the gate for you."

"James—"

"Goodnight, my dear. As I said, you haven't really changed
at all. It's a pity."

Chapter Seven

ON THE MORNING following her arrival Mrs. Voycey took her friend Miss Silver shopping. Melling had a butcher, a baker who also sold buns, cake, biscuits, fruit preserved in glass bottles and sweets, and a grocer whose groceries merged by tactful degrees into the appurtenances of a general shop. You could, for example, start at the left-hand side of the counter and buy bacon, coffee and semolina, and work gradually to the right through apples, potatoes and root vegetables, till you arrived at twine, garden implements, shopping-bags, and boots and shoes hanging like strings of onions from a nail high up on the wall. Somewhere midway there was a stand of picture-post cards and a blotting-pad, the latter an advertisement of the fact that the shop was also a branch post office, and that stamps and telegraph forms could be obtained.

With so many different attractions, it was naturally a very general meeting-place. Miss Silver was introduced to Miss Ainger, the Vicar's sister, a formidable lady with iron-grey hair, a Roman nose, and the sort of tweeds which suggest armour-plating. It might have been the size of the check, black and white upon a ground of clerical grey, or it might have been something about Miss Ainger's figure, but the suggestion was certainly there. She was scolding Mrs. Grover about the bacon, and detached herself with difficulty.

"Yes, much too thick, and with far too much fat— Did you say a school friend? Oh, how do you do?—Don't let it happen again or I shall have to tell the Vicar."

Mrs. Grover's colour rose. She pressed her lips together and restrained herself. Mrs. Voycey moved a step nearer the post cards and caught Miss Cray by the arm.

"Rietta, I want to introduce you to my friend Miss Silver. We were at school together."

Rietta said, "Oh—" She was in a hurry, but, with twenty years' experience, she knew that it wasn't any use being in a hurry with Mrs. Voycey. The large, firm hand upon her arm would remain there until she had done her social duty. She said, "How do you do?" to Miss Maud Silver, and was invited to tea that afternoon.

"And it's no use saying you can't come, Rietta, because I know perfectly well that Carr and Miss Bell have gone up to town for the day. The baker saw them start. He mentioned it when he called, because there was a very black cloud overhead at the time and he noticed that Miss Bell hadn't got an umbrella so he hoped she wouldn't get wet. He said he told her she'd better take one, but she only laughed. How long are they staying with you?"

"I don't quite know. Carr has brought down some manuscripts to read."

"He looks as if he needed a good long holiday. Then you'll come to tea this afternoon? I'll ring Catherine up and ask her too. I want Maud Silver to meet you both." She leaned closer and said in a throaty whisper, "She's quite a famous detective."

Miss Silver was examining the stand of post cards. She looked so much less like a detective than anything Rietta could have imagined that she was startled into saying,

"What does she detect?"

"Crime," said Mrs. Voycey right into her ear. She then let go of the arm she had been holding and stepped back. "I'll expect you at half past four. I must really have a word with Mrs. Mayhew."

Mrs. Mayhew was buying onions, and a stone of potatoes.

"I'm sure I never thought I'd come to having to get either from anywhere else except the garden, but it's all Mr. Andrews can do to keep the place tidy, and that's the truth, Mr. Grover—indeed he can't, and there's no getting from it. So if Sam can bring them up after school—" She turned, a little meek woman with a plaintive manner, and was immediately cornered by Mrs. Voycey.

"Ah, Mrs. Mayhew—I suppose you're very busy with Mr. Lessiter back. Quite unexpected, wasn't it? Only last week I said to the Vicar, 'There doesn't seem to be any word of Melling House being opened up again,' and I said it was a pity. Well, now he's back I hope he isn't going to run away again."

"I don't know, I'm sure."

Mrs. Voycey gave her hearty laugh.

"We must all be very nice to him, and then perhaps he'll stay." She came a step nearer and dropped her voice. "Good news of your son, I hope."

Mrs. Mayhew darted a frightened glance to the right and to the left. It was no good. She was in the angle between the counter and the wall, and get past Mrs. Voycey she couldn't. Her own tone was almost inaudible as she murmured,

"He's doing all right."

Mrs. Voycey patted her kindly on the shoulder.

"I was sure he would—you can tell him I said so. Things are different to what they used to be thirty or forty years ago. There wasn't any second chance then, whether it was a boy or a girl, but it's all quite different now. He'll be coming down to see you, I expect."

Mrs. Mayhew had turned dreadfully pale. Mrs. Voycey meant well—everyone in Melling knew how kind she was —but Mrs. Mayhew couldn't bear to talk about Cyril, not right here in the shop with people listening. It made her feel as if she was in a trap and couldn't get out. And then the little lady who looked like a governess coughed and touched Mrs. Voycey's arm—"Pray, Cecilia, tell me something about these views. I should like to send a card to my niece, Ethel Burkett" —and she was free. Her heart was beating so hard that it confused her, and she was half-way up the drive before she remembered that she had meant to buy peppermint flavouring.

When the two ladies came out of the shop and were walking home across the Green, Mrs. Voycey said,

"That was Mrs. Mayhew. She and her husband are cook and butler at Melling House. Their son has been a sad trouble to them."

Miss Silver coughed and said,

"She did not like your talking about him, Cecilia."

Mrs. Voycey said in her hearty way,

"It's no good her being so sensitive. Everyone knows, and everyone feels kindly about it and hopes that Cyril has made a fresh start. He was their only one and they spoilt him—a dreadful mistake. Of course it makes it hard for Mrs. Mayhew the Grover boy having turned out so well—that was Mrs. Grover serving Dagmar Ainger at the end of the counter. Allan and Cyril used to be friends. They both took scholarships, and Allan went into Mr. Holderness's office—a very good opening. But Cyril took a job in London, and that's what did the mischief. He isn't a bad boy, but he's weak and they spoilt him. He ought to have been where he could keep in touch with his home. It's terribly lonely for boys like that when they first go out into the world, and the only company they can get is just the sort that isn't likely to do them any good. You

know, Maud, I used to be dreadfully disappointed about not
having children, and I dare say I missed a great deal, but it's a
tremendous responsibility—isn't it?"

Miss Silver coughed and said it was.

"Even a satisfactory boy like Allan Grover," pursued Mrs.
Voycey. "Well, I wouldn't say it to anyone but you, and of
course it's too silly for words, to say nothing of being exceed-
ingly presumptuous—"

"My dear Cecilia!"

"I was really shocked. And I can't—no, I really can't believe
that she gave him any encouragement. Of course at that age
they don't need any, and she is a very pretty woman—"

"My *dear* Cecilia!"

Mrs. Voycey nodded.

"Yes—Catherine Welby. Quite too absurd, as I said. It
began with his offering to go and put up shelves in her house,
and then he said he would plant her bulbs, and she lent him
books. And when she wanted to pay him he wouldn't take a
penny, so of course she couldn't let him go on. He isn't
twenty-one yet, so she is more than old enough to be his
mother."

Miss Silver coughed indulgently.

"Oh, my dear Cecilia, what difference does that make?"

Chapter Eight

JAMES LESSITER SAT back in his chair and looked across the
table at Mr. Holderness, who appeared to be considerably
perturbed. A flush had risen to the roots of the thick grey hair,
deepening his florid complexion to something very near the
rich plum-colour achieved by the original founder of the firm,
a three-bottle man of the early Georgian period whose portrait
hung on the panelling behind him. He stared back at James
and said,

"You shock me."

James Lessiter's eyebrows rose.

"Do I really? I shouldn't have thought anyone could practise
as a solicitor for getting on for forty years and still retain a
faculty for being shocked."

There was a moment's silence. The flush faded a little. Mr. Holderness smiled faintly.

"It is difficult to remain completely professional about people when one has known them as long as I have known your family. Your mother was a very old friend, and as to Catherine Welby, I was at her parents' wedding—"

"And so you would expect me to allow myself to be robbed."

"My dear James!"

James Lessiter smiled.

"How very much alike everyone is. That is exactly what Rietta said."

"You have spoken to her about this—distressing suspicion of yours?"

"I told her there were a good many things missing, and that it wouldn't surprise me to find that Catherine knew where they had gone, and—what they had fetched. Like you, all she could find to say was, 'My dear James!'"

Mr. Holderness laid down the pencil he had been balancing and placed his fingertips together. It was a pose familiar to any client of long standing, and indicated that he was about to counsel moderation.

"I alluded just now to this idea of yours as a distressing suspicion. You cannot wish to precipitate a family scandal upon a mere suspicion."

"Oh, no."

"I was sure of it. Your mother was extremely fond of Catherine. If there is no evidence to the contrary, there would be a strong presumption that the furniture at the Gate House was intended to be a gift."

James continued to smile.

"My mother left Catherine five hundred pounds. By a few strokes of the pen she could have added, 'and the furniture of the Gate House,' or words to that effect. Yet she did not do so. If it comes to presumptions, that would be one on the other side. The will never mentions the furniture. Did my mother ever mention it to you?"

"Not precisely."

"What do you mean by not precisely?"

The fingertips came apart. The pencil was taken up again.

"Well, as a matter of fact, I mentioned it to her."

"And she said?"

"She put the matter aside. She could be very peremptory, you know. I cannot pretend to give her exact words. The will was drawn more than ten years ago, but my recollection is that she said something like 'That doesn't come into it.' Considered in the light of what you have been saying, it might be argued that her will had no concern with the furniture because she had already given it to Catherine—"

"*Or* because she had no intention of giving it to her. You didn't ask her what she meant?"

"No—she was being extremely peremptory."

James laughed.

"I've no doubt of it! What I shall continue to doubt is that my mother had any intention of letting Catherine get away with so much valuable stuff."

Mr. Holderness rolled the pencil meditatively to and fro between finger and thumb.

"You may have some grounds for such a doubt, but you have no certainty. I dare say, if the truth were known, that your mother never defined the situation very clearly. When she told Catherine that she might have this or that from Melling House she may have intended a loan, or she may have intended a gift, or she may have had no very clear intention. Catherine, on the other hand, might naturally have concluded that the things were being given to her. I think, if I may say so, that it would be a pity to encourage a suspicion which you cannot prove."

James Lessiter sat up straight and formidable.

"Who says I can't prove it? I will if I can."

Mr. Holderness looked shocked all over again. His colour did not mount so vigorously as before, nor did it attain to quite so deep a shade. He stopped rolling the pencil and said,

"Really—"

James nodded.

"I know, I know—you think I ought to let it slide. Well, I'm not going to. I have an extreme dislike for being taken for a fool, and an even more extreme dislike for being done down—I can assure you that very few people have ever got away with it. I've got an idea that there's been quite a lot going on behind my back. Well, I mean to get to the bottom of it, and when I do, anyone who thought he could take advantage of my absence is going to find himself in Queer Street."

Mr. Holderness put up a hand.

"My dear James, I hope you don't mean that you suspect the Mayhews. Your mother had every confidence—"

James Lessiter laughed.

"If there weren't so much confidence, there would be no room for the confidence trick, would there? Now I'm going to tell you something. You say I can't prove my suspicions because my mother held her tongue and didn't put anything in her will. What she did do was to write to me a couple of days before she died. Would you like to know what she said?"

"I should indeed."

"I can give it to you verbatim. 'I have not troubled you with letters about business as I hope you will soon be coming home. Meanwhile, in case of accident, I should like you to know that I have kept a careful note of everything.' A careful note of everything—that should tell us what we want to know, shouldn't it?"

"It might," said Mr. Holderness slowly.

"Oh, I think you are too cautious. I think we may assume that it would. I haven't found the note yet. My mother, like so many women, had a profound distrust of banks and office safes. It would, of course, have been a great deal more sensible—and convenient—if she had left this memorandum in your hands, but she didn't. I have been through the drawers of her writing-table and a filing-cabinet which she had in the library, but for a special paper of this kind she may have had some special hiding-place. I have every hope that I shall find it, and when I do—"

Mr. Holderness lifted his eyes and looked steadily and gravely across the table.

"You sound vindictive."

James laughed easily.

"Oh, yes."

"You would really proceed to extremes?"

"I should prosecute."

Chapter Nine

MRS. VOYCEY'S TEA-PARTY went off as tea-parties do. Home-made scones were partaken of, and home-made quince preserve offered with modest pride.

"My dear mother's recipe. A lovely colour, isn't it? It reminds me of that deep red dress of yours, Rietta. But what I would like to know is how to keep the pale green colour of the

fruit as they do in Portugal. I stayed out there for a month
when I was a girl, and they made a most delicious quince
cheese which they called marmalada, the colour of green
grapes and turned out of a jelly-mould. You ate it in slabs, and
it was crystallized all over the top—quite terribly good. But I
never met anyone who could tell me how it was done. The
minute I boil quinces with sugar they behave like traffic lights
—first they go amber, and then they go red."

Mrs. Voycey laughed very heartily at her own joke and
proceeded to terrible disclosures about Portuguese plumbing.
Whilst Miss Silver shared her views as to up-to-date sanita-
tion, it was, in her opinion, a subject not at all suited to the
tea-table. She coughed and endeavoured to change the topic,
but it was some time before she was able to do so, and then, a
good deal to her distaste, she found her professional activities
the next topic on Cecilia's rattling tongue. The whole story of
the extraordinary affair of the Eternity Earring as retailed by
Miss Alvina Grey was poured out.

No use for Miss Silver to say with her slight admonitory
cough, "I prefer not to talk about it," or even, "My dear
Cecilia, I never discuss my cases." Even as a schoolgirl it had
always been very difficult to stop Cissy Christopher. As an
elderly woman in her own house it was quite impossible to
check or deflect Cecilia Voycey. Miss Silver sighed and gave
up the attempt. At the earliest possible opportunity she
introduced the subject of education, and found herself able to
exchange views in a very interesting manner with Miss Rietta
Cray.

"I spent twenty years in the scholastic profession."

Something stirred at the back of Rietta's mind and vanished
again in the shadows. A little later it was there again—
something just on the edge of being remembered. And then
all at once, in the middle of Catherine being plaintive about
the cost of living, Mrs. Voycey urging everyone to have more
tea, and Miss Silver interrupting a quotation from Tennyson to
say, "No, thank you, dear," it came to her.

"'Knowledge comes, but wisdom lingers,' as Lord Tennyson
so aptly says."

Rietta said, "Oh—" And then abruptly, "Are you Randal
March's Miss Silver?"

Miss Silver smiled in a gratified manner.

"He and his sisters were pupils of mine. The friendship has,

I am glad to say, been maintained. Do you know the Marches?"

"I was at school with Isabel and Margaret. They were big girls when I was a little one. Miss Atkinson always said how well grounded they were. Randal was younger of course —about my age. He's Chief Constable of the county now."

"Yes. I had the pleasure of lunching with him in town not long ago. Isabel has married, you know. A widower with several children—extremely suitable. In my experience these late marriages are often very happy. People have learned to appreciate companionship. Margaret, of course, married in her early twenties, but it has turned out very well."

They went on talking about the Marches.

Catherine and Rietta walked home together. It was deep dusk. There were no lights except a distant yellow gleam here and there where a curtain had been carelessly drawn in one of the cottages which bordered the Green. When they had gone a little way Catherine said with a sudden energy,

"Rietta, what did James say to you last night? Did he talk about me?"

Rietta considered. There seemed to be no reason why she should hold her tongue. She said,

"He asked me whether I know what arrangement his mother had made with you about the Gate House."

"What did you say?"

"I said I didn't know."

Catherine took a quick breath.

"Anything else?"

"He asked me about the furniture."

"What about it?"

"Whether it was given or lent."

"And what did you say?"

"Just what I said before—I didn't know."

Catherine brought her hands together in sharp exasperation.

"Aunt Mildred gave me the furniture—you know she did —I've told you a dozen times! Why couldn't you say so?"

Rietta said in her brusque way,

"What you've told me isn't evidence."

"You mean you don't believe me when I tell you—when I *tell* you that she gave me the things?"

"No, I don't mean that. I mean just what I said—what you told me isn't evidence."

"And what evidence do you want?"

How exactly like Catherine to make a scene about nothing. Rietta wondered, as she had often wondered before, whether the old friendship was really worth while. Only when you have known someone all your life and you live practically next door each other in a village, there isn't much you can do about it except to try and keep your temper. She said as coolly as she could,

"It isn't what *I* want—it's James. And what he wants is evidence—something to show his mother's intention. He asked whether she had ever said anything."

"What did you say?" The words came quick and angry.

"I said your mother told me, 'I'm letting Catherine have the Gate House. I've told her she can have the two groundfloor rooms knocked into one, and I suppose I shall have to let her have some furniture.'"

"There—you see! What did he say to that?"

"That it might mean anything," said Rietta drily.

"*Oh!*" It was a gasp of pure rage, followed by a sharp, "How perfectly outrageous!"

They were in the middle of the Green on the narrow footpath which cuts across it. Rietta stopped.

"Catherine, don't you see you can't take James like that? You'll only get his back up. He looks on the whole thing as a business transaction—"

Catherine broke in with an edge to her voice.

"Of course you would stand up for him—we all know that!"

Rietta's temper rose. She restrained it.

"I'm not standing up for him—I'm telling you how he looks at the thing. Opposition always put his back up. Unless he has changed very much, the best thing you can do is to lay your cards on the table and tell him the exact truth."

"What do you think I've been telling him—lies?"

"Something betwixt and between," said Rietta in a blunt voice.

"How dare you!" She began to walk on quickly.

Rietta caught her up.

"Well, you asked me. Look here, Catherine, what's the good of going on like this? You know, and I know, what Aunt Mildred was like, and what is more, James knows too. She had spasms of being businesslike, but most of the time she couldn't be bothered. She was an autocrat to her fingertips, and she was as changeable as a weathercock. If she told you

you could have something, she might have meant it for a present one day and not meant it the next, or she might never have meant it at all. And if you want to know what I really think, well, I don't believe she did mean to give you the things outright—some of them are too valuable. But I didn't say that to James."

"But you will."

"No. He didn't ask me, and I shouldn't have said it if he had. It's just what I think."

They walked along in silence for a minute or two. Then Catherine's hand came out and caught at Rietta's arm. She said in a trembling voice,

"I don't know what to do."

"Do what I said, put your cards on the table."

"I can't."

"Why can't you?"

"I can't—he might turn nasty."

A little contempt came into Rietta's tone.

"What can he do? If you don't make him angry, he'll probably take back the half dozen things which are really valuable and let you keep the rest."

Catherine's grip became desperate.

"Rietta—I'd better tell you—it's worse than that. I—well, I sold some of the things."

"Oh!"

Catherine shook the arm she was holding.

"You needn't say 'Oh!' at me like that. They were mine to do what I like with. Aunt Mildred gave them to me—I tell you she gave them to me."

"What did you sell?"

"There were some miniatures, and—and a snuffbox—and a silver tea-set. I got three hundred for one of the miniatures. It was a Cosway—really very pretty—I'd liked to have kept it. And the tea-set was Queen Anne. I got quite a lot for that."

"Catherine!"

Catherine let go and pushed her away.

"Don't be a prig—one must dress! If you're going to blame anyone, what about Edward, never telling me he was head over ears in debt and leaving me practically without a penny! And now, I suppose, you'll go and tell James!"

"You don't suppose anything of the sort," said Rietta coolly.

Catherine came close again.

"What do you think he'll do?"

"I should think it would depend on what he finds out."

"He knows the things have gone—the snuffbox, and the miniatures, and the tea-set. I mean, he knows they're not at Melling House, and Mrs. Mayhew told him Aunt Mildred let me have the tea-set. He said last night that he hoped it wouldn't inconvenience me, but of course it was an heirloom and he must have it back. As if it mattered whether it was an heirloom or not! He hasn't any children."

After a moment's silence Rietta said,

"You've got yourself into a mess."

"What's the good of telling me that? What am I to *do*?"

"I've told you."

There was a pause. Then Catherine said under her breath,

"He says his mother made out a—a memorandum of everything she'd done—all the business things, you know —while he was away. It hasn't turned up yet, but when it does —" Her voice petered out.

Rietta finished the sentence.

"When it does, you don't think there will be anything about giving you the Cosway miniature and the Queen Anne tea-set."

"She might have forgotten to put them down," said Catherine in an extinguished tone.

They had reached the edge of the Green. As they stood, the Gate House lay to the left, and the White Cottage to the right. Catherine turned to where the tall pillars loomed up in the dusk. She said, "Goodnight," and went across the road.

Rietta took her own way, but before she could reach the Cottage gate she heard quick footsteps on the path. Catherine came up with her and put out a hand.

"I want to ask you something—"

"Yes?"

"It would make a lot of difference if you could remember Aunt Mildred saying she had given me those things—"

"I don't remember anything of the sort."

"You could if you tried."

Rietta Cray said, "Nonsense!" She made a movement to go, but Catherine held her.

"Rietta—listen a minute! After he came back last night James was—" she caught her breath—"rather frightening. Polite, you know, but in that sort of icy way. He talked about things missing—oh, it wasn't so much what he said, it was a sort of undercurrent. I thought he wanted to frighten me, and

I tried not to show it, but I think he saw I was frightened, and I think he enjoyed it. I haven't ever done anything to make him feel like that, but I got the most horrid sort of impression that he would hurt me if he could, and that he would enjoy doing it."

Rietta stood perfectly still. The shadow which she had shut away all those years ago came out and stood at her shoulder.

Catherine spoke in a whispering voice.

"Rietta—when you and James were engaged—was he like that? It would come out if you were engaged to someone. Did he like—*hurting*?"

Rietta stepped back. She said, "Yes," and then she walked quickly away, lifted the latch of her own gate, and went in.

Chapter Ten

JAMES LESSITER DROVE back from Lenton. He liked driving at night in these country lanes, where the headlights made a bright path for the car and all you had to do was to take your way along it. It gave him a sense of effortless power. He did not make the conscious comparison, but he had a sense of life stretching before him just like that. He had made a great deal of money, and he expected to make a great deal more. When you had made a certain amount it went on making itself. Money was power. He thought of the boy who had left Melling more than twenty years ago, and his sense of well-being became something very like triumph. How right he had been. Instead of allowing himself to go down with a ship which had been foundering for three generations he had cut loose and made for the shore. He had no regrets. The house could go. If he wanted a place in the country, there were more amusing spots than Melling. Nowadays you didn't want a great big barrack of a place built for the days when house-parties lasted for weeks and large staffs could be counted upon. Something modern and labour-saving—a big room where you could throw a party—half a dozen bedrooms. Meanwhile he rather thought he was going to enjoy himself. He had a score or two to pay off, and he was looking forward to the payment. Something very pleasing about being able to arrange one's own private day of judgment.

He turned in between the tall pillars of Melling House and saw the beam of the headlights slide in front of him up the drive, whitening the neglected gravel, striking bright patches of green from holly and rhododendron. All at once the light picked up a movement in the crowded undergrowth. He thought someone had stepped aside into the bushes, but he couldn't have sworn to it. It might have been a tradesman's boy getting out of the way of the car, or it might have been someone coming up to see the Mayhews. Then he remembered that it was their half day out and that they would be in Lenton. Mrs. Mayhew had asked if it would be all right for them to go. There was to be cold supper left ready for him in the dining-room.

He drove right on into the garage, rather pleased at the idea of having the house to himself. It would be a good opportunity for a thorough search of his mother's bedroom and sitting-room. He meant to find that memorandum. He had made up his mind that it would be somewhere in one of those two rooms. She had been getting feeble—not going downstairs any more.

He let himself in by the front door and clicked on the lights in the hall. The person who was just emerging from the drive stood still and saw the two hall windows spring into sight.

A good deal later the telephone bell rang in Catherine Welby's charming room. She put down her book and lifted the receiver. Her hand tightened on it when she heard James Lessiter's voice.

"Is that you, Catherine? I thought you would be glad to know that I have found that memorandum."

"Oh—" For the life of her she couldn't think of anything to say.

"I was afraid it might have been destroyed, because of course Mr. Holderness collected all the papers he could find, and Mrs. Mayhew tells me that you were in and out a good deal."

Catherine's left hand came up to her throat.

"I did what I could."

"I've no doubt of it. But it was—where do you think?"

"I've no idea."

Her mouth was dry. She mustn't let her voice sound different.

"You'll never guess—you didn't guess, did you? It was in a volume of the late Vicar's sermons. I remember when he had them printed and gave her the copy—don't you? She could be perfectly certain no one would meddle with it there. I only found it because after I'd looked everywhere else I took all the books out of her bookcase and shook them. Perseverance rewarded!"

Catherine said nothing at all. She took a quick breath. The sound of it reached James Lessiter and gave him a lively pleasure.

"Well now," he said briskly, "you'll be delighted to hear that the memorandum makes your position perfectly clear. You were originally supposed to pay a nominal rent of ten shillings a month, but after one or two payments nothing more was said about it and the rent question lapsed. Then as regards the furniture— Did you say anything?"

"No—" She got the one word out, but she couldn't have managed another.

"Well, as regards the furniture the memorandum is quite explicit. My mother says, 'I am not quite sure what furniture Catherine has at the Gate House. I have let her have things from time to time, but of course it was clearly understood that they were only lent. It was better that they should be used, and she is very careful. I think you might let her keep enough for a small house if it does not suit you to let her stay on at the Gate House. Nothing valuable of course, just useful things. She has the small Queen Anne tea-set which I lent her during the war when china was so difficult to get. It was, of course, understood that it was only a loan.' "

Catherine spoke from a tight throat.

"That isn't true. She gave it to me."

"Well, well. Do you know, if this case came into court, I'm afraid the memorandum would be taken as evidence that she didn't do anything of the sort."

Again Catherine only got out the one word.

"Court—"

"Certainly. You see, this is a business matter, and I am a business man. I don't want there to be any mistake about that. I have just informed Holderness—"

With shock of terror Catherine came to herself. The fear that had paralysed her became a driving force.

"James—you can't possible mean—"

He said, "Can't I?" And then, "I advise you to believe that I do."

Chapter Eleven

CARR AND FANCY came back by the six-thirty and took a taxi from Lenton. They were hungry and cheerful. Fancy had had a marvellous time, because she had met a friend who had not only taken her out to lunch but had introduced her to three separate people, each one of whom had declared that he or she could get her a job with simply no difficulty at all.

"And one of them was in films. He said I'd be too photogenic, and I told him I was, because I do take marvellously. So I showed him the photos I had in my bag—wasn't it lucky I got them—only I shouldn't dream of going up to town without them, because you never can tell, can you? And he said he'd show them to a friend of his who is the big noise at the Atlanta Studios, and of course what he says goes. Wouldn't it be simply marvellous if I got a job in films?"

Carr put his arm round her shoulders quite affectionately and said,

"Darling, you can't act."

The big blue eyes opened in surprise.

"How do you know?"

"I've seen you try."

"So you have." There was no rancour in her voice. "Do you think it matters? And, you know, you're sort of funny that way —a lot of people liked me. And it wasn't a proper part either —I only had two sentences to say."

He laughed again.

"Darling, you were rotten."

Rietta, helping sausage loaf and a mixed salad, thought, "I haven't heard him laugh like that since I don't know when. I wonder if they're engaged. She isn't the right sort for him. I wonder how it will turn out. I think she's got more heart than Marjory had—she couldn't very well have less. Oh, God—why does one bring up children!"

Whatever the future was going to be, there was no doubt about Carr's access of spirits in the present. He had been into the office and found Jack Smithers elated over a very advantageous sale of film rights. He also described, with a good deal of verve, a manuscript which they had had pressed upon them as a discovery of the age by a pontifical gentleman with something of a name in politics.

"It's written by a child of ten without stops or capitals, and he says it's absolutely *the* last word in the pure genius of simplicity. Smithers says it's tripe, but of course you never can tell whether that sort of thing mayn't come off. There's a sort of borderline between tripe and genius, and there have been hits before now which have had a foot on either side of it."

He and Rietta produced instances and wrangled joyously about them. It was all very much like the old times before Marjory happened. If Fancy felt left out in the cold she didn't show it, and acquired merit with Rietta, who conceded that she seemed to be very sweet-tempered. As a matter of fact Fancy was quite pleased not to have to talk, her mind being entirely taken up with a model she had seen at Estelle's —twenty-five guineas, and it looked every penny of it, but she knew one of the girls who modelled there, and if she could coax the coupons out of Mum, and Maudie could give her the low-down on how the pleats went, she thought she could copy it. And talk about hits, it would be just about smashing.

She was still thinking about it when they had finished the washing up and Henry Ainger came in, as he did a dozen times a week for the perfectly simple reason that he couldn't keep away from Rietta Cray. It was a reason which was patent to everyone in the village. Henry himself displayed it with perfect simplicity. He loved Rietta, and if she ever consented to marry him, he would be the happiest of men. He didn't mind who knew about it, which was one of the things that exasperated his sister. She had tried scolding him as she had scolded Mrs. Grover about the bacon, but you cannot really make a success of scolding a man who merely smiles and says, "I shouldn't worry, my dear."

Henry came in cheerfully, put down a bundle of picture-papers—"Had them sent to me—thought you'd like to see them"—wouldn't take coffee because he was on his way to see old Mrs. Wingfold at Hill Farm, wouldn't sit down for the same reason, and ended by taking the cup which Rietta put into his hand and drinking from it standing up in front of the fire.

"She thinks she's dying. Of course she isn't. It happens about three times a month, but I must go or she might, and then I'd never forgive myself. You make the best coffee I know, Rietta."

She smiled, her face softening. It is agreeable to be loved when the lover demands nothing except the privilege of worship, and she was very fond of Henry Ainger. He was, as she had once said, so very nearly an angel. Not that he looked like one, or like a parson either, in a pair of old grey flannel slacks, a thick white sweater, and a disreputable raincoat. Above it his rosy face, round blue eyes, and thick fair hair gave him rather the look of a schoolboy in spite of his forty-five years. In daylight you could see that there was a good deal of grey in the hair, but the look of youth would be there when he was ninety. He finished his coffee, had a second cup, and said goodnight.

At the door he turned.

"Mrs. Mayhew's back early. I came out in the bus with her from Lenton. I thought she looked worried. I hope it isn't Cyril again."

Carr came back from the bookcase where he had been dallying.

"I saw Cyril Mayhew at the station. He came down on the same train that we did."

Rietta held out a cup of coffee to him.

"Did you speak to him?"

"No—I was going to offer him a lift, but he slipped away."

"He may not have been coming here. He doesn't—" she paused and added, "officially."

Carr raised his eyebrows.

"Anything the matter?"

She said, "Some trouble—I don't want to rake it up." She turned to Henry Ainger. "Mrs. Mayhew couldn't have known he was coming, or she'd have met the train and they'd have come out together."

"She might. I hope there's nothing wrong. I was surprised to see her hurrying back like that on her evening out. Mayhew wasn't with her."

Rietta frowned a little.

"James Lessiter's up at the House. I expect she felt she had to come back and give him something to eat. I don't suppose he's in the way of doing anything for himself."

Henry agreed.

"I don't suppose he is. He seems to have made a lot of money. There's a picture of him in one of those papers. He's just pulled off some big deal. I must see if I can get something out of him for the organ fund."

The door slammed after him—the banging of doors was one of Henry's less angelic habits—and almost at the same moment the telephone bell clamoured from the dining-room. As Rietta went to answer it she saw Carr stretch out his hand to the pile of picture-papers.

She shut both doors, picked up the receiver, and heard Catherine's voice, blurred and shaken.

"Rietta—is it you?"

"Yes. What's the matter? You sound—"

"If it was only sounding—" She broke off on a choked breath.

"Catherine, what is it?"

She was beginning to be seriously alarmed. None of this was like Catherine. She had known her for more than forty years, and she had never known her like this. When things went wrong Catherine passed by on the other side. Even Edward Welby's death had always been presented as a lack of consideration on his part rather than an occasion for heartbreak. The ensuing financial stringency had not prevented her from acquiring mourning garments of a most expensive and becoming nature. Rietta had listened to her being reproachful, complacent, plaintive. This was something different.

"Rietta—it's what we were talking about. He rang up—he's found that damned memorandum. Aunt Mildred must have been out of her mind. It was written just before she died. You know how forgetful she was."

"Was she?" Rietta's tone was dry.

The line throbbed with Catherine's indignation.

"You know she was! She forgot simply everything!"

"It's no use your asking me to say that, because I can't. What does the memorandum say?"

"It says the things were lent. She must have been mad!"

"Does it mention them by name?"

"Yes, it does. It's completely and perfectly damnable. I can't give them back—you know I can't. And I believe *he* knows too. That's what frightens me so much—he knows, and he's enjoying it. He's got a down on me, I'm sure I don't know why. Rietta, he—he said he'd rung up Mr. Holderness."

"Mr. Holderness won't encourage him to make a scandal."

"He won't be able to stop him. Nobody ever could stop James when he'd made up his mind—you know that as well as I do. There's only one thing—Rietta, if you went to him—if you told him his mother really didn't remember things from one day to another—"

Rietta said harshly, "No."

"Rietta—"

"No, Catherine, I won't! And it wouldn't be the least bit of good if I did—there's Mr. Holderness, and the doctor, to say nothing of the Mayhews and Mrs. Fallow. Mrs. Lessiter knew perfectly well what she was doing, and you know it. I won't tell lies about her."

There was a dead silence. After it had gone on for a long minute Catherine said,

"Then anything that happens will be your fault. I'm *desperate*."

Chapter Twelve

As Rietta came back into the sitting-room she saw Carr Robertson on his feet. Her mind was full of her conversation with Catherine—what she had said, what Catherine had said, what James Lessiter might be going to do. And then she saw Carr's face, and everything went. One of the papers which Henry Ainger had brought lay open across the table. He stood over it now, his hand on it, pointing, every muscle taut, eyes blazing from a colourless face. Fancy was leaning forward, frightened, her red mouth a little open.

Rietta came to him and said his name. When she touched his arm it felt like a bar of steel. She looked where the hand pointed and saw the photograph which Mrs. Lessiter had been so proud of—James as she had seen him last night at Catherine Welby's.

In a voice that was just above a whisper Carr said,

"Is that James Lessiter?"

Rietta said, "Yes."

Still in that dreadful quiet tone, he said,

"He's the man I've been looking for. He's the man who took Marjory away. I've got him now!"

"Carr—for God's sake—"

He wrenched away from her hand and went striding out of the room. The door banged, the front door banged. The striding steps went down the flagged path, the gate clapped to.

Fancy said something, but Rietta didn't wait to hear what it was. She caught up an old raincoat from the passage and ran out by the back door and through the garden to the gate which opened on the grounds of Melling House. She got her arms into the coat sleeves somehow and ran on. How many hundred times had James Lessiter waited for her just here in the shadow of the trees?

With the gate left open behind her she ran through the woodland and out upon the open ground beyond. Her feet knew every step of the way. There was light enough when memory held so bright a candle.

She struck through shrubs into the drive and stood there, quieting her breath to listen. If Carr was making for the House he must come this way. He could not have passed, because he had to follow two sides of the triangle while she had cut across its base. She listened, and heard her own breath, her own thudding pulses, and as these died down, all the little sounds which go by unnoticed in the day—leaf touching leaf in a light breeze, the faint rub of one twig against another, a bird stirring, some tiny creature moving in the undergrowth. There were no footsteps.

She walked quickly up the drive, not running now, because she was sure that Carr could not be ahead of her and it would not serve her purpose to arrive out of breath. The more reasonable pace allowed thought to clear and become conscious again. Everything between this moment and that in which Carr had banged out of the house had been governed by pure panic instinct. Now she began to take order of what was in her mind, to sort out what she was going to say to James Lessiter. She thought back to last night at Catherine's. He hadn't remembered Margaret's married name—and if he had, the world was full of Robertsons. Carr Robertson had meant nothing to him. Mrs. Carr Robertson had meant Marjory, a pretty blonde girl bored with her husband. No connection at all with Melling and Rietta Cray. But last night—last night he must have known. Their words came back to her:

"Carr Robertson . . . How old is the boy?"

"Beyond being called one. He's twenty-eight."

"Married?"

"He was. She died two years ago."

And Catherine leaning sideways to put down her coffee-cup and saying,

"None of us really knew Marjory."

He must have known then. James Lessiter must have known then.

She came out on the gravel sweep at the front of the House. The huge square building stood up black against the sky, the light wind moved in the open space before it. All the windows were dark—not an edge to any blind, not a glow behind any curtain.

She turned the near corner of the House where a flagged path ran between a narrow flower-bed and the hedge which presently bent back to enclose a small formal garden. Here the flower-bed ended and a clump of shrubs took its place beside the glass door leading from the study. Passing them, Rietta drew a breath of relief. The study curtains were drawn and a red glow came through them. It was plain that the room was lighted. Two steps led up to it. Rietta stood on the bottom one and knocked upon the glass. There was a moment in which she listened and heard a chair pushed back. Steps came to the window, the curtain was held aside. She could see the room brightly and warmly lit—the writing-table facing her—the hand which held the curtain back.

As the light fell on her face, James Lessiter came from behind the heavy red drapery, turned the key in the lock, and opened the door. She stepped in, shutting it behind her. The curtains fell again in their accustomed folds. Outside among the bushes someone moved, came up the two steps, and stood there pressed close against the glass, all without a sound.

James stared in astonishment and some admiration.

"My dear Rietta!"

Her colour was bright and high, her breath a little uneven. The room was very warm. She let the raincoat slip down upon a chair. He exclaimed,

"What have you done to your hand?"

She looked down, startled, and saw the blood running from a scratch on her wrist.

"I must have done it coming through the wood—I didn't know."

He offered his handkerchief, and she took it.

"It's nothing at all—I didn't know I'd done it. I ought to have a handkerchief somewhere, but one has no pockets."

She wore the dark red dress she had worn last night. There was a small triangular tear near the hem.

"There must have been brambles in the wood—I didn't notice."

He laughed.

"In such a hurry?"

"Yes."

She came round the table to the hearth behind it and stood there. He had been burning papers. The grate was full. Heat came from it, but no glow. It was strange to be here in this room with James. Everything in it was familiar. Here they had kissed, agonized, quarrelled, parted. Here they met again. Nothing in the room had changed—the massive table; the old-fashioned carpet; the wallpaper with its sombre metallic gleams; the family portraits, rather forbidding. A handsome half-length of Mrs. Lessiter with an ostrich-feather fan over the mantelpiece, and on the black marble shelf below, the heavy ormolu clock. Two on either side of it, the golden Florentine figures which she had always loved. They represented the Four Seasons—Spring, with a garland trailing across her slim body—a naked Summer—Autumn, crowned with vine-leaves and holding up a bunch of grapes—Winter, catching a wisp of drapery about her. Even now she could think them lovely. Some things perished, but others endured. The room was hot, but everything in her shivered with cold. She looked at him and said gravely,

"Carr has found out."

James leaned back against the writing-table, handsome, sure of himself, not exactly smiling but with a definite hint of amusement.

"That sounds intriguing. What has Carr found out?"

"That you ran away with his wife."

He raised his eyebrows slightly.

"Didn't he know?"

"Of course he didn't. Nor did you until last night at Catherine's."

He reached into his pocket for a gold cigarette-case, opened it, selected a cigarette, and then, as if suddenly recollecting himself, held out the case to her.

"My dear Rietta, forgive me."

She shook her head.

"I don't smoke."

"Quite right!" The case went back into his pocket, he struck a match. "It would be quite out of character—" he drew at his cigarette, blew out a mouthful of smoke, and added—"Pallas Athene!"

She was suddenly, sharply angry. Colour burned in her cheeks. Her voice hardened.

"I've come to warn you. It was a frightful shock—I don't know what he might do."

"Really? May I ask why?"

"Do you have to ask? I didn't like Marjory very much, but she was quite young—only twenty-four when she died. You took her away from her husband and her home, you left her penniless in France. She had to sell nearly everything she had in order to struggle back. She travelled in bitter weather without a coat, and died two days later of pneumonia. Carr didn't know the name of the man she'd gone off with, but he found your photograph in the back of her powder-compact. He saw a reproduction of the same photograph with your name under it in a picture-paper this evening. He regards you as Marjory's murderer, and I'm afraid of what he may do."

James had his cigarette held lightly between the second and third finger of a well groomed hand. He sketched a salute with it.

"And you came here to protect me? How extremely charming of you!"

Her dark brows drew together. She said,

"Don't!"

"Don't what?"

"Don't talk to me like that. Carr rushed out of the house. I don't know where he is, and I don't know what he may do. He thinks you murdered his wife."

"Then he ought to have gone to the police station."

Rietta stamped her foot. In a stormy voice which obliterated more than twenty years of separation she said,

"Stop it, James!"

He stood up, came over to her, and tossed his cigarette into the fire.

"All right. Now suppose you listen to a few facts. You're forty-three years old, and if you don't know what Marjory was like you've been wasting your time. I don't pretend to morality, but I shouldn't have wasted *my* time over a girl who wasn't easy money. Marjory was dead easy. She was bored with her life, she was bored with her husband—and she was fed to the teeth with being a grass widow, she wanted to have a good time. I took her to France and I gave her a rattling good time. Then I had to fly over to the States on business, and she got bored again. She walked out of the flat where I'd left her and moved in on a gentleman who had been running after her a good deal—wealthy international financier. I could have told her he wasn't a good investment. I imagine he found her out doing something he didn't care about and pitched her into the street. He was perfectly capable of it. It may surprise you, but I'm not. I should at least have given her a third-class ticket back to London."

"Is that the truth—all that about her leaving you and going to someone else?"

"Gospel, my dear."

She said bitterly, "When you talk like that you make everything sound like a lie."

He said quite soberly, "It's true nevertheless."

He went back to the table and stood half turned away, fingering the papers which lay there. Presently he lifted one of them, looked at it, laughed, and turned to face her.

"Your young firebrand hasn't turned up here, so I imagine he's walking his feelings off. When he comes home you can administer those cooling facts. He can't have been married to Marjory for three years without finding her out. I think you'll be able to get him to see reason. I've got a good deal of business on hand just now—I don't particularly want to be murdered!" He laughed a little. "Funny you should come along tonight, Rietta. I've been burning your letters."

"My letters?"

"Love's young dream! Most instructive—a little black ash in the fireplace. But they made a very hot fire—that's why the room is so warm."

She looked down at the heaped ash which choked the fireplace. Some of it still kept the shape of those folded letters. The curled edges wavered in the chimney-draught, a few red sparks ran to and fro, hurrying to be gone. She frowned at them, stern and pale.

James was speaking.

"I had to turn everything out because I was looking for a memorandum my mother left me—a very interesting memorandum." He laughed a little. "Everyone is going to hear a good deal more about it before we are through." Malice sparkled in his eyes. "Here it is, on the table, and some people would be glad if it wasn't. It would reassure them a good deal if they could be certain that it was in ashes like your letters. I found them, you know, when I was looking for it. They were locked up where I left them when I went away. And this with them."

He put the paper he was holding into her hand—an old will form, yellowing. She stared at it, uncomprehending at first, then with surprise and discomfort.

"James—how absurd!"

He laughed.

"It is rather, isn't it? 'Everything to Henrietta Cray, the White Cottage, Melling.' My mother had the life-rent of what my father left, and a power of disposal, so at the time I made this will I was leaving you some school prizes, a valued collection of football groups, and my not very extensive wardrobe. The comic thing is that I have never made another will, so if young Carr were to murder me tonight, you would come in for quite a tidy fortune."

She said quietly, "I don't like that kind of talk. Anyhow, here it goes—"

The paper dropped from her hand on to the piled ash, but before it had time to catch James Lessiter snatched it back.

"No, you don't, my dear! That's my property. Don't you know it's a criminal offence to destroy a will? I don't know how many years penal servitude it lets you in for—you might ask Holderness next time you see him."

She said in a tone of dislike,

"James, it's ridiculous. Please burn it."

He stood there half laughing with the paper in his hand held up high as if they were boy and girl again and she might catch at it. In a moment his expression changed. He reached across the table and put the will down on the blotting-pad. Then he turned back to her and said soberly,

"I don't know anyone I'd rather leave it to, Rietta."

"That's nonsense."

"Is it? I don't think so. I've no relations except a distant cousin or two about the same degree as Catherine—and you. They don't interest me. I shan't marry—I have no qualifications for the domestic hearth, and no desire to found that tiresome thing a family." His tone lightened again. "What would you do if it came to you? It's quite a packet."

She stood up straight and frowning.

"I don't want to talk about it. Please put that paper on the fire."

He burst out laughing.

"You don't get much fun out of life—do you? Relax and

discuss a hypothetical case with me—a purely hypothetical case, because I assure you that I mean to live to be a hundred, and a conscience like yours will nag you into your grave long before that. But it would interest me very much to know just how you would react to—well, to coming into a packet."

They had to talk about something. She wanted to be reasonably sure that Carr was only walking off his passion. She allowed herself to relax, and said,

"That would depend—"

"How truly cautious! It would depend on what I mean by a packet? Well, let us say enough to run this place on quite a lavish scale. Would you want to live here?"

She laughed frankly.

"I should hate it. I like my cottage."

"No urge to go elsewhere and make a splash?"

"My dear James!"

He was leaning back against the table again, his eyes bright, his lips smiling.

"Then what would you do with it? You've got to do something—in my hypothetical case."

She said in a considering voice,

"There are such a lot of people who haven't any homes. Nobody wants them. They drift into cheap bed-sitting rooms and shrivel up. I thought some of the big country houses might be run on communal lines—a lot of comfortable bed-sitting rooms, and the big public rooms for meals and recreation—"

He nodded, and then laughed.

"A hennery! I don't envy you the running of it. Just think how they'd scratch each other's eyes out!"

"Why should they? And I wouldn't only have women. Men want homes even more—they can't make them for themselves." She held out her hand. "And now, James, please burn that paper."

He shook his head, smiling.

"It's *my* will, and none of your business. If I'd ever cared enough, I'd have made another years ago. I just haven't bothered. But if I did bother, I've an idea that I should do the same thing all over again."

He got a very direct look.

"Why?"

"I'll tell you. Stand by to receive a bouquet. There was love's young dream, as I said—and, believe it or not, I never managed to repeat it. I've made love to quite a number of charming women, and I've enjoyed myself, but if I may say so, the contacts were—on a different plane. The idyllic note was —well, lacking. The other ladies bore no resemblance whatever to Pallas Athene. Without any desire to return to the uncomfortable period of youth, it has in retrospect a certain charm. You, as it were, personify that charm."

"You know perfectly well I've never had an atom of charm."

"*Ars est celare artem*. Do you know, when you said that you made me feel like a boy again."

She laughed.

"You used to tell me I was as blunt as a poker. I am still. I never did have any tact, so you must just take me the way I am. There's something I want to say to you. It's about Catherine."

Outside upon the steps, leaning against the glass door, Catherine Welby heard her own name. At the top of the window above her head there was one of the old star-shaped ventilators dating from the discovery round about 1880 that fresh air was not necessarily lethal. The ventilator was open, the voices of the two people in the study were vigorous and resonant. She had heard a good deal. She now heard James Lessiter say,

"What about Catherine?"

Rietta took a step forward.

"James—don't harry her."

"My dear girl, she's a thief."

Catherine was wrapped in a long black cloak. It was very warm, because it was lined with fur. Mildred Lessiter had given it to her long ago. The fur was still good and warm. Inside it her body shrank with cold.

"She's a thief."

"You've no right to say that!"

"I think I have. Here's my mother's memorandum—you can read it if you like. She's put everything down on it. Catherine was lying when she said the things were given to her. If she can't or won't produce them, I shall prosecute."

"You can't do that!"

"I can, and will."

"Why?"

"Because she's a thief."

Rietta shook her head.

"It isn't that. You've got something against her. What is it?"

"You don't need me to tell you that. She broke our engagement—lied about me to you—"

"James, they weren't lies!"

"She lied about both of us to my mother."

She came up quite close to him and stood there at the side of the table, her right hand resting on it.

"James, those were not the things which broke our engagement. I broke it—when you killed your dog."

A dark flush of anger had come up into his face. His jesting manner had gone.

"Did you expect me to keep a brute that had turned on me?"

"You frightened him and he snapped. You killed him —cruelly."

"I suppose Catherine told you that."

"No, it was one of the gardeners—he saw it. Catherine didn't know. I've never told anyone."

He said moodily, "What a fuss about a dog." Then, with a resumption of his earlier manner, "I told you I paid my scores. I think I'm going to enjoy settling with Catherine."

"James—*please*—"

As she met his look she knew just how useless it was. He laughed lightly.

"It's going to give me a good deal of pleasure to see Catherine in the dock."

The words hit her like a blow. He had stirred the past, played on her feelings, even for a moment reached out to touch her with the old charm. And now this. If he had actually struck her in the face, it would have been no more of a stinging shock. Rietta's anger broke. Afterwards she couldn't remember what she said. The words sprang up out of her anger and she flung them at him. If she had had anything in her hand she might have flung that too.

And then suddenly she was afraid of her own anger. It came up out of the past, and she was afraid of it. She said in a choked voice,

"I'll go."

When she had said that, Catherine drew back from the glass. She stepped down into the bushes out of which she had come. She saw the curtains pulled back and the door wrenched open. Rietta Cray ran down the steps, bare-headed, in her red dress.

Chapter Thirteen

SHE OPENED HER own door and went in. All the way back she had met no one, heard nothing. Her anger was so hot in her that she did not miss the coat, lying where she had dropped it in the study at Melling House. She did not remember it or think of it at all. She thought about Carr, she thought about Catherine, she thought about her own quick anger and was aghast.

She opened the door of the living-room and went in. Fancy looked up, yawning.

"You've missed the nine o'clock news."

Instinctively Rietta glanced at the clock, an old round wall-clock hanging on the chimney breast. It was twenty past nine. A dance band was swinging the latest song hit. She put out her hand and switched it off.

"Has Carr come back?"

Fancy yawned again. She really had lovely teeth, as white as milk and as even as peas in a pod.

"No, he hasn't. What's the matter with him, Miss Cray?"

Rietta came and stood over her, tall and frowning.

"I want you to tell me what happened—when I was out of the room."

The large blue eyes blinked up at her. There was an obvious attempt to control another yawn. Rietta thought with exasperation that the creature looked exactly like a sleepy child. You couldn't blame her for it, but it wasn't a situation in which a child was going to be much use. She said,

"I want you to tell me just what happened whilst I was at the telephone."

"Well—" the eyes remained wide and a little unfocussed—"I don't know that anything happened—much. Not till the end."

"What happened then?"

"Well, we were looking at those papers—the ones Mr. Ainger brought—and I'd seen a hat I liked, and I was thinking about how I could copy it, so I wasn't taking a lot of notice —you don't when you're thinking about something special. And all at once there was Carr, calling out. I thought he must have been stung or something. He looked awful, Miss Cray, he really did. And he said, 'The damned swine!' and I said, 'Where?' because I didn't know what he meant—I don't see how I could. And then you came in, and he said that piece about its being the man who took Marjory away—in the picture he was looking at—and he asked you if it was James Lessiter. Marjory was his wife, wasn't she? I mean, she was Carr's wife, and that James Lessiter went off with her. Carr won't do anything silly, will he?"

Rietta said, "No," in a deep, determined voice. It seemed to surprise Fancy a little. She blinked.

"Well, you can't pick up spilt milk again, can you?"

Rietta said, "No."

Fancy yawned.

"By what I've heard she wasn't much loss, was she?" Then she blinked again. "Perhaps I oughtn't to have said that. You weren't fond of her, were you?"

"No, I wasn't fond of her."

"By all accounts nobody was. I expect Carr got a bit of a jolt with her. He's kind of—nice, isn't he? When I told Mum about him she said she reckoned he'd had his feelings pretty badly hurt. She told me to look out and be careful. Have him if you want to, Ducks, or don't have him if you don't want to, but don't play him up.' That's what Mum said."

"And which are you going to do?"

At any other time there might have been sarcasm in the question. At this moment Rietta put it with complete simplicity, and with equal simplicity Fancy answered her.

"He doesn't want me. He said we wouldn't fit in. I think he likes that girl where he took me to tea—that Elizabeth Moore. He was fond of her, wasn't he?"

"A long time ago."

"Why didn't he marry her?"

"He met Marjory."

Fancy nodded.

"She was the sort who'd snatch. I only really met her once, but you could see how she was. Oh, Miss Cray, whatever have you done to your hand—it's all over blood!"

Rietta glanced down at her right hand. It was astonishing how much blood had come from that small scratch. Up at Melling House she had wrapped James Lessiter's handkerchief about it. It must have dropped whilst they were talking, and the bleeding had started again. It was dry now, but what a mess. She went down the passage to the lavatory and held it under the cold tap until the stain was gone.

Chapter Fourteen

ELIZABETH MOORE SAT with a book on her lap, but she wasn't reading. She had turned off the wireless after listening to the headlines of the nine o'clock news. Her mind refused to leap the Atlantic, the Channel, traverse the wastes of Europe and Asia, and concern itself with the follies which men were perpetrating hundreds of thousands of miles away. There are moments when the world contracts to what is happening to one person. Elizabeth's world had so contracted. There was only one person in it—Carr. She herself was present only as a striving against pain. Fancy hovered vaguely as a threat. But Carr wandered alone in that small, empty world. He was in torment, and she couldn't go to him, or touch him, or help him. A line came to her from her schooldays:

> "Yes: in the sea of life enisl'd . . .
> We mortal millions live alone."

And it was true—when it came down to brass tacks you had to work things out for yourself. Another line came to her, from the Bible this time, full of haunting melancholy beauty: "No man can save his brother, nor make agreement unto God for him, for it cost more than that to redeem their souls, so that he must let it alone for ever."

It was on this that she stretched out her hand to the bookcase without even looking to see what book it was that she had taken. It lay open upon her lap, and it was just white paper and black print, as dead to her as if the script had been Phoenician.

She did not know whether the time was long or short before she heard the tapping on the window. The room was at the back of the house. She lifted the curtain and saw only the black night pressing up against the glass like another curtain. Then in the dark something moved. A hand came up to knock again. Carr said her name.

It was a casement window with a low sill. She threw it wide, and he came in and pulled it to behind him. She let the curtain fall into its place, and saw his ghastly look, his shaking hands. They caught at her and held her, weighing her down until she came to a chair and dropped upon it. Then he was on his knees, his head against her, his whole body shaken. It was as if they had stumbled through the everyday crust into a dream where the most fantastic things are as natural as the drawing of one's breath. She put her arms round him and held him until the shuddering died down and he was still, his head against her breast, her arms holding him. She knew that she had said his name, and that he had repeated hers over and over like a cry for help. If there had been other words, she did not know. They were in her thought, they beat with her blood, but she did not know if they passed her lips, or whether they reached him without sound on a pure tide of comforting love.

"What is it, my darling?"

She heard herself say that, and felt him shudder.

"Don't let me go!"

"Carr—what is it?"

He told her then, lifting his head and speaking just above a whisper, as if the breath had gone out of him and he had to struggle for it.

"That man—I told you about—the one who took Marjory away—and left her—I saw his photograph—in a paper. It's James Lessiter—"

She said with a gasp, "Carr, what have you done?"

"I haven't—I thought I should if I stayed."

The fear which had touched her was still cold at her heart.

"What happened?"

"Henry Ainger came in—he brought some papers for Rietta. Afterwards Fancy and I were looking at them—Rietta had gone to the telephone. I saw that man's picture with his name under it—James Lessiter. I told you Marjory had kept his photograph—it was the same one. Rietta came in—I asked her, 'Is this James Lessiter?' After that I don't quite know what happened. She said, 'Yes,' and I went out of the house—I wanted to get my hands on him—I knew I'd kill him if I did. I've been walking—I don't know how long—"

She looked across his shoulder to the grandfather clock with its slow, solemn tick.

"It's getting on for half past nine."

"I can't have taken an hour to get here—I suppose I did—I think I started out the other way—then I thought about you. It's all I did think about after that—to get to you. I've made a damned fool of myself—"

"It doesn't matter."

It came to him that what she had just said was the underlying fact in their relationship. It didn't matter what he did or said, or what anyone else did or said, whether he went away and forgot or came back and remembered, wet or shine, day or night, year in year out, the bond between them held. He couldn't put it into words. He could only say, "No, it doesn't matter," and lay his head against her shoulder again.

The passion of the last hour had gone out of him, it already seemed remote and far away. There was a renewing. They stayed like that without any sense of time.

At last she said, "They won't know where you are—they'll be worried about you."

Elizabeth's world had come back to the normal again. It held other people—Rietta Cray, who must be terribly worried, and Jonathan Moore, who would be coming home after an evening's chess with Dr. Craddock. She got up and began to make tea, fetching the kettle from the kitchen, moving about the small domestic tasks as if they were the whole of love and service. It was perhaps the happiest hour that she had ever known. To receive back all that you have lost, all that you have not even hoped for, to be allowed to give again what you have kept unspent, is joy beyond words. She had not many words.

Carr was silent too. He had travelled a long way—not the two and a half miles from Melling, but the five years through which he had come to reach this place again. When she said, "You must go," he put his arms round her and said her name.

"Elizabeth—"

"Carr—"

"Elizabeth—are you going to take me back?"

"Do you want me to?"

"You know."

There was a little pause before she said,

"Can you—come back?"

"Do you mean—about Fancy?"

"You said you didn't know whether you were engaged to her."

He gave a shaky laugh.

"That was just talking. We had it out on the way home. She's a nice kid really—quite sensible and matter-of-fact. 'No offence meant, and none taken,' as her estimable Mum would say, so that's all right. I've come back like a bad shilling. Are you going to have me?"

Elizabeth said, "I can't help it."

Chapter Fifteen

HE TOOK A sober pace back to Melling. The feeling of fighting time and space was gone. His mind was anchored and safe. Everything on the far side of the storm that had swept him seemed a little unreal, like a dream when you have waked up with the daylight round you. It might have happened a long time ago to someone else. He had Elizabeth again. It seemed the most amazing thing that he could have let her go. He began to plan their life together as he walked.

He came out on to the edge of the Green and saw it like a soft dark smudge under the night sky. There was neither moon nor star, but after the lane with its high banks and tangled hedgerows it seemed by comparison light. He could see the row of cottages away on the far side, and the black, crouched outline of the church. He lept the left-hand path and came up with the Gate House. Light showed through the curtains. Catherine was still up.

Such a little thing can decide so much. If Catherine Welby had gone to bed a little earlier, a lot of things would have been different. The light shining through her pale brocade curtains broke Carr's train of thought and started another. If Catherine was up, other people would be up. In a flash "other people" became James Lessiter. He could hear Rietta saying, "Mrs. Lessiter never destroyed anything. He'll have a mass of papers to go through."

James Lessiter would be up. He could get the whole sordid business between them finished and start fresh. He wasn't afraid of himself any longer. He could walk in, tell the swine what he thought of him, and walk out again. It was fixed in his mind that he must do that before the whole unhappy business of his marriage could be put away. It had robbed him of every illusion, every happiness. But Marjory was dead. He had to close her account with James Lessiter. As to touching him, he would as soon touch carrion. He turned in between the tall pillars and went up the drive.

The wall-clock at the White Cottage struck its three soft notes. Rietta Cray looked up incredulously. That it should be no more than a quarter to eleven seemed to give the whole lie to time. It was an hour since Fancy had gone up to bed, a quarter over two since Carr had flung out of the house. On any ordinary evening the time would have gone too fast. She worked hard all day, but once the supper things were washed up she could step aside out of this hard post-war world and become a leisured woman, with a concert, a play, waiting for her at the turn of a switch, or a book to take her here and there in time, or anywhere in space. But this evening there were none of these things. No enchantment has power on the racked mind. She did not know when so heavy a fear had weighed her down. It was past all reason, but she could do nothing to lift it. She told herself that she would laugh at it tomorrow, and tomorrow seemed very far away.

The house was dreadfully still. She missed the old dog who had died a month before, friend and companion of fifteen years. She would have to get a puppy, but she had put off for the old dog's sake. It was too quiet here alone at night.

Then, into the quiet, there came footsteps—not in front from the path skirting the Green, but from the back, coming up the garden. Like Catherine's the room ran through the house, windows at either end. She heard the click of the garden gate, she heard the steps come right up to the back door and come in. She would have locked the door before she went to bed, but she hadn't locked it yet. While she was up and about it would never have occurred to her to lock her door.

But the footsteps frightened her now. They had come down through the wood, as she herself had come an hour and a half ago. They had come down from Melling House. They were in the passage now, and the door opened. Carr came in and shut it behind him. He leaned against it and said,

"He's dead."

Rietta stood looking at him. His face was pale and stern —dreadfully pale, dreadfully stern. There was no wildness in his eyes. They looked at her, and she looked back, whilst everything in her froze. When she said nothing, Carr raised his voice to her as if she were deaf. He said,

"Do you hear?—James Lessiter is dead."

She said, "No!"—not because she didn't believe him, but because she did. It was the last hopeless protest against something too dreadful to be accepted.

His next words cut across the numb surface of her mind like a knife.

"Why did you do it?"

"Carr!"

He left the door and came forward. She saw then that he had the raincoat bundled up on his arm. It was the first moment that she had thought about it since she had dropped it across a chair in the study at Melling House. She thought of it now, and remembered that she had left it there.

Carr thrust it at her.

"What sort of a fool do you think you are to leave it there with his blood on it?"

Rietta lifted her head. It was like a nightmare—nothing made sense. But the numbness was going.

"It's my own blood. I scratched my wrist going up through the wood." She turned it for him to see—a scarlet line like a hair, already healing.

Carr gave an angry laugh.

"Don't be a fool, Rietta—not with me! We've got to think."

"I scratched myself—"

He shook out the coat, held up the right sleeve, and heard her gasp. The cuff was drenched and soaked. The red, wet stain ran up almost to the elbow, the breadth below it was splashed and streaked.

"You scratched your wrist— Oh, my God, talk sense!"

There was a moment when the room shook under her feet and the red stains spread in a milky mist. Then she had hold of herself again and her sight cleared.

"Carr, look at me!"

He was looking.

"And listen! I don't know anything about this. After you went out I was afraid of what you might do. You'd had a shock. I—well, I was afraid. I took the first coat I touched and ran up the back way to Melling House. When I got there the room was hot—I dropped the coat on a chair and never thought of it again. I talked to James—in the end we quarrelled. No, it wasn't exactly a quarrel. He said something I resented very much, and I walked out. I never thought about the coat."

He was holding up the sleeve.

"That's his blood."

She said, "I did scratch my wrist—it bled. He lent me his handkerchief—I must have dropped that too."

"What's the good of telling me all this came from a scratch on your wrist?"

"I don't tell you that—it didn't. But I did catch my wrist on something in the wood. It bled quite a lot for such a little scratch." A shudder went over her. "Not like that!" She paused for a moment, drawing hard upon her self-control. Then she came up to him. "Carr, put that dreadful thing down and tell me what's happened. We're talking in the dark. And for God's sake tell me the truth, because nothing else is going to be the slightest bit of use."

He let the coat fall down in a heap on the floor. It lay there with a broken look. But Rietta had no eyes for it. They were fixed on Carr's hard, dark face. He said,

"Very well, I'll tell you. When I went out of here I didn't know what I was doing. I walked myself pretty well off my legs, because if I hadn't I was going to go up to Melling House and smash James Lessiter. I must have walked for an hour, and I fetched up at Jonathan Moore's. Elizabeth was there by herself. I stayed there until I'd got hold of myself. We—" his face changed—"she's taken me back. When I came away I didn't want to kill him any more—I just wanted to be quit of the whole thing. That's the truth, Rietta. When I got to the Gate House Catherine's light was on. I thought, then it wasn't so late—Lessiter would be up—I could get quit of it all and start fresh. I wasn't going to touch him. I was going to let him know that I knew, and I was going to tell him what I thought of him. Stupid of me, I expect, but that's how I saw it. I went up to the house, and the front was all dark. I thought if he was up he'd be in the study, so I went round to the glass door, and found it ajar."

Rietta took her breath quickly.

"I can't remember—I can't remember whether I shut it. I don't suppose I did—I was too angry—"

He gave a sort of half laugh.

"Angry! I shouldn't say too much about that!"

"It was about Catherine—it doesn't matter. Carr, go on."

"I opened the door and went in. The curtains were drawn

behind it. The overhead light was on. He was lying slumped forward over the table with his head smashed in."

"Carr!"

He nodded.

"It wasn't pretty. It looked as if he had been sitting in his chair and had been hit from behind. The poker was lying on the hearthrug. There wasn't any doubt about what he'd been hit with."

She said, "Horrible!"

"Not nice to look at. Probably instantaneous. You're not expecting me to be sorry for him, are you? If we're not careful we may have to be uncommon sorry for ourselves."

"Go on."

"I had that cheering thought in the first five seconds. When I saw the raincoat it got a lot stronger. It was turned over, so a bit of the lining showed, and I thought I'd seen the stripe before. I went and had a look and found my initials on the neckband. After that I wiped the handle of the poker with a bloodstained handkerchief which seemed to have dropped on the hearth."

She shuddered.

"He lent it to me for my wrist. You shouldn't have wiped the handle."

He stared at her accusingly.

"Why shouldn't I have wiped it? If my raincoat was there, someone brought it, didn't they? It wasn't I. And that left you."

"Carr!"

"It's no use saying 'Carr!' If you'd had a row and hit him, it would be a hundred to one you'd rush off and never think about fingerprints. But if it was someone else, and someone clever enough to make use of my raincoat, then it was a hundred to one he'd have dealt with the handle of the poker already—anyhow that's what I thought at the time. I wiped the handle, and I put the handkerchief on the fire, which was practically choked with ash. I don't know if it'll burn or not—it doesn't really matter. Then I wiped the edge of the door with my own handkerchief, got the raincoat, and came away."

She took another of those quick breaths.

"You ought to have rung up the police."

He said, "I may be a fool, but I'm not a damned fool." Then he picked up the raincoat. "We've got to get the blood off this. What's the best way?"

"Cold water . . . Carr, I don't like it. We ought to send for the police—we haven't done anything wrong."

He touched her for the first time, taking her shoulder in a bruising grip.

"You've got a good headpiece—use it! On the evidence, do you think you could find a dozen people who would believe I didn't do it?"

"*You?*"

"Or you."

A dazed feeling came over her. She put up her hand to her head.

"A dozen people—"

He turned at the door.

"There are twelve people on a jury, Rietta."

Chapter Sixteen

MR. STOKES STARTED his milk round at seven in the morning. He reached Melling House at twenty past, and found what he afterwards described as a very horrid state of things. The back door stood open. Nothing unusual about that. All in the day's work that he should take the milk through to the kitchen and say "I don't mind if I do" when Mrs. Mayhew offered him a cup of tea. But this morning there wasn't any tea—only Mrs. Mayhew sitting up straight in a kitchen chair with her hands gripping the seat on either side. Looked as if she was afraid she'd fall off if she was to let go. She sat up straight, and looked at Mr. Stokes, but he wouldn't like to say she saw him —face all white like wet curds, and her eyes set in her head. Mr. Stokes didn't know when he'd had such a turn.

"Why, Mrs. Mayhew—what's up?" he said, and didn't get a word or anything except that stare. He put down the milk on the dresser and looked round for Mayhew, because for certain sure there was something wrong, and he couldn't go away and leave her like that.

He went across the kitchen to the door on the far side and opened it. There was a darkish bit of passage, and the door of the butler's pantry standing wide. He could see Mayhew's shoulder and right arm, and his hand holding the telephone receiver. The hand shook, the arm and shoulder shook. When his head came into the picture it shook too—not as if Mayhew was shaking it, but as if the whole of him was quivering like one of his wife's jellies. His teeth chattered. Mr. Stokes was of the opinion that nobody couldn't make head nor tail of what he was trying to say. He was probably right, because it became obvious that he was being adjured to speak up, and to speak distinctly. He said, "I'll try," and shook all over again and said, "It's the shock—I found him—he's a dreadful sight—oh dear!"

Mr. Stokes had a well founded local reputation as a nosy parker. He could contain himself no longer. It was obvious to the meanest intelligence that Something had Happened. Mr. Stokes did not think at all meanly of his intelligence. It immediately suggested that the Something, if not Murder, was at the very least of it Sudden Death. In a friendly and sociable manner he came up to the shaking Mr. Mayhew and laid an arm across his shoulders.

"What's up, chum? Who are you talking to—the police? Here, have a drink of water and see what that'll do."

Having filled a cup at the tap, he removed the receiver from Mr. Mayhew's nerveless hand, pressed it to his own ear, and stooped to the mouthpiece.

" 'Ullo! This is Stokes speaking—milk roundsman. Are you police?"

The sort of voice which suggests a large policeman said it was. It also asked what Mr. Stokes was doing on the line.

"Just happened to come in with the milk, and seeing Mr. Mayhew wasn't in shape for what you might call making a statement, I've given him a drink of water and told him I'll hold the line. Lenton police station, is it?"

The voice said it was. It also said it wanted Mayhew back on the line.

"Easy does it," said Mr. Stokes. "Bit of dirty work been going on, if you ask me—Mrs. Mayhew next door to a faint in the kitchen, and this pore chap looking as if someone had got him up to be shot at dawn. He's spilling half the water I give him instead of getting it down. Here, hold on a jiff and I'll see if I can get out of him what it's all about."

Constable Whitcombe waited impatiently. A number of disconnected and extremely irritating sounds reached him. There was some gasping, some choking, and, superimposed on these, an impression of Mr. Stokes administering a mixture of soothing syrup and encouragement. Then, very distinct and sharp, Mr. Stokes saying, "Gosh!" and then a pause which went on for so long that Constable Whitcombe flashed the exchange and wanted to know why he had been cut off. Exchange said he hadn't, and was rather crisp about it. After that there were one or two gasps, and then the sound of running feet. Mr. Stokes was back on the line, his voice risen in key and all detachment gone.

"It's Mr. Lessiter," he said—"murdered—in his own study! Bin hit over the head with the poker something crool! That's what Mr. Mayhew was trying to tell you, only he couldn't get it out, and no wonder. It fair turned me up! I've just been along to have a look. . . . No, of course I haven't touched anything! What d'you take me for? Children five year old know enough not to disturb nothing on the scene of the crime. . . . No, I didn't touch the door, and didn't need to. Standing wide open it was, the way Mr. Mayhew left it after he looked in and seen the horrid sight. Couldn't get back to his pantry fast enough, and I don't blame him. And if you ask me, the sooner you get someone out here the better. . . . All right, all right, all right, I didn't say you did! No need to take me up like that —I'm only trying to be helpful."

Everyone got their milk very late that morning. There was not only the delay caused by the interlude at Melling House, but it was obviously impossible for Mr. Stokes to call anywhere else without making the most of the dramatic fact that he had practically been on the spot when the murder was discovered. By the time he reached Mrs. Voycey's on the other side of the Green he was not only word-perfect, but he was also in a position to retail some first-hand observations on the manner in which the news had been received.

"Mrs. Welby, she put her head out of the window to ask for another half pint, and when I told her, she must have sat down sudden, because there she was one minute and there she wasn't the next, so I thought maybe she'd gone off in a faint with the shock. I called up to the window and asked if she was all right, and she looks out again as white as death and says, 'Are you sure?' And when I told her I seen him with my own eyes she says, 'Oh, my God—what a horrible thing!' "

Variants of this remark seem to have been made at every house. To his own regret, and to that of all his listeners, he had no knowledge of how the White Cottage had reacted, since he had most unfortunately delivered the milk at Miss Rietta Cray's before going up to Melling House.

Cecilia Voycey's stout, elderly housekeeper listened with

the same amiable interest which she had accorded during the past year to the birth of twins in the Stokes family and the decease of an uncle of Mrs. Stokes who had married for the fourth time in his eighty-ninth year and left his house and a nice little sum in the bank to the designing widow. "Yellow hair, and makes out she's under thirty!" had been Mr. Stokes's embittered conclusion. Upon all these items of news Mrs. Crook had had the same comment to make—a slow "Fancy that!" followed by "Who'd ha thought it!" The murder of James Lessiter provoked her to no higher flights, but having absorbed all that Mr. Stokes could tell her and shut the back door after him, she went through into the dining-room where Mrs. Voycey and Miss Silver were partaking of breakfast. With slow and lumbering accuracy she repeated her garnered news.

"Mr. Stokes, he waited till the police came. He don't know if there's anything missing, but the grate was fair choked with burned paper, and the poor gentleman sitting there with his head smashed in, and the poker on the hearthrug. Mr. Stokes was able to leave us two pints this morning, but he doesn't know if he'll be able to keep it up."

Miss Silver said, "Dear me!"

Mrs. Voycey waved away the milk.

"Good gracious, Bessie—don't talk about food! Have the police got any clue?"

"Not that they told Mr. Stokes. There was a Constable, and an Inspector, and a Superintendent, taking photographs and fingerprints and all sorts when he come away. He did say it looked like someone had tried to burn the poor gentleman's will. All scorched down one side it was."

"His will!" exclaimed Mrs. Voycey in what was almost a scream.

Mrs. Crook gazed at her in a ruminative manner and said placidly,

"They do say that everything was left to Miss Rietta Cray."

Chapter Seventeen

SUPERINTENDENT DRAKE OF the County Police sat in one of the tapestry-covered armchairs in the housekeeper's room at Melling House. Mrs. Mayhew sat in the other. Constable Whitcombe had made her a cup of tea, and Mayhew had laced it with whisky out of the case which James Lessiter had brought down with him. If she had been capable of coherent thought on any but the one dreadful subject, she would have been very much shocked at the idea of taking spirits so early in the morning. She had come out of that deathlike rigor. The whisky had got into her head and confused it. It had also loosened her tongue. But there was one thing she wasn't ever going to say, not if they burnt her at the stake. The improbability of this form of persuasion did not present itself. Nobody wasn't going to hear from her about Cyril coming over from Lenton on the bike he borrowed from Ernie White. If it wasn't for no other reason, whatever was Fred going to say? Fred didn't know, and he wasn't going to know. What was the use of saying he'd done with Cyril and he wouldn't have him coming about the place? You can't be done with your own flesh and blood, any more than you can cut off your hand and say you'll do without it. She'd got to manage so that Fred didn't know about Cyril coming down and—all the rest of it.

The terror began to come over her again. He mustn't know —the police mustn't know—nobody mustn't know—not *ever*.

She sat in the tapesty chair, not leaning back against the comfortable patchwork cushion which had been a legacy from her aunt Ellen Blacklock, but sitting straight up in her blue overall, which was very clean and a little faded, her hands clasping one another tightly, her eyes fixed upon the Superintendent's face. He hadn't been very long in Lenton, and she hadn't seen him before. If she had passed him in the street she wouldn't have thought about him one way or another except for his having red hair, which was a thing she didn't care about. Red hair and red eyelashes, they gave a man a kind of a foxy look. They'd never had them in their family, but of course it wasn't her business what other people had—she wasn't one for meddling with other people's affairs like some. It wasn't

anything to her whether Superintendent Drake was fair or
dark or foxy. Only no matter what he looked like, he was the
police, and she'd got to keep him from knowing about Cyril.
The terror in her took hold of her body and shook it.

The Superintendent said, "Now, Mrs. Mayhew, there's no
need for you to be nervous. You've had a shock, and I'm sorry
to trouble you, but I needn't keep you long. I just want you to
tell me what time you got home last night. It was your half day
off, wasn't it?"

"Yes, sir." She was looking at him, but without shifting her
gaze she could see that the young man sitting up to the table
had written that down. They would write everything down.

It didn't matter what they wrote just so long as she didn't say
a word about Cyril.

The Superintendent was speaking again.

"And on your half day, what do you generally do?"

"We go into Lenton."

"Every week?"

"Yes."

"What do you do when you get there?"

The dreadful grip of the terror had relaxed. He wasn't
asking her anything about Cyril—only what they'd done week
in, week out for more years than she could count, when they
had their day off.

"We do a bit of shopping, and then we go round to tea with
Mr. Mayhew's sister, Mrs. White."

"Yes—your husband gave us the address."

Ernie—Ernie and the bicycle—she didn't ought to have
mentioned Emmy White. But it wasn't her—it was Fred, and
Fred had given the address. She stared at the Superintendent
as a rabbit stares at a stoat.

"And after tea, Mrs. Mayhew?"

"We go to the pictures."

"You do that every week?"

"Yes, sir."

"Well, it's a great thing to have regular habits. I'm that way
myself—when I get the chance. Now, Mrs. Mayhew, why
didn't you go to the pictures last night? Your husband says you
came back by the early bus. He kept to the regular programme, but you didn't. why was that?"

"I came out by the six-forty bus."

"Yes—it reaches Melling at seven, doesn't it? Why did you

come back early instead of going to the pictures with your husband?"

"I'd a bit of a headache."

"Have you ever come back like that by yourself before?"

"Mr. Lessiter was here—"

"Yes?"

There wasn't any answer. The Superintendent said,

"You'd left him a cold supper, hadn't you?"

"Yes, sir."

"Then you didn't come back on Mr. Lessiter's account."

She couldn't turn any paler, but a sweat broke upon the skin.

"My head was bad."

"I see. Now, will you just tell me what you did after you got back."

Her hands clutched one another. She must tell him everything just like it happened, only nothing about Cyril—nothing about going to the back door and Cyril saying, "Well, I made it. Ernie lent me his bike. If I'd come by the bus, every dog and cat in Melling 'ud know." She's got to leave out all the bits about Cyril and tell the truth about the rest. She moistened her stiff lips.

"I come in, and I made me a cup of tea—"

She mustn't say nothing about giving Cyril his supper, and his saying right in the middle of it, "I've *got* to have some money, Mum. I'm in trouble."

The Superintendent's voice made her jump.

"Did you see Mr. Lessiter at all? You say you came home partly because he was here. Did you go to the study and see if he wanted anything?"

He saw her wince, and thought, "She's hiding something."

Instinct prompted her, as it will pompt any terrified weak creature. She said on a panting breath,

"Oh, yes sir."

"What time would that be?"

"It was just before the news."

"Just before nine?" He frowned.

"That's right."

"You were in before a quarter past seven, weren't you?"

"Yes, sir."

"But you didn't go and see if Mr. Lessiter wanted anything until just before nine."

She said very faintly, "My head was bad—I had to sit for a bit—I didn't rightly know what I was doing."

"It's a long time from a quarter past seven till nine o'clock."

A long time—a terrible long time . . . Cyril with his head in her lap—crying . . . She said in a weak voice,

"I didn't hardly know how it went. Then I made me some tea and went along to the study."

"And you saw Mr. Lessiter?"

There was a little colour in Mrs. Mayhew's cheeks, a flush born of whisky and desperation. She said,

"No, sir—I didn't see him."

The eyes behind the foxy lashes bored into her like gimlets.

"You went to the study, and you didn't see him?"

Mrs. Mayhew nodded, sitting up straight and pinching her left hand with her right till it felt quite bruised.

"I went along to the study like I said, and I opened the door, but I didn't open it no more than a little."

"Yes?"

She caught her breath and said in a fluttering voice,

"Miss Rietta Cray was there."

"Who is Miss Rietta Cray?"

"Lives at the White Cottage—just to the left outside the gates."

"Go on."

"I didn't mean to listen—I wouldn't do anything like that—I just wanted to know whether to go in. People don't thank you if they're talking private."

"Were they?"

Mrs. Mayhew nodded with emphasis.

"Mr. Lessiter was saying he didn't particularly want to be murdered."

Superintendent Drake said, *"What!"*

Mrs. Mayhew repeated her nod.

"That's what he said. And then he went on, 'Funny you should come along tonight, Rietta. I've been burning your letters.' That's when I knew it was Miss Cray he was talking to. And then he said something about love's young dream."

"Were they engaged?"

She nodded again.

"A matter of twenty years ago—getting on for twenty-five. So I thought I'd better not go in."

"Did you hear any more?"

She said, "I'm not one to listen."

"Of course you're not. But you might have happened to hear something before you shut the door. You did, didn't you?"

"Well, I did. There was a piece about his turning everything out, looking for a memma something or other his mother left him. I remember that because it rhymed with Emma."

"Memorandum?"

"That's right."

The terror in her was lulled. All this was easy, and no more than gospel truth. She was all right so long as she told the truth and kept away from Cyril. She had a picture in her mind of Cyril in the kitchen fiddling with the knobs of the wireless, and herself a long way off at the study door. Instinct told her to stay there and make as much of it as she could—the same instinct which sets a bird to trail a wounded wing and trick a cat away from its nest. She repeated the Superintendent's suggestion.

"Memma-randum. Something his mother left for him, and when he was looking for it he'd found Miss Rietta's letters and —something else."

"What else?"

"I couldn't see—the door wasn't open more than an inch. By what he said, it was a will, sir. Seemed he was showing it to Miss Rietta. And she said, 'How absurd!' and Mr. Lessiter laughed and said it was rather. And then he said, 'Everything to Henrietta Cray, the White Cottage, Melling.'"

"You definitely heard him say that to Miss Cray?"

"Oh, yes, sir." Her look was unwavering and truthful.

"Did you hear anything more?"

"Yes, sir. I wouldn't have stayed, but I was that taken aback. I heard him say he'd never made another will. 'So if young Carr was to murder me tonight you'd come in for quite a tidy fortune.' That's what he said, and it give me the creeps all down my back—I don't know what I felt like. And I pulled the door to and come back to the kitchen."

The Superintendent said, "H'm—" And then, "Who is young Carr?"

"Miss Rietta's nephew, Mr. Carr Robertson."

"Why should he want to murder Mr. Lessiter—do you know of any reason?"

"No, sir, I don't."

"You don't know of any quarrel between them?"

"No, sir—" She hesitated.

"Yes, Mrs. Mayhew?"

"Mrs. Fallow—she helps here, and she goes to Miss Cray Saturdays—she passed the remark only yesterday that it was funny Mr. Lessiter never coming down here these twenty years and not knowing scarcely anyone in the village, after being born and brought up here. And I said there wasn't hardly anyone would know him by sight, and she said, 'That's right,' and she brought in Mr. Carr's name. Seems she'd heard him say he wouldn't know Mr. Lessiter if he was to meet him —but I don't know how he come to say it."

The Superintendent said "H'm—" again. He may have suspected a red herring. He brought Mrs. Mayhew firmly back to the events of the night before.

"You returned to the kitchen without hearing any more. That would be at something after nine?"

"Yes, sir—the news was on."

Sweat broke on her temples. She didn't ought to have said that, she didn't. Cyril fiddling with knobs—Cyril turning on the news—

"You'd left the wireless running?"

The flush burned in her cheeks, her feet were like ice. She said,

"Yes, sir—it's company."

"Did you go back to the study again later?"

She nodded.

"I thought I would."

"What time would that be?"

"A quarter to ten. I thought Miss Rietta would be gone."

"Did you see Mr. Lessiter then?"

"No—" It was just a whisper, because it came over her that when she opened the study door that second time Mr. Lessiter might have been dead, and if she had opened it a little farther and gone in she might have seen him lying there across the table with his head smashed.

It wasn't Cyril—it wasn't Cyril—it *wasn't* Cyril!

"What did you do?"

"I opened the door like I did before, quiet. There wasn't anyone talking. I thought, 'Miss Rietta's gone,' and I opened the door a little farther. Then I see Miss Rietta's coat lying across a chair."

"How do you know it was hers?"

"There was a bit of the lining turned back—a kind of a plaid with a yellow stripe. It's Mr. Carr's coat really—an old one he leaves at the Cottage. Miss Rietta will wear it if she feels that way."

"Go on."

"I shut the door and come away."

"Why did you do that?"

"I thought Miss Rietta hadn't gone. The room was all quiet. I thought—"

It was plain enough what she had thought. Everyone in the village knew that James Lessiter and Rietta Cray had been young lovers. Everyone would have thought it quite right and proper if they had come together again. The Superintendent decided that Mrs. Mayhew was speaking the truth. He wondered if she had anything more to tell. She had an uncertain look, her hands fidgeted in her lap. He said,

"Well—what is it?"

Mrs. Mayhew moistened her lips.

"It was the raincoat, sir—I couldn't help but notice—"

"What did you notice?"

"The sleeve was hanging down so I couldn't help but see it."

"What did you see?"

Mrs. Mayhew said in a trembling voice,

"It was the cuff—it was all over blood—"

Chapter Eighteen

BETWEEN ELEVEN AND twelve o'clock Superintendent Drake made his way to the White Cottage. Miss Cray was at home. She received him in the dining-room, very pale, very much under control. Sizing her up from between his red eyelashes, he considered that she might have done it, but if she had, he would have expected her to keep her head and not go leaving her raincoat for anyone to see. If she *had* left it. Perhaps she hadn't—perhaps she was still in the room when the housekeeper opened the door the second time. Mrs. Mayhew said she had seen the coat at a quarter to ten with blood on the sleeve, but it wasn't there in the morning when Mayhew discovered the body. It might have been removed at any moment between those times. If Miss Cray was still in the room at a quarter to ten she could have taken it when she left.

If she had already gone she could have come back for it later
—she, or the nephew.

He had these things in his mind as he took the chair she
offered him and sat down. Constable Whitcombe sat down too,
took out a notebook, arranged himself for writing.

Drake watched her closely when he introduced James
Lessiter's name. Her face did not change.

"You have heard of Mr. Lessiter's death?"

He got a quiet, rather deep-toned "Yes."

"When did you hear of it, Miss Cray—and how?"

"Mrs. Welby came over. She had heard of it from the
milkman."

"He hadn't let you know?"

"He calls here before he goes to Melling House."

"You were very much shocked and surprised?"

"Yes."

The dining-table was between them. His chair was turned
sideways. He shifted it now so as to face her more directly.

"Miss Cray, can you give me an account of your movements
last night?"

"My movements?"

He was conscious of a slight feeling of satisfaction. When
anyone repeated what you had said, it meant just one thing,
whether it was man or woman. It meant that they were rattled,
and that they were playing for time. He thought Miss Rietta
Cray would do with a bit of jolting. He proceeded to jolt her.

"You have your nephew staying with you—Mr. Carr Robertson? And a friend of his—?"

Rietta Cray supplied the name.

"Frances Bell."

"I'd like to know what you were all doing last night."

"We were here."

"You didn't leave the house—are you quite sure about that?
Mrs. Mayhew states that she heard Mr. Lessiter address you
by name when she went to the study door just before nine."

The bright colour of anger came into her cheeks. Her grey
eyes blazed. Had the Superintendent been a student of the
classics, he might have been reminded of Virgil's famous line
about the "very goddess." Not knowing it, he nevertheless
received a general impression that Miss Cray was a high-
tempered lady and a surprisingly handsome one. And he
thought he had jolted her all right. But she fixed a steady gaze
on him as she said,

"Mrs. Mayhew is perfectly right. I went up to see Mr. Lessiter between half past eight and a quarter past nine."

"You were back here at a quarter past nine?"

"Miss Bell will tell you so. She remarked when I came in that I had missed the news."

"Miss Bell? What about Mr. Robertson?"

"He wasn't in the room."

"Was he in the house?"

"No—he had gone for a walk."

The Superintendent lifted his reddish eyebrows.

"At that hour!"

Miss Cray replied, "Why not?"

He left it at that.

"Miss Cray, I must ask you about this visit of yours to Melling House. You are an old friend of Mr. Lessiter's?"

"I haven't seen him for more than twenty years."

"You were engaged to him?"

"More than twenty years ago."

"There was a breach—a quarrel?"

"I wouldn't call it that."

"Who broke off the engagement?"

"I did."

"Why?"

"I think that's my business."

The grey eyes were angry, scornful, and very fine. He didn't know when he had seen a finer pair of eyes. He thought a woman who could get so much angry scorn into a look might very well do murder if she was put to it. He said,

"Miss Cray, were you aware that Mr. Lessiter had made a will in your favour?"

"He showed it to me last night. I told him it was absurd."

"He had been burning your letters, hadn't he?"

"If Mrs. Mayhew was listening at the door she will have told you that."

"He had been burning your letters, and then he showed you the will—it's dated twenty-four years ago. And he threw that on to the fire too."

She said, "No—it was I who put it on the fire."

"Oh, it was you?"

"The whole thing was absurd—a will made during a boy-and-girl engagement. I put it on the fire, but he took it off again. If Mrs. Mayhew was listening she ought to be able to confirm that. I would like you to understand that Mr. Lessiter was—" she hesitated, and then said, "amusing himself."

"You mean he wasn't serious?"

"Of course he wasn't serious. He was teasing me. He saw that I was vexed, and it amused him."

"You were vexed?"

"I disliked the whole thing very much."

He leaned towards her, an elbow on the table.

"Was Mr. Lessiter amusing himself when he spoke of the possibility of his being murdered by Mr. Carr Robertson?"

She could control her voice, but not her angry blood. She felt it burn her face as she said,

"Of course!"

"You mean that he was joking. But there must be some reason even for a joke. Why should he make a joke like that?"

"I can't tell you."

"Mrs. Mayhew states that she heard him say at one time that he didn't particularly want to be murdered. And later on, after he had shown you the will and read out from it, 'Everything to Henrietta Cray, the White Cottage, Melling,' she heard him say, 'If young Carr was to murder me tonight, you'd come in for quite a tidy fortune.' He did say that, Miss Cray?"

"Something like it. I've told you he wasn't serious. People don't say that sort of thing seriously."

"There's many a true word spoken in jest. Murder is serious, Miss Cray. Mr. Lessiter was murdered last night. As far as we have any evidence, you were the last person to see him alive. Why did you go and see him?"

She said with composure, "Why should I not?"

"I was asking you why you did."

"Why does one do anything? I thought I would."

"It was a sudden impulse?"

"You may call it that."

"Were you wearing a coat?"

"Certainly."

"What kind of a coat?"

"I took one that was hanging in the hall."

"Was it a coat belonging to your nephew?"

"It may have been—I took the first one I touched."

"You were wearing it when you went?"

"Naturally."

"And when you came back?"

Her colour rose again. She looked at him.

"Superintendent Drake, what is all this about my coat? I wore it, and it's back on its hook in the hall."

"Then I should like to see it, Miss Cray."

If she had kept a brave front it covered a bitter cramping fear. She had made up her mind to tell the truth as far as she could, and when she got past that point to hold her tongue. There was more than one old coat hanging up in the hall—she could say that she had worn one of the others. . . . She couldn't do it. If you have been brought up to tell the truth, it is very difficult indeed to tell a lie, and next door to impossible to make it convincing. Rietta Cray had a direct and simple nature and a truthful tongue. She couldn't do it. In a moment she was to be glad of this, because Inspector Drake walked down the line of coats, turning each one back so as to see the inner side. When he came to a plaid lining with a yellow stripe, he stopped, unhooked the coat, and turned back to the dining-room.

She followed him with a cold drag at her heart. If he had recognized Carr's raincoat, it was because someone at Melling House had seen it and described it to him. Mrs. Mayhew had been listening at the door. If she had opened it a little way she might have seen the coat. That wouldn't matter, because the Superintendent already knew that she had talked with James Lessiter. But suppose Mrs. Mayhew had come back later and seen the coat as it was when Carr brought it home—the sleeve soaked with blood, the whole right side of it splashed and stained—

It was a darkish morning. He took the coat to the window and examined it by touch and eye. He exclaimed,

"It's damp!" And then, "This coat has been washed." He held it at arm's length with his right hand and pointed with his left. "All this right side has been washed—you can see the watermark. Why did you wash it, Miss Cray?"

She wasn't angry now, she was controlled and pale. She made no answer.

"Was it to wash the bloodstains out? Mrs. Mayhew saw the sleeve hanging down, and the cuff was stained with blood."

"I scratched my wrist."

It was the truth, but it sounded like a lie, and not even a good one. She pulled away the sleeve of the jumper, and he said what Carr had said last night,

"That little scratch!"

Those were the words, but the tone added something. It said plainly and scornfully, "Can't you do better than that?"

She made up her mind that she wouldn't answer any more questions. She was perfectly plain about it, standing up straight and looking him in the face.

"I've told you the truth, and I have no more to say. . . . Yes, I'll sign a statement if you want me to, but I won't answer any more questions."

He folded up the raincoat, put it down on the window-seat, and asked to see Miss Frances Bell.

Chapter Nineteen

FANCY CAME INTO the room, her blue eyes very wide. They observed the Superintendent, and didn't think much of him. Like Mrs. Mayhew, Miss Bell had no affection for a foxy man. The young man with the notebook at the end of the dining-table was better—quite nicelooking in fact. She wondered, as she always wondered about any new young man, whether he could dance. Such a lot of nice boys couldn't, and the boys that could weren't always the nice ones. With these simple thoughts in her mind she sat down in a chair which faced the window, thus affording both men an unshadowed view of her quite incredible complexion.

Constable Whitcombe was not unaffected. He gazed, at first in doubt, but later with heart-felt appreciation. If Superintendent Drake had any such feelings he concealed them perfectly, and produced his questions in the impersonal manner of a conjurer pulling rabbits out of a hat.

They began by being very small rabbits, and Fancy received them in an amiable manner. She agreed that she was Miss Frances Bell, and that she was a friend of Mr. Carr Robertson's. She was staying at the White Cottage on a short visit. Oh, no, she wasn't engaged to Mr. Robertson—nothing like that—they were just friends. She didn't know Mr. Lessiter at all. She didn't even know him by sight—not till she saw his picture in the paper.

"And when was that, Miss Bell?"

"Oh, that was last night."

He leaned towards her across the table.

"Now, Miss Bell, I want you to tell me just what happened last night."

The blue eyes opened slowly.

"How do you mean, happened?"

"Well, just what you did, all three of you—you, and Miss Cray, and Mr. Robertson."

"Well, Carr and I were up in town for the day. We got back a little before seven, and we had supper, and Mr. Ainger came in with some picture-papers. Is that what you want?"

"Yes. What time would that be?"

"Well, it would be about a quarter past eight."

"Go on."

"Mr. Ainger went away—he had to go and see an old woman who was ill. And then Miss Cray went to the telephone—it's in here. Carr and I looked at Mr. Ainger's papers."

"Was that when you saw Mr. Lessiter's picture?"

"Yes—only it was Carr that saw it, not me. I can show it to you if you like."

He said, "Presently will do for that. So Mr. Robertson saw this picture. What did he say when he saw it?"

The blue eyes wavered from his. It is a fact that not till this moment did it occur to Fancy that what Carr had said could have any possible connection with James Lessiter's death an hour or two later. If Carr himself or Rietta Cray had pointed out the connection by asking her to forget what had happened between Henry Ainger's agreeable departure and Carr's tempestuous one, she would doubtless have done her best to comply, and under expert cross-examination she would almost certainly have failed. But neither Carr nor Rietta had been able to bring themselves to suggest any such thing. To each of them it would have looked like an admission of guilt. The mere possibility was dismissed with angry pride. Fancy was therefore left to her own direction. A bewildered, frightened feeling swept over her. Carr's voice rang harshly in her memory: "So it's you—you swine!" She couldn't tell the Superintendent that. But what was she to tell him? When you can't tell the truth and you haven't had any practice in telling lies, what do you do? She hadn't the faintest idea. An exquisite flush rose and glowed under the fine skin, the blue eyes slowly filled. Constable Whitcombe found himself quite unable to look away. The Superintendent remained unaffected. He thought the girl was a fool, and he thought he was going to get something out of her. He repeated his question rather sharply.

"What did he say?"

There was a pause. The blush faded. Fancy said,

"Miss Cray came back, and Carr went out for a walk."

Drake rapped on the table.

"You haven't answered my question, Miss Bell. Mr. Robertson saw this picture of Mr. Lessiter. What did he say when he saw it—did he appear to recognize it?"

"Well, sort of—"

"You'll have to explain that. I want to know what he said."

Fancy did the best she could.

"He—he seemed surprised."

Drake was quick.

"Do you mean that he recognized the picture, but he was surprised to find it was Mr. Lessiter?"

"Yes—sort of."

"He was surprised. Was he angry?"

What could she say to that? Angry wasn't the word. She didn't know what to say. She didn't say anything. Her silence gave consent.

"He was angry when he recognized Mr. Lessiter—very angry?"

She sat looking down at the table, damp lashes shading her eyes.

Drake rapped again.

"He recognized Mr. Lessiter, and he was angry. Why? I think you know. If you don't tell me, someone else will."

Fancy's head came up with a jerk. She whisked away two angry tears. Her eyes blazed.

"Then you can go and ask them!" she said. Her native Stepney rose vigorously.

"Miss Bell—"

She pushed back her chair and jumped up.

"It's no use your asking me a lot of questions I can't answer. If you've got other people who can answer you, go and ask them. If you want to know what Carr said, ask him—he can tell you a lot better than me!"

The Superintendent maintained his poise. He said,

"I can't force you to answer my questions, Miss Bell, but when the inquest is held you will be obliged to attend and give your evidence on oath. Meanwhile it is of course your duty to assist the police in every way you can."

She stood there. Now that he had made her angry, she wasn't frightened any more. He couldn't make her speak—he had said so himself. She wouldn't answer anything she didn't want to. She wouldn't answer anything about Carr being angry.

Now he was speaking again.

"Mr. Robertson went out, and then Miss Cray went out?"

"Yes."

"How long were they away?"

"They didn't go together. He went out of the front door, and she went out at the back."

"All right, we'll take them one at a time. When did Miss Cray come in?"

What did he want with all these silly questions? What was he getting at? She said,

"It was a quarter past nine—the news had just finished."

"And Mr. Robertson?"

"I don't know—I went to bed."

"You didn't hear him come in?"

"No, I didn't. I can't tell you any more about anything."

He said, "Just a minute, Miss Bell—it was after Mr. Robertson had recognized the picture that he went out, didn't he?"

"I told you he did."

"What time was that?"

"It was half past eight. I looked to see because of the wireless programme."

"Mr. Robertson recognized this picture and almost immediately went out of the house. He was angry, wasn't he? Did he bang the door?"

He'd trick her, would he? Fancy's temper boiled over.

"Ask him!" she said and ran out of the room. The dining-room door fell to behind her with a resounding slam.

Constable Whitcombe so far forgot himself as to whistle.

Chapter Twenty

CARR HAD WALKED into Lenton at very much the same pace as he had used the night before. He found Jonathan Moore in his shop discoursing at leisure with old Lady Fitchett. The contrast of her square bulk and gruff manners with Jonathan's distinguished height and polished courtesy would have entertained him at any other time. As it was, he chose the other side of a Chippendale bookcase and made for the door at the back of the shop.

It took more than a bookcase to deflect Lady Fitchett's interest. Her attention wandered from the Hispano-Mauresque plates which were under discussion. She demanded with energy,

"Who was that?"

Jonathan Moore looked vague.

"I really couldn't say."

"Well, he's just walked through your private door as if it belonged to him."

"One of the men perhaps—"

"One of the men, my foot! It looked like Carr Robertson."

"Then it probably was."

Lady Fitchett snorted. Nothing made her so angry as an attempt at concealment.

"Jonathan, you are prevaricating! Is Carr back?"

"I believe so."

"High time, if you ask me! Has he made it up with Elizabeth?"

She got a most charming smile.

"You had better ask him."

There was a second snort.

"You want a great deal too much for these plates."

"Think of my income tax."

"Think of mine!"

Carr went through the private door and whistled. The sound made Elizabeth's heart turn over. This was what he had always done—come through the door and stood just inside it whistling, so that if she was upstairs she would hear him and come down, and if she was in the parlour she had only to call, "Come in!"

She called, and next moment there he was, and she was in his arms. Something about the way he held her set her wondering. Then all in a minute she was afraid. He didn't kiss her, he only held her as if he couldn't bear to let her go.

"Carr—what is it?"

She had to say it again. Even then there was a pause before she got her answer. The hard grip relaxed. He set her away at arm's length, his hands heavy upon her shoulders, and said,

"You'll have to chuck me again."

"Carr!"

"Somebody murdered James Lessiter last night, and they'll be pretty well bound to think it was me."

She kept her eyes very steadily on his face.

"And was it?"

He laughed harshly.

"There—you see—you'd believe it yourself for twopence!"

Elizabeth's eyes were very bright—hazel eyes as clear as water.

"Not for twopence—only if you said so."

"Well, I didn't. I might have before I saw you, not afterwards. And anyhow I shouldn't have gone up behind him and brained him with a poker."

"Carr!"

"Somebody did. I found him—"

"You didn't go there!"

"Oh, yes, I did. It's no good telling me I was a fool—I know that now. I didn't know he was going to be murdered. I was going to see him and have a show-down and bang the door on the whole thing—finish—new book, chapter one—wedding-bells and a happy-ever-after story. It seemed like quite a good idea. You see if he was going to be up and down to Melling House, and I was going to be to and fro to the Cottage, we were more or less bound to meet. I thought it would be better to have a show-down in decent privacy. We could then cut each other at leisure, and Melling would stop asking us anywhere together. It did seem a good idea."

She stood there, her head with its windblown hair a little tilted back on the long, slender throat, her eyes never wavering from his face.

"What happened? Tell me."

He told her about seeing Catherine's light and going on up

to the house, then round the corner, up the two steps, and in through the door that stood ajar, and the drawn curtains. He spared her nothing—the man lying dead across his desk, the stained poker, the raincoat with its drenched sleeve and splashed skirt.

When he had finished she said,

"It's a pity you wiped the poker."

"I had to—in case—"

She shook her head.

"It was a pity. You said you wouldn't have come up behind anyone and hit them over the head with the poker. Did you think Rietta would?"

The colour came up into his face.

"I didn't begin to think until a lot later than that. That damned coat was there—the next I knew I was wiping the poker. I don't suppose it made a ha'p'orth of difference. The murderer had been thinking all right. He either slipped on that coat to do the job, or else he messed it up afterwards—on purpose. Do you think he would have overlooked the poker?"

"No—" She thought for a moment. "Carr, if you took the raincoat away and didn't leave any fingerprints yourself, I don't see what there is to make anyone think it was you."

He said grimly, "There's our little Fancy—that's all. She and I were looking at Henry Ainger's papers together, when I turned up James Lessiter's picture. I can't remember what I said, but she will. Something on the lines of 'I've got you, you swine!' After which I proceeded to bang out of the house."

"Won't she hold her tongue? Couldn't you have asked her—"

He was frowning fiercely.

"No!"

Then all at once he relaxed.

"It wouldn't be a bit of good if I did. The child is quite artless, and they'd have it out of her. Better let her say her piece and take the line that we haven't got anything to hide."

The telephone bell rang. Elizabeth walked over to the table and lifted the receiver. He heard her say, "Yes, he's here." Then she looked over her shoulder.

"Carr, it's Rietta. She wants to speak to you."

Rietta Cray's deep voice came to him along the wire. She was speaking German. She said,

"It's not too good, Carr. They have taken away the coat. We didn't wash it well enough. Mrs. Mayhew knows I was there.

She listened. She heard him speak about his will and say, 'If young Carr murders me tonight, you'll come in for a tidy fortune.' It's not so good, is it? I thought you had better be warned."

There was a click as she hung up. He did the same, and turned, repeating what she had said. At the end he used the words Rietta had used.

"Not so good is it?"

She said soberly, "They'll find out who did it. But you ought to have legal advice."

"Yes—I'll go and see old Holderness."

"He's not—a criminal lawyer."

His mouth twisted.

"Gosh—that rubs it in!"

"I'm sorry."

"You needn't be—we're going to have to go through the mill all right. To come back to Holderness. He knows us all, and if we're too criminal for him, he can turn us over to somebody else. He'll know who we'd better have. I'll go round and see him."

"Come back and tell me what he says."

He nodded, went a step or two towards the door, and came back.

"Elizabeth, last night is washed out. We're not engaged."

Her eyes were brighter than ever. She was tall enough to put her arms round his neck without standing on tiptoe. Her locked hands drew his head down until she could lay her cheek against his.

"Aren't we?"

"No."

"All right, darling, I don't mind—we'll get married instead."

"Elizabeth!"

She said, "Don't be silly! Run along and see Mr. Holderness!"

Chapter Twenty-one

MR. HOLDERNESS SAT back in his chair. His florid colour stood high, but the black brows which made such a handsome contrast with his thick grey hair were drawn together in a frowning line, and the eyes they shaded had a worried look. It had become more and more pronounced as Carr's story proceeded. He drew in his breath now and let it out again in gusty protest.

"My dear Carr!"

Carr's lip twitched.

"Damnable—isn't it?"

Mr. Holderness drummed on his knee with big white fingers.

"You realize, of course, that if all this comes out, you'll be in very serious danger of arrest."

"I've done nothing else but realize it."

"Of course there is no reason why it should all come out."

"How do you mean?"

"Who knows that you went up to Melling House last night? How many people have you told?"

Carr jerked a shoulder.

"Rietta—Elizabeth—you—"

"Then don't tell anyone else. They must hold their tongues, and you must hold yours."

He said slowly, "I'm not sure about that."

"You'd better be."

"I'm not sure. You see, they know Rietta was there—they'll say she had a motive. She went up to warn him that I'd found out about him and Marjory. He told her some cock-and-bull story to soothe her down. Then he produced a will he had made in her favour when they were engaged—and Mrs. Mayhew was listening at the door! She heard him say, 'If young Carr murders me tonight, you'll come in for a tidy fortune.' That puts it fair and square on Rietta—or me. If I back out, it just leaves Rietta. Besides, everything else apart, Fancy will tell them about my recognizing his photograph and slamming off in a blazing rage."

Mr. Holderness set his jaw in a very obstinate manner.

"There will be time enough for you to commit suicide if it proves that Rietta is in real danger. I really must insist that you hold your tongue."

Carr cocked an eyebrow.

"Suicide?"

Mr. Holderness stared at him angrily.

"You might just as well, if you propose to tell the police, firstly, that you recognized James Lessiter's portrait last night as that of the man who seduced and deserted your wife, and secondly, that you were present on the scene of the crime at or about the time it was committed. You can do as you like, but I refuse to be associated with any such folly. Rietta is not, to my mind, in anything like so serious a position as you are. No one who knew her would believe that she would commit a sordid crime for money."

Carr gave a half absent nod, and then came out with,

"I wonder who did do it—"

The large, well kept hand rose and fell upon Mr. Holderness's knee.

"James Lessiter had made a great deal of money. That kind of fortune is often made at the expense of somebody else. It seems improbable to me that it was a local crime, though quite possibly pains may have been taken to make it look like one. I wonder, now, whether there is anything missing. I had a very careful inventory taken after Mrs. Lessiter's death. I think the first thing for me to do will be to communicate with the police and suggest that they should check on it. There were some valuable things in that house. If any of them are missing—well, that will be something for the police to follow up. And meanwhile I insist that you keep your own counsel. If you are asked to make a statement you will say that, acting under the advice of your solicitor, you prefer to say nothing until the inquest. That will give me time to find out how the land lies."

Carr nodded briefly, his mind elsewhere. He appeared to be debating something. An air of hesitation in the end resolved itself. He said,

"Do you know anything about Cyril Mayhew?"

The hand on Mr. Holderness's knee jumped slightly.

"Why do you ask that?"

"Idle curiosity. I asked Rietta about him the other day, and she shied off the subject. What has he been up to?"

"I believe he has been in trouble."

"With the police?"

"I am afraid so. He was bound over."

"What had he done?"

"Theft from his employer, I believe. The Mayhews felt it very much. It's hard when an only son goes wrong. They are most respectable people."

"Only children get spoilt. Cyril was a horrid little squirt."

"Parents are often extremely unwise. What made you ask about Cyril Mayhew?"

Carr looked at the ceiling.

"Nothing—except that I saw him at Lenton station last night."

Mr. Holderness knit his brows.

"Are you sure?"

"Absolutely."

"Did you speak to him?"

"No. I only saw him by accident. He got out of the last carriage and cut away behind the booking-office. It didn't strike me he wanted to be spoken to. I've been wondering if he went home last night."

Mr. Holderness said,

"I think we will ask the police."

Chapter Twenty-two

WHEN RIETTA CRAY had finished her telephone call she remained sitting at the writing-table upon which the instrument stood. She liked a good-sized table, and was grateful for the room afforded by a bulging bay which broke the front wall of the dining-room. She stayed there, the dining-table at her back—one of the old-fashioned Victorian kind built to take a family and much too large for its present surroundings. Neither it nor the heavy upright chairs with imitation Sheraton backs and seats of faded brocade were in the least suited to a cottage, but Rietta had grown up with them, and it would never have occurred to her to change them. They belonged to the time when her father had the leading practice in Lenton and they lived in a big house on Main Street. That time seemed very far away. Dr. Cray died, and they came to live at the White Cottage. Nearly thirty years ago. A long time.

She sat looking at the telephone for some minutes before

she stretched out her hand and again lifted the receiver. The voice which answered her from the exchange was not Gladys Luker's, as it had been when she rang up Carr. It was Miss Prosser who said, "Hullo!" and that made everything a great deal easier. Everyone in Melling knew that Gladys listened in if she thought there was going to be anything worth listening for, but Miss Prosser couldn't be bothered. She was not deaf but a little hard of hearing, and as she put it herself, "I've got enough to do getting hold of what I've got to."

Rietta gazed at the number she wanted and had to repeat it —"21 Lenfold." She wondered whether Miss Prosser would remember that it was Randal March's private number. On being made Chief Constable of the county he had bought an agreeable small house some miles out of Lenton, installed an elderly married couple to do for him, and developed an interest in the garden, which boasted a tiny stream, a water-lily pond, and a patch of woodland.

As she waited for the call to come through she told herself that she was a fool to ring up, but that she would probably be preserved from the consequences of her folly because as likely as not Randal wouldn't be there. He might if he was coming home to lunch. But then it was quite likely that he wouldn't be coming home to lunch. He might even be coming over here —if Superintendent Drake had had time to make his report.

Someone lifted the receiver at the other end. Randal March said, "Hullo!" The colour ran hot to the roots of Rietta's hair. Why in the world had she rung him up? A most preposterous piece of folly. She heard her own voice say in deep, calm tones,

"Is that you, Randal?"

He sounded warm and pleased as he said, "Rietta!"

Her flush died down. She thought, "He hasn't heard yet —it's all right." She said,

"I just wanted to ask you something. It's about your Miss Silver. You know she's staying here with Mrs. Voycey who is an old school friend of hers—"

"So I gathered. Have you met her? Unique, isn't she?"

"Yes. Randal, how good is she—at her job, I mean?"

He laughed.

"Oh, definitely top of the class! No, that's the wrong simile. She's the teacher up at the desk, with the rest of us sitting in a row in the infants' class."

Her voice went deeper, slower.

"Do you really mean that? Seriously?"

"Quite seriously. Rietta, why do you ask? Is there anything wrong?"

"Quite a lot." She slipped into French just in case. "James Lessiter was murdered here last night."

"So I am informed. I haven't had a report yet."

Rietta Cray said, "I'm the chief suspect, Randal," and rang off.

Chapter Twenty-three

RANDAL MARCH LOOKED up from the typewritten sheets which he had just been reading. He went through them without comment until he came to the end. When he let the last page fall Superintendent Drake said,

"Well, sir, there you have it. There's no denying there's quite a serious case against Miss Cray."

March smiled.

"My dear man, it's absurd. I've known Miss Cray since she was a child. She is quite incapable of hitting anyone over the head with a poker."

Drake stiffened. So that was going to be the way of it. Class-consciousness rose in him, bitter as brine. He had known her since she was a child—so she couldn't do murder! All these people hung together! His thin nose had a pinched look as he said,

"That's what somebody always says until it's proved. A murderer is just like anyone else until you get him on the end of a rope."

Randal March had the pleasant, even temper which goes with a good physique, good health, and a good conscience, but at this moment a jag of pure rage went through him. It surprised him a good deal. He found it uncomfortably revealing. He was, fortunately, able to control any outward manifestation and merely repeat his former assertion.

"Miss Cray is quite incapable of murdering anyone."

That pinched look extended to the rest of Drake's features. One might have said a hungry fox.

"What we have to look at is the evidence, sir. If you will just cast your eye over those statements again you will see that

Miss Cray has quite a strong motive. She was engaged to this Mr. Lessiter a matter of twenty years ago or more. She says she broke off the engagement herself, but she declines to say why, and the local opinion is that he treated her badly. I don't say there's actual evidence that she bore him any grudge, but she might have done. On the top of that he comes back here twenty years later full of money. Then we come to the events of last night. Mr. Carr Robertson refuses to make any statement. That, to my mind, is a very suspicious circumstance. I wouldn't think so much of it if he was older. It's more natural for a middle-aged person to be cautious, but it isn't natural for a young man of twenty-eight. It's highly suspicious. He knows something, and he's afraid it's going to look bad, either for himself or for Miss Cray, so he's holding his tongue. But look at Miss Bell's statement. She makes it perfectly clear that Mr. Robertson went banging out of the house because he had just seen a photo of Mr. Lessiter in a picture-paper with the name underneath. I find they had never met or seen each other, but the minute Mr. Robertson sees this photo with the name under it he recognizes it and rushes off out. Now the local talk is that Mr. Robertson's wife ran off to France while Mr. Robertson was in Germany. Nobody knew who it was she'd run off with. Then Mr. Robertson is demobbed and comes home. Presently his wife turns up ill. The man she went away with has left her flat. Mr. Robertson takes her in and nurses her, and she dies—a matter of two years ago. The talk is he's set himself to find out who was responsible. Mrs. Fallow that works for Miss Cray, she's got some story about a photo—says she heard Mr. Robertson tell his aunt he'd know the man if he saw him because Marjory—that's his wife—had a photo. Well, that's just local talk, but it fits in. Now come back to Miss Bell's statement and you'll see that no sooner has Mr. Robertson gone out by the front than Miss Cray goes out by the back. She picks up the first coat she comes to—it happens to be her nephew's—and she goes off up to Melling House, where Mrs. Mayhew hears Mr. Lessiter tell her about the will he made when they were engaged—'Everything to Henrietta Cray,' etc. And she hears him say, 'If young Carr was to murder me tonight, you'd come in for quite a tidy fortune.'" Drake paused, pleased with what he felt to be an efficient and convincing exposition.

Randal March said, "Well?"

"Well, sir, does that leave any doubt in your mind that Miss

Cray's reason for hurrying up to Melling House was to warn Mr. Lessiter that he might apprehend some act of violence on the part of Mr. Carr Robertson?"

Randal March smiled a little more pleasantly.

"If she took the trouble to go and warn him, then she didn't murder him. You're trying to have it both ways, Drake. I'm afraid you can't do that."

Drake's eyes narrowed between the red lashes.

"Wait a minute, sir—I don't think you've got the point. When she came up to warn him she didn't know about that will. They say he's worth the best part of half a million. You might come up to warn a man, and change your mind about it if it was going to mean half a million in your pocket."

Randal March had himself very well in hand. He maintained the exact shade of attention due to an efficient subordinate with whose conclusions it is impossible to agree. He had the air of giving due weight to the supposition that a hypothetical half million might have inspired Rietta Cray to hammer out a man's brains with a poker. Attention having been given to this theory, he shook his head.

"Not in character, I'm afraid."

Superintendent Drake pursued the theme.

"There's evidence which is going to take a lot of explaining away, if you don't mind my saying so. After refusing to explain why she was in a such a hurry, Miss Cray says in her statement that she picked up the first coat she came to—they hang in the passage, and she went out by the back door. The coat she did take was an old one of Mr. Robertson's. It has a plaid lining with a yellow stripe in it. Mrs. Mayhew's statement refers to this. When she went back to the study the second time and opened the door this coat was hanging over a chair. A bit of the lining showed, and she describes it. One of the sleeves was hanging down, and she says the cuff was all over blood. Miss Cray explains this by saying she scratched her wrist coming up through the wood. But mark this, sir—all the right side of that coat had been sponged down. It was hanging in among the others in the passage, and all one side of it still wet. I sent it right away to see what a test could make of it, and this is what I've got. I was on the phone to them, the last thing before coming out, and they say there are traces of human blood over the whole damp area. The right cuff must have been fairly drenched—there's quite a lot left along the stitched seam and where the lining is doubled over. There's no doubt at all that the staining was very extensive, and a great deal more than could be accounted for by a surface scratch. Miss Cray showed me her wrist, and the scratch theory just won't wash."

March turned over the sheets in front of him and picked one up.

Drake went on speaking.

"The only thing that would account for the condition of the coat is that it was worn by the murderer."

March looked up from the sheet he was holding.

"Mrs. Mayhew particularly says in her statement that she heard no sound in the room on this second occasion. That would point to Miss Cray having left. There is no proof that she was wearing the coat when it became so deeply stained. If she scratched her wrist as she says, there might have been enough superficial staining to attract Mrs. Mayhew's attention. And the murderer's. Somebody else's coat with somebody else's blood on it would be a bit of luck, not to be counted on, but certainly not to be overlooked."

"You are putting forward the theory that Miss Cray went home without her coat—it was a very cold night—and that someone else put it on to murder Mr. Lessiter. If that is so, how do you account for the fact that the coat was hanging up in her hall and had been washed? There is, of course, just one thing that would account for it—I've thought of that myself. If Mr. Carr Robertson came up to Melling House after Miss Cray had left he could have slipped on the coat—it was an old one of his own, you remember—and when he had done the murder he would only have to walk back to the cottage and make the best job he could of cleaning up the mess he had got it into. There's no doubt where that job was done. There's a little wash-place at the end of the passage. We found a smear on the underside of the basin, and a couple of splashes of blood on the floor—there's a dark linoleum and they didn't show. The coat must have been reeking wet when it was taken in there. I suppose they thought they had cleaned up, but there's usually something gets overlooked."

Randal March sat appalled. This was evidence which couldn't be dismissed with a shake of the head. Not evidence against Rietta—there reason continued to block the way—but the possibility of a strong case against Carr Robertson. If last night he had really identified James Lessiter with the seducer of his wife, it might prove to be a damnably strong case.

And Carr wasn't making any statement.

Chapter Twenty-four

"MAY I COME in, dear?"

Mrs. Voycey, who was doing accounts, turned her head. She beheld Miss Silver attired for walking, in her second-best hat which resembled her best so closely that it would have been indistinguishable from it but for the fact of being trimmed with a band of plain petersham instead of an abundance of satin loops. In either case there was a small nosegay of flowers on the left-hand side, but the everyday bunch was smaller, older, flatter, and consisted of a tired wallflower in a pale circle of mignonette, repeating the tones of the elderly fur neck-tie much treasured for its draught-excluding qualities. The black cloth coat remained the same whether it was Sunday or weekday, and so did the neat black laced shoes and black woollen stockings which it was Miss Silver's habit to wear from October to April, and sometimes beyond if the spring was a cold one.

Having entered and closed the door gently behind her, Miss Silver coughed. A capacious handbag depended from her wrist, and she wore black knitted gloves. She said,

"Such a terribly raw day. I hope I do not disturb you, Cecilia, but I have just received an invitation to lunch. I thought that you would have no objection to my accepting it."

Mrs. Voycey was amiable but surprised.

"An invitation to lunch?"

"Yes, Cecilia—from Miss Cray."

Mrs. Voycey said, "Oh—"

Since the arrival of the milkman with the first intelligence of James Lessiter's death the village news-service had been extremely active. Mrs. Crook had "popped out" to the general shop for a packet of cake-mixture, a thing which she ordinarily despised, and had there encountered a niece of Mrs. Fallow's who had almost, if you might put it that way, seen Mrs. Mayhew. The niece had been inspired to "step up" to Melling House with an offer of neighbourly assistance, and if she hadn't actually seen Mrs. Mayhew, she had seen and talked to Mrs. Fallow who had only just left her.

"Can't hardly lift her head, pore thing," said Mrs. Crook,

retailing the interview to Mrs. Voycey and her guest. "They've had the doctor to her, and he says it's the shock, and Mrs. Fallow's to stay and not to let her set her hand to anything. And from what Mrs. Fallow says there's been enough to give her a shock—blood everywhere, and Miss Rietta Cray's coat soaked with it up to the elbow."

Mrs. Voycey said, "Nonsense, Bessie!"

Mrs. Crook stood her ground.

"That's what Mrs. Fallow told her niece, and she come straight from Mrs. Mayhew that saw it. And they do say the pore gentleman left everything to Miss Cray, and the will lying there right under his hand with his blood on it. Mr. Mayhew seen it when he found the body, and he says it's right enough someone had been trying to burn it, because it was scorched all down one side."

"Rietta Cray wouldn't harm a fly," said Mrs. Voycey.

Mrs. Crook maintained an immovable front.

"Flies don't make wills," she said darkly. "But they do say there was maybe more in it than that. It seems Mr. Carr, he comes bursting out of the Cottage round about half past eight. Jim Warren that goes with Doris Grover, he happened to be passing, and he tells Doris that if ever he sees anyone in a passion it's Mr. Carr. Pretty well beside himself, he says, and goes past him like anything wound up, and he hears him say Mr. Lessiter's name swearing-like. Horrid, Jim says it was —made him think of a dog that's got something between its teeth worrying it. Doris says he come in looking all anyhow, and she says, 'What's up, Jim?' and that's what he tells her. Always a bit soft Jim was from a child. Doris says she had to get him a nip of her father's whisky, and Mr. Grover didn't half carry on."

At this point Miss Silver intervened.

"Which way was Mr. Carr Robertson going?"

Mrs. Crook stared in a contemplative manner. Miss Silver phrased her question again.

"Was Mr. Carr going in the direction of Melling House?"

Mrs. Crook considered. She took her time.

"Couldn't have been," she said at last—"not if Jim met him. Up from the other side, that's the way Jim would come. First of the small cottages on the left, that's where the Warrens live, and that's the way Mr. Carr must have gone, because Jim says their dog run out and barked at him as he went past. But they do say it could have been Mr. Lessiter that ran off with Mr.

Carr's wife, and that maybe it all come out and Mr. Carr killed him for it."

It was with all this in the background that Mrs. Voycey heard Miss Silver say that she was going out to lunch with Rietta Cray and said, "Oh—" It was so very unlike her to have no more than that to say that Miss Silver instinctively paused for what would come next.

An expression of lively interest overspread Mrs. Voycey's face, and she exclaimed,

"Maud! Has she consulted you? Professionally, I mean. Oh, I do wish she would!"

"She has asked me to lunch," said Miss Silver.

Mrs. Voycey clasped her hands. Three handsome rings which were a little too tight for her gleamed under the pressure.

"Then you must certainly go. Really, you know, it is quite providential that you should be staying here, because nothing will ever make me believe that Rietta would do anything like that. It's really too shocking and it only shows what a dreadful thing gossip is. The breath is hardly out of that poor man's body before everyone in the village is saying he ran away with Carr's wife, and that Rietta murdered him because he had left her a fortune. I mean, it isn't sensible, is it? I don't suppose he ever set eyes on Marjory. I'm sure I only saw her half a dozen times myself, and if I ever did see a young woman whom I disliked—dreadfully pretty and not a bit of heart. And Carr was engaged to such a nice girl before he met her. Marjory simply grabbed at him and he went down like a ninepin, and that nice Elizabeth Moore went off and joined the A.T.S. I believe she commanded an anti-aircraft battery or something like that. And Marjory ran away like I told you, but I can't see why it should have had anything to do with James Lessiter."

Miss Silver coughed.

"Perhaps, dear, I should be going—"

It took her another ten minutes to get away.

At the White Cottage she found that Miss Cray was not alone. Mrs. Welby was with her but almost immediately rose to go. Miss Silver, observing her with attention, took note of the fact that her make-up, discreet and carefully applied as it was, had as its foundation that rather ghastly pallor which no make-up can quite conceal. No one seeing Miss Silver would have supposed her to possess the eye of an expert where cosmetics were concerned, or indeed in any other direction, yet at a single glance she was aware of that underlying pallor, and of the fact that the foundation cream, the powder and the rouge with which Mrs. Welby had done her best to conceal it were the best and most expensive of their kind. They had been applied with a high degree of art, and, for a woman who had run over before lunch to see an old friend and country neighbour, Catherine Welby had taken a good deal of trouble with her clothes. Whereas Rietta Cray was in a short brown tweed skirt and an old sweater of natural wool, both very well worn, Catherine looked as if everything she had on had been most carefully chosen. There was nothing that was not suitable, but the general effect was that everything was a little too new. She might have taken part just as she was in the mannequin parade of some house which specialized in country clothes. The grey tweed coat and skirt were perfectly cut. The jumper, of a paler shade, displayed the very latest neckline, her smart brogues the very latest heel. If she was bareheaded, it was not from informality, but because it was the fashion. Not a wave of the golden hair was out of place.

Had her acquaintance with Mrs. Welby been less recent, Miss Silver would have recognized that she had somehow passed the intangible line which separates enough from too much. Even without this longer acquaintance she was aware of something of the sort. It seemed to her that there was an indefinable hardening, the failure of something which might have given life and freshness to the whole.

In the few minutes which elapsed between greeting and goodbye Miss Silver dealt with the impressions she was receiving. She was too intelligent herself not to recognize intelligence in others. She recognized it in Catherine Welby, and a quotation from an older poet than her favourite Lord Tennyson presented itself:

> "Still to be neat, still to be drest,
>   As you were going to a feast . . .
> Lady, it is to be presumed . . .
>   All is not sweet, all is not sound."

There was intelligence up to a point, but to overdo an effect is not intelligent. Perhaps it was only against this background of sudden tragic death and gathering scandal that the effect appeared in this instance to be overdone. Perhaps—

Her eyes followed Catherine Welby thoughtfully as she left the room.

Chapter Twenty-five

WHEN THE DOOR closed there was a little pause. To Rietta Cray it was like the moment when you stand above an icy pool and brace yourself to take the plunge. There came to her the thought that it need not be taken. Her confidence was still her own. She had only asked Miss Silver to lunch. If anything more had been implied, it could still be ignored. She became aware of Miss Silver's regard, and lifted her eyes to meet it.

Something incomprehensible happened. She experienced what many of Miss Silver's clients had experienced. When she thought about it afterwards the image which presented itself was that so often seen during the war, the spectacle of a house with the front ripped right off and every room on every floor open and bare to the passing eye.

Miss Silver's eye did not pass. It dwelt upon her, calmly and thoughtfully exploring. A smile changed the small, neat features. It imparted confidence, it diffused reassurance, and above all it charmed. Then the whole astonishing experience was over. It was the little dowdy ex-governess who said,

"How can I help you, Miss Cray?"

Rietta had no answer ready. She found that she was being invited to sit down in her own house. A feeling of beneficent authority diffused itself. She leaned forward and said with a child's simplicity,

"We are in great trouble."

Miss Silver coughed gently.

"I believe I know something about it."

"Everyone does. I suppose it is always like this, only you don't think about it until it happens to yourself. Anyone can ask you anything. If you don't answer, they make something up. There's no privacy any more."

"Does that matter so much, Miss Cray?"

"You mean have I got anything to hide? I suppose I have. I suppose everyone has things that they would rather not have trampled upon—" On the last words her voice went down into the depths.

Miss Silver looked at her with concern. She saw painful evidences of a sleepless night and continuing strain. The fine eyes had marks like bruises under them. She said in her most practical voice,

"What did you have for breakfast?"

"I don't know."

Miss Silver coughed.

"It is just one o'clock. You have asked me to lunch, and I think we will defer our talk until we have had something to eat. Perhaps you will allow me to help you."

Rietta felt surprised and relieved. She wouldn't have to talk about it yet. The thought of lunch was rather dreadful, but it deferred the moment when she would have to talk about James Lessiter. She said,

"Everything is ready—Fancy will help me bring it in. That's the girl who is staying here—Frances Bell. You will meet her, and Carr. I expect that's a good thing."

In the course of her professional activities Miss Silver had become accustomed to the kind of meal in which she now participated. The general feeling of gloom and apprehension, the sporadic outbursts of conversation checked and impeded by the fear of saying something which would better have remained unsaid, the alternating patches of silence during which no one can think of anything to say—all these were perfectly familiar. She herself could always produce a small even trickle of talk, but she did not always choose to do so. She sometimes found it instructive to watch how people behaved under the stress of silence. Today she made it her concern to see that Miss Cray partook of a sufficient meal, and in this she ultimately succeeded. It became easier to eat something than to keep on saying no, and after the first few mouthfuls Rietta was aware of her own need for food.

Observing Mr. Carr Robertson, Miss Silver could not fail to be aware of his disapproval. Men, she reflected, had so little power of hiding their feelings. From the earliest stage they presented their frame of mind to the world in a manner which was often sufficiently naïf to be engaging. She could have no doubt at all that Mr. Carr thought her a meddling old maid. He reminded her of more than one little boy who considered himself affronted at having to share his sisters' lessons. She regarded him with indulgence.

For Fancy Bell in her scarlet suit she had a faint kind smile. A guileless creature, and an open book to a tactful and experienced questioner. She had no doubt that if Fancy knew anything, she herself would know it before very long. As to Mr. Carr—well, her immediate business was not with him.

To Rietta the time passed at once slowly and too fast. Since Carr and Fancy volunteered to wash up, she could count on no more delays. She found herself in the sitting-room with Miss Silver, who had the air of being quite at home there. She had removed her tippet and laid aside her coat, revealing beneath it a dress of sage-green wool with some odd little bits of embroidery down the front. Her favourite brooch, a rose carved in black bog-oak with an Irish pearl at the centre, fastened the neck of this garment and slightly dragged it down. A fine gold chain looped up on the left-hand side supported the pince-nez used for small print or in a bad light. The capacious black bag reposed on the floor beside her open, and served to confine the ball of pale blue wool from which she was knitting a cosy coat and knickers for her niece Ethel Burkett's little Josephine. She kept her hands low in her lap, holding the needles after the Continental fashion as she and Cecilia had been taught by the German mistress, Fraülein Stein, when she was at school. It has the great advantage of making it almost impossible to watch either one's hands or the work. Miss Silver rarely glanced at the rapidly clicking needles or the lengthening strip of blue. She gazed placidly at her hostess and said,

"Before you tell me anything I must ask you in what way you think I may be able to help you."

Rietta felt the icy shock which she had been anticipating. She heard herself say in a lost voice,

"I don't know—" And then, "I hoped—"

Miss Silver said in a grave manner,

"I must ask you to think clearly about this. I can take no case with any other object than that of discovering the truth. I cannot undertake to prove anyone innocent, any more than I would undertake to prove anyone guilty. I feel obliged to make this perfectly clear to an intending client. Perhaps you would like a little more time to think it over."

Rietta's shivering reluctance was gone. The plunge had been taken. She looked steadily at Miss Silver and said,

"No—the truth is what I want."

The needles clicked, the pale blue strip revolved.

"Then, Miss Cray, perhaps you will tell me just what happened last night."

Rietta put up a hand and pushed back her hair.

"I don't quite know where to begin. . . . James Lessiter was an old friend—at one time we were engaged. I broke it off, and until the day before yesterday I hadn't seen him for twenty-three years. I met him then in the evening after supper at Catherine Welby's—she lives in the Gate House at the entrance to the drive of Melling House. James was perfectly easy and friendly. He walked home with me and discussed one or two things about which he thought I might have known his mother's intentions. I couldn't help him, but it was all quite easy and friendly. Then last night—"

She broke off, because now she had to speak, not about herself, but about Carr. If he were to be left out of it, she might as well not speak at all. But if he were to be brought in, how could she be sure that she would not be bringing him into danger? The answer to that came flat and practical—"You can't keep him out."

Her distress evoked a look of reassurance and a "Pray continue, Miss Cray."

She went on in short, bald sentences—things like "Mr. Ainger came in and left some papers. . . . After he had gone I went to the telephone. . . . When I came back Carr went out. . . ."

That wasn't any good. She knew that it wasn't.

Miss Silver said gently,

"I think you will have to tell me why he went out." Then, after a pause, "Miss Cray, you will have to make up your mind whether you intend to trust me. Half measures are quite useless. As Lord Tennyson so beautifully says, 'And trust me not at all, or all in all.'"

"It isn't—for myself—"

Miss Silver coughed.

"Consider what you imply. You can lay your own thoughts and motives bare to me because you know that you are innocent. When it comes to Mr. Carr, are you not so sure?"

Rietta cried out. It was a sound without words, sharp with pain and protest.

Miss Silver said with quiet authority,

"You must make up your mind."

There was a silence. Rietta got up and went to the window. Standing there with her back to the room, she said,

"When you've said a thing you can't take it back. He didn't do it. It's not true to say that I'm not sure, but things can be made to look—as if—he had a motive."

Miss Silver knitted. After a little while she said,

"Come and sit down. Emotion is a distorting factor. We need to be practical and clear. Here is a point I would like you to consider. If Miss Bell was present when Mr. Carr left the house so suddenly, she as well as yourself is aware of why he did so."

"Yes."

"How long do you suppose she would withstand a cross-examination? You know her better than I do."

Rietta said, "No—you're right—I had better tell you. Carr saw James Lessiter's picture, and when he saw it he recognized the man who had seduced and deserted his wife. I suppose you have heard about that."

"Yes."

"I think there may have been extenuating circumstances. James says she left him and had been living with another man. It's quite likely. But Carr didn't know that. He rushed out, and I went up to Melling House to warn James." She told the rest of the story simply and clearly. He had been burning her letters. He had shown her the old will made when they were engaged. She had scratched her wrist going up through the wood. It had bled a good deal and stained the cuff of her raincoat. James had lent her his handkerchief to staunch the blood. . . . No, she hadn't brought it away with her. And she hadn't brought the raincoat either. She had taken if off when she went in, and had forgotten it when she came away.

Miss Silver listened with close attention. At this point she coughed.

"How did you come to forget your coat, Miss Cray? It was surely a very cold night."

The fine grey eyes met hers with perfect candour.

"I never thought about it."

"You came out into the cold and forgot that you had left your coat?"

"Yes, I really did."

"I am not doubting that, but I should like to know what made it possible for you to forget. You left Mr. Lessiter and came out into the cold without noticing it. Did you leave him alive?"

The angry colour came to Rietta's face.

"Of course I did!"

"Did you part on friendly terms?"

Rietta's head was high.

"No, we didn't. I was angry. That's how I came to forget my coat."

"What were you angry about?"

"He made me angry. It was nothing to do—with this, or with Carr."

Miss Silver gazed at her with mild persistence.

"Did he make love to you?"

"No—no—it wasn't anything like that. It was a business matter—not even my own business. It concerned a friend."

Miss Silver continued to gaze for a moment. Then she stooped down and unwound some lengths of pale blue wool from the ball lying beside her chair. Resuming her knitting, she enquired with the air of one who changes an unwelcome subject,

"You say that you were called to the telephone while Mr. Carr and Miss Bell were looking at the papers left by Mr. Ainger. Since the question of time may be involved, perhaps the person who called you up could corroborate you on this point."

"Fancy says it was twenty past eight. She listens incessantly to the wireless, so she always knows the time. She says Carr and I went out at half past eight."

Miss Silver beamed.

"Your caller could corroborate that. Who was it?"

"It was Catherine Welby."

Miss Silver coughed.

"And you were talking for ten minutes. Miss Cray—what were you talking about?"

Rietta felt as if she had missed a step in the dark. There should have been something solid under her foot, but it wasn't there. The colour drained away from her face. Concealment is an art which requires much practice. She had never acquired it. She looked helplessly at Miss Silver and beat about in her mind for something to say. She found nothing better than,

"We were talking."

"On a matter of business?"

"I suppose you might call it that."

"Connected with Mr. Lessiter?"

Rietta said, "Oh—"

She was so plainly taken aback that Miss Silver was answered. She knitted rapidly whilst a number of small circumstances came together in her mind—Catherine Welby's pallor and her look of strain; the fact that James Lessiter had walked home from the Gate House with Rietta Cray and talked, not about old times, but about his mother's intentions with regard presumably to some disposition of her effects; the ten minutes' conversation with Mrs. Welby about business; the angry parting between Rietta Cray and James Lessiter after a conversation on business—business which involved a friend.

From this train of thought the word business emerged with a good deal of emphasis—business connected with James Lessiter and his mother's effects. Scraps of Cecilia Voycey's gossip came back in an illuminating manner. Her needles clicked busily. When she spoke again it was to return to an earlier topic.

"You say that you came away from Melling House and left your raincoat behind you?"

"Yes."

"Then I presume that it is in the possession of the police."

Miss Cray's hesitation in answering this question was so marked that when she did at last say, "Yes," she encountered a look of the most stringent enquiry. With a hortatory cough Miss Silver said,

"Just why did you find that question so difficult to answer? Are you not sure whether the police have the coat?"

This time there was no hesitation. Rietta said,

"Oh, yes, they have it."

"They informed you of that?"

"They took it away—from here."

"Did you go back for it?"

Rietta's lips moved, but no sound came from them. She shook her head.

Miss Silver stopped knitting for a moment and leaned forward.

"Miss Cray, you possess information which is vital to your case. You can impart or withhold it, but if you do not trust me, I cannot help you." Then, after a slight but significant pause, "If you did not bring the raincoat back, it is quite plain that it was Mr. Carr who did so."

Rietta turned as pale as if she had been struck. Then the colour rushed into her face.

"Yes—you're right. I must tell you. It's no use thinking that everything won't come out. Carr walked into Lenton. He went

to see Elizabeth Moore. They were engaged before he met
Marjory—his wife. I hoped they would make it up some day
when they met again. They are really suited, and they cared
very much. Marjory was a madness—a very tragic one for all
three of them. Last night Carr went straight to Elizabeth. I
think he was afraid of what he might do. I'm trusting you—I
think he might have done something dreadful when he first
rushed out of the house. But he didn't, he went to Elizabeth.
She has taken him back. Don't you see he wouldn't do
anything violent after that? He was happy and satisfied. You
don't do murder when you're feeling like that. All he wanted
to do was to close that chapter of his life and have done with it.
He went up to Melling House, and found James lying there
dead."

"Why did he go to Melling House?"

"I asked him that. He said it seemed the natural thing to do.
He wanted to close the whole thing down and be done with it,
and to do that he felt that he had to see James and tell him that
he knew. Then they could avoid each other, as he put it,
decently."

Miss Silver said, "I see."

Rietta put up her hand to her head. The long, beautifully
shaped fingers pressed against her temple.

"He went up there and found James. My raincoat was lying
over a chair. It was most horribly stained. The right cuff and
sleeve were soaked." Her voice had become strained and
toneless. "Miss Silver, you asked me if I was sure that Carr
didn't do it. I am quite, quite sure, and I can tell you why I am
sure. He thought I had done it. He came down here with the
raincoat and asked me why." Her hand fell into her lap again.
"I'm not sure—I'm really not sure—whether he thinks so still.
I don't think he does with his feelings, but I think he does with
his mind. That's why he tried to get the stains out of the coat."

Miss Silver said, "Dear me!" The words, mild in themselves,
carried a considerable weight of disapproval.

Rietta drew in her breath.

"All the right side of the coat was wet when the police came
this morning. They took it away."

Miss Silver coughed.

"Unless the washing was extremely thorough, traces of
blood will be found. You are quite clear that the stains were far

more than could be accounted for by the fact that you had scratched your wrist?"

Rietta shuddered. She said,

"The sleeve was *soaked*."

Chapter Twenty-six

MISS SILVER STAYED until after three o'clock. By the time she resumed her coat, her yellow fur tippet, and her warm black woollen gloves, one whole side of little Josephine Burkett's woolly jacket had been completed and cast off. At least an inch of the second front had made its appearance as a pale blue frill. In her professional capacity it may be said that she now possessed quite an accurate picture of what had taken place the previous evening, in so far as this was known to Rietta Cray. A very short conversation with Fancy had elicited a few extra details. Fancy was, in fact, only too anxious to talk to someone who wasn't the police and who was trying to help Carr and Miss Cray. In the circles of her origin there had been a wary feeling that however respectable you were you didn't get matey with the police. When people live packed together in very crowded districts their lives and interests are closely knit. A touch upon one part of the fabric is felt throughout the whole—people hold together. It would never have occurred to Fancy that a friend might betray you to the police. She talked freely.

Miss Silver came away with quite a factual impression of Carr Robertson's behaviour when he had recognized James Lessiter's photograph.

"He did look dreadful—" Fancy thrilled in retrospect— "white as a sheet. I'm sure he could have gone on as a ghost without a bit of make-up. He regularly frightened me. Miss Cray came into the room, and said, 'Carr!' She was frightened too, you know. He did look dreadful. And she put her hand on his arm, but he didn't take a bit of notice, just went on pointing at the picture. And then he said, 'Is that James Lessiter?' and she said, 'Yes.' And he said, 'He's the man I've been looking for—he's the man who took Marjory away.' She was his wife, you know, and if you ask me, he was well rid of her, but that's what he said—'He's the man who took Marjory

away. I've got him now!' and off out of the room and out of the
house, and the door banging. I knew he'd got a temper, but I'd
never seen him like that before."

Miss Silver coughed, and enquired whether Fancy had
communicated these interesting particulars to Superintendent
Drake. An outraged flush deepened the wild rose colour under
the delicate skin.

"Oh, no, Miss Silver, I didn't! They've got a way of making
you say things before you know you've done it, but I didn't tell
him what Carr said—I wouldn't do that!"

Carr Robertson having gone out directly after lunch, Miss
Silver had no opportunity of interviewing him. She considered
that on the whole she had enough to think about. Making her
way across the Green, she observed that Mr. Ainger had
emerged from the Vicarage gate and was taking the path which
skirted the village pond and came out a mere stone's throw
from the gate of the White Cottage. He might be going to visit
someone in the row of cottages alluded to by Bessie Crook, or
he might be going to call upon Miss Rietta Cray. If this were
the case, she hoped he would be tactful. In her experience
men were very rarely tactful—men in love practically never.
The Vicar was said to be in love with Miss Cray. If she had
been in love with him, it was probable that they would have
married years ago. If she were not, then the last thing she
would desire at this moment was an emotional scene. Miss
Silver shook her head slightly as she walked. With every
esteem for the manly virtues, and a good deal of indulgence
toward the manly failings, it had often occurred to her that in
moments of stress a man could be dreadfully in the way.

Something of the same feeling afflicted Rietta Cray as she
opened the door to her visitor. He had made for it in a
purposeful manner, sounded a vigorous tattoo with the
knocker, and immediately upon Rietta making her appearance
he had taken her by the arm and marched her into the
sitting-room, enquiring in a loud and angry voice,

"What is all this nonsense?" Then, as the light fell upon her
face and he saw how blanched and strained it was, he caught
her hands in his and went on more gently, "My dear, my dear
—you mustn't take it like this. No one but a preposterous
blundering fool could possible connect you in any way—"

His voice had mounted again—a fine organ well suited to
the pulpit. At such close quarters Rietta found it a little

overpowering. He was still holding her hands. She withdrew them with difficulty and said,

"Thank you, Henry."

"I never heard anything so outrageous! Just because you knew the man a quarter of a century ago!"

The words sounded bleakly on Rietta's ear. A quarter of a century—how sere, how dry, how melancholy it sounded. She forced a faint smile.

"You make me feel like Methuselah."

He brushed that aside with an emphatic gesture.

"Just because you knew the fellow all those years ago!"

"Not quite that, Henry. I'm afraid there's more to it than that. You see, I was there talking to him not very long before it must have happened. We—" she hesitated—"well, we quarrelled, and I came away and left my coat behind me. When I saw it again it was—rather horribly stained. A stupid attempt was made to get the stains out, and—well the police found it all wet, and they have taken it away. I don't see how they can help suspecting me. Poor James made a will in my favour when we were engaged. He showed it to me last night and told me he had never made another. Mrs. Mayhew was listening at the door, and she heard what he said. You see, they were bound to suspect me. But I didn't do it, Henry."

"You don't need to tell me that." He ran his hands through his thick fair hair and made it stand on end. "You must have the best advice—you must see a solicitor at once. You say your coat was stained when you saw it again. How did you see it again? Someone must have brought it to you. Was it Carr?"

"Henry, I can't tell you anything more."

"You're shielding someone. You wouldn't shield anyone but Carr—not in a murder case. Do you know what they're saying? Mrs. Crockett told my sister. Dagmar knows how much I object to gossip, but she thought she ought to tell me. They're saying that it was James Lessiter who ran away with Carr's wife. Is that true? Are you shielding Carr?"

"Henry—*please*—"

"Is it true?"

Those bright blue eyes of his were fixed upon her in a very angry and compelling manner. She said in a tired, flat voice,

"Carr didn't do it, and I didn't do it. I can't tell you any more than that."

She stepped blindly back until she arrived at a chair. If she had to go on standing she would fall. The room and Henry were beginning to come and go in a baffling mist. She sat down and closed her eyes.

And then in a moment Henry was on his knees beside her, kissing her hands, accusing himself, protesting his undying devotion.

"You've never wanted it, but you need it—Rietta, you do need it now. You want someone to stand up for you and fight your battles. If you'll only give me the right—let me give out our engagement and stand by you openly. It would knock out this stupid will motive if it didn't do anything else. I've got quite a lot of money, you know—from my old Uncle Christopher. It really is quite a lot. That would cut out any question of motive. And I wouldn't ask you to live with Dagmar—I know she's difficult. I could make her an allowance. Perhaps she could have this house if you came to the Vicarage."

Well might Miss Silver reflect upon the male lack of tact, but on this occasion it had a most salutary effect. The thought of Dagmar Ainger moving into the White Cottage and running it with iron efficiency warmed Rietta with a glow of restorative anger. The mist cleared, the floor became stable, the colour came into her cheeks. She sat up and pushed Henry Ainger away.

"Henry, for heaven's sake! You can't propose when I'm fainting!"

He wasn't really abashed. He let go of her hands, but remained upon his knees.

"Well, it seems to have brought you round." And then, "Oh, Rietta—won't you?"

The momentary force went out of her. She spoke the bitter, honest truth.

"I ought to say thank you, but I can't. I'm fond of you, but I don't love you. I can't even feel grateful to you—I can't feel anything—I'm too tired. Please go away."

He stared at her, dismayed, obstinate.

"There must be something I can do. Why won't you let me help you? You must have someone, and there isn't anyone else. Even if you hate me you might let me help you."

That "there isn't anyone else" bit deep. How deep, she didn't know till afterwards when the sharp hurt of the moment settled into a desolate aching. She caught her breath.

"*Please*, Henry—"

He got to his feet and stood there looking down on her, bewildered and thwarted.

"Even if you hate me you might let me help you."

Her mood changed. He did want to help her. Why should she hurt him? She said,

"Oh, Henry, don't be silly. Of course I don't hate you —you're one of my very best friends. And I'm not—not ungrateful—really not. If there's anything you can do, I'll let you do it. It's just that I'm so tired—I'm really too tired to talk. If you would please understand and—and go away—"

He had just enough sense to go.

Miss Silver received a telephone call that evening. Mrs. Voycey, answering the insistent bell, encountered a pleasant masculine voice.

"I wonder if I could speak to Miss Silver. I am an old pupil of hers—Randal March."

Miss Silver put down her knitting and approached the instrument.

"Good evening, Randal. It is nice to hear your voice. A very distinctive one, if I may say so."

"Thank you— I will return the compliment. I rang up to say that I have business in Melling tomorrow. I should not like to be there without paying my respects. It is a little difficult for me to fix an exact time, but it would not, I think, be earlier than half past three."

"I shall be at home. Mrs. Voycey, I believe, has to go to a meeting in the village hall. She would, I know, be very glad if you would have a cup of tea with me."

He said, "Thank you," and rang off without giving time for the affectionate enquiries for his mother and sisters with which she had been about to round off the conversation.

Returning to the drawing-room and resuming her knitting, she acquainted Mrs. Voycey with the substance of the call. She was obliged to exercise a good deal of delicate tact. There was nothing that Cecilia Voycey would have liked better than to throw over her meeting, remain at home, and entertain the Chief Constable at tea. She had to be dissuaded from this course without allowing it to appear that Randal March's visit was anything but a respectful gesture to the preceptress of his childhood's days.

Knitting briskly and completing the second side of little Josephine's jacket, Miss Silver condoled with her hostess.

"It is always so difficult when one would like to be in two places at once. You are the chairman of the Women's Entertainments Committee, I understand. So important, of course, with the Christmas season coming on, and you would be extremely difficult to replace in the chair. Unless perhaps Miss Ainger—"

Cecilia Voycey coloured quite alarmingly.

"My dear Maud!" she exclaimed.

Miss Silver coughed.

"I thought, dear, you mentioned that she was efficient."

"She is a complete kill-joy," said Mrs. Voycey in a tone of Christian forbearance. "I have never said that she wasn't efficient, and I never will, but you can't entertain people by being efficient, and when we get up a play or an entertainment we like to be able to enjoy ourselves and get some fun out of it. Dagmar Ainger's idea is to scold everyone till they are sulky, and then organize everything until you might just as well be a lot of chessmen on a board for all the life and go there is left in you. No, no—however much I should like to stay, I can't risk it. I am the only one who really stands up to her."

She continued for some little time to discourse upon the fruitful subject of Miss Ainger, finishing up with,

"And how Henry stands it, I can't imagine. But of course he can always say he has got to write a sermon and lock the study door!"

Miss Silver remarked mildly that interference in other people's affairs was a sad fault. She then steered the conversation into a channel which led in the most natural manner to Catherine Welby.

"A very pretty woman. She was with Miss Cray when I arrived this morning. Has she been a widow for long?"

"Oh, yes." Mrs. Voycey was full of information. "Of course everyone thought she was settled for life when she married Edward Welby. And then he died and left her with nothing but debts. I really don't know what she would have done if Mrs. Lessiter hadn't let her have the Gate House."

Miss Silver coughed.

"I should have thought she might have found Melling dull."

"My dear Maud, I have no doubt she does, but there is nowhere else where she could live so cheaply. She did go away during the war, and I believe she had a very pleasant job, driving for someone at the War Office. She used to drive Mrs. Lessiter's car a good deal. Of course we all thought she would marry again, and I believe she was practically engaged. But she had very bad luck—the man went abroad and was killed —at least that's the story. And then her job petered out and she came back here. Doris Grover tells Bessie she still gets quite a lot of letters from India, so perhaps something may come of that. And she goes up and down to town quite a lot. It would really be very much better if she were to marry again."

Miss Silver began to cast off her neat pale blue stitches.

Chapter Twenty-seven

THE CHIEF CONSTABLE laid down the papers submitted by Superintendent Drake. He saw before him an unpleasant and harassing day. He found Drake zealous, efficient, and extremely uncongenial. He allowed none of these things to show in face or manner.

Drake, always ready to break a silence, took up his tale.

"As you see, the medical report puts the time of death anywhere between nine and eleven. Well, we know he was alive at nine, because Mrs. Mayhew heard him speak about then. If we knew when he had his last meal we could narrow it down a bit, but with a cold supper left, we can't do better than that. They think it couldn't have been later than eleven. Well now, Mrs. Mayhew saw that raincoat with the blood on it at a quarter to ten. That means he was dead within half an hour of the time at which Miss Cray admits she was there. If he was dead then, Miss Moore's statement gives Mr. Robertson an alibi—he was with her until nine-fifty. But I've seen Mrs. Mayhew again, and I don't make out from what she says that there was all that blood on the sleeve when she saw it. She says it was stained round the cuff and she saw the stain. But when I put it to her, was it soaked, she said no it wasn't, it was just stained. And that would tie up with the scratch Miss Cray had on her wrist. The way I see it now is this. Miss Cray goes home, like she says, at a quarter past nine. Miss Bell corroborates this. We don't know why she left the raincoat, but leave it she did. My guess is, either there was a quarrel and she came away too angry to notice, or maybe he started to make up to her and she got nervous and cleared out. Now to my mind one of two things happened. Either Miss Cray gets thinking about that old will and the half million it would bring her, and then she remembers her raincoat and goes on up to get it back. Mr. Lessiter is sitting there at his table. She puts on her coat, goes over behind him to the fire as if she was going to warm herself, picks up the poker and—well, there you are. Then she comes home and washes the coat. It must have needed it!"

The Chief Constable shook his head.

"Impossible."

"Oh, I wouldn't say that, sir. It's one of the things that might have happened. The other is that Mr. Robertson took Melling House on his way back from Lenton. He gets there about half past ten, goes in, and sees the raincoat lying there—it's an old one of his own, you'll remember. He recognizes it, as Mrs. Mayhew did, by the lining. Remember too that he isn't wearing a coat himself. He picks it up and puts it on. He has only to make some excuse to go over to the fire. It was a bitter night, and he had been walking in the wind, so it would be easy enough. Well, there he is, with the poker to his hand, as you might say."

Randal March leaned back in his chair.

"Isn't all this a little too easy, Drake? Do you know what strikes me?"

"No, sir."

"I'll tell you. It's what you might call the supine acquiescence of Mr. Lessiter. Here is a young man with quite a bitter quarrel against him— I am assuming that it really was James Lessiter who had seduced Marjory Robertson—that's your theory, isn't it? Well, if you assume that, you also assume that Miss Cray's object in going to Melling House was to warn James Lessiter. Now on the assumption that Carr had just found out who was his wife's seducer, and that James Lessiter had just been warned that Carr had found him out, do you really think that an interview between them would have been conducted on the lines you indicate—Carr Robertson strolling in, putting on his raincoat, going over to the fire to warm himself, with James Lessiter just sitting at the table with his back to him? I'm afraid I find it quite incredible."

"Then it was Miss Cray."

"Who has a witness to prove that she returned home at a quarter past nine, and Mrs. Mayhew to prove that the coat was only slightly stained at a quarter to ten."

"That leaves more than an hour for her to go back, kill him, and bring the coat away."

"And no evidence to prove that she did any such thing."

Drake looked at him with narrowed eyes.

"That raincoat was hanging in her hall, sir. It didn't walk there."

A short silence ensued. Drake thought, "Set on getting her out of it, that's what he is. All the same these people —whoever's done murder, it can't be one of them. But you can't hush things up like you used to—not nowadays." He went on with his report.

"Mr. Holderness—he was Mrs. Lessiter's solicitor, and he's acting for Mr. Robertson, and I suppose for Miss Cray—"

"Yes, I know him."

"He was on to me this morning. It seems Mr. Robertson mentioned a circumstance to him which he thought we ought to know about. The Mayhews have a son, a lad of about twenty. He's been working in London. Mr. Robertson says he saw him get off the six-thirty at Lenton the evening of the murder. He and Miss Bell were on the train too. Well, it might be he'd made a mistake, or it might be he'd made it up, but as it happens, there's corroboration. The Mayhews go to relations in Lenton on their day out—name of White—tobacco and sweets, 16 Cross Street. We checked up on them for the Wednesday of the murder. You remember Mrs. Mayhew came home early, on the six-forty bus—well Whitcombe checked up on that. There's a boy there, Ernie White —seventeen—helps his father in the shop. When Mr. Holderness handed us this about young Mayhew I sent Whitcombe along and told him to find out if Ernie White had seen his cousin. You see, if he came down on the six-thirty he'd have to get out to Melling or find someone to put him up in Lenton. As it turns out, Whitcombe finds out that Cyril Mayhew had borrowed young Ernie's bike. Told him his father had forbidden him the house, but he was going to pop over and see his mother."

The Chief Constable straightened up.

"Why had Mayhew forbidden him the house?"

"Oh, he'd been in trouble. Spoilt only child brought up in a big house. Got a job in London. Caught taking money out of the till—put on probation. The officer got him a job. Mayhew wouldn't have him about the house. He's a very respectable man—and I don't mean just the ordinary respectable kind —he's something rather out of the way—very much respected in Melling. I suppose he felt it was a bit of a responsibility. Well, there you are—Cyril Mayhew came down on Wednesday night and borrowed his cousin's bike. And Mrs. Mayhew took the six-forty bus. There wasn't much doubt why she went home early. Mr. Holderness and his clerk are out at the House now with Whitcombe checking over the inventory. I looked in on my way, and they say there are some figures missing from the study."

"Figures?"

Drake consulted a note.

"Four figures—The Seasons—"

"Seems an odd sort of thing to be taken. What were they —china?"

"No, sir, gilt. I asked Mrs. Mayhew about them, and she says she thinks they were there Wednesday morning. She says they were after the style of those statues you see in a museum —not much in the way of clothes. About ten inches high."

If the Chief Constable felt inclined to smile he did not permit himself to do so. He said,

"They might be valuable, but it would be a connoisseur's value, and a strictly limited market. Of course there are people who specialize in that sort of thing. The boy might have been got hold of. What does Mrs. Mayhew say about his being there on Wednesday night?"

"Oh, she denies it—she would of course. Cries and says she hasn't seen him for six months. Well, everyone knows that isn't true. It's common talk he's been up and down, and Ernie White admitted it wasn't the first time he'd lent his bike."

March frowned.

"Look here, Drake, Mrs. Lessiter must have had an insurance policy. It was probably used as a basis for probate. What were those figures insured for?"

Drake looked alert.

"I put that point to Mr. Holderness, but it doesn't get us anywhere. The only separate items in the insurance were some of the old bits of furniture and the jewelry. Everything else was just lumped together and not put very high. The total amount including the house was ten thousand."

March said, "I think we might ask Miss Cray about those figures. She would know if they were still there when she left at a quarter past nine."

"That's what I thought, sir. Meanwhile I've taken steps to find out whether this young Mayhew is back at his job. I got the address from Mrs. Mayhew—a firm of house agents in Kingston. I've been on to the local people and asked them to keep an eye on the boy without letting him know. I thought better not startle him till we knew a little more."

"No—quite right, Drake." March glanced at his wrist-watch. "Well, if we are to see Miss Cray before we go up to the House we'd better be off."

Chapter Twenty-eight

AFTER ANOTHER NIGHT, sleepless except for indeterminate stretches of time in which there was a vague sense of half-recognized calamity, Rietta Cray was paler than yesterday but steadier—nerves taut and rigidly controlled. She opened the door to the Chief Constable and Superintendent Drake, and needed no reminder that this was an official visit. To the end of her life there would be nightmare moments when she would re-live that interview.

It was circumstance rather than detail which made the nightmare. They went into the dining-room, and Drake produced a notebook. Randal sat on one side of the table and she on the other. She had known him since she was ten years old. Lately, with Lenfold only five miles away, they had seen a good deal of one another, and the friendship of slow years had deepened into something closer. Each had felt a growing awareness of the other, and each had known where this was leading them. Now, with the table between them, they were strangers—the Chief Constable of the county and a pale, strained woman who was the leading suspect in a murder case. The position came near to being intolerable. Being what they were, they kept their dignity and observed the social forms. Mr. March apologized to Miss Cray for troubling her, to which Miss Cray replied that it was no trouble.

Horrified at his own feelings, Randal March continued.

"We thought you might be able to help us. You know Melling House well, don't you?"

Her deep voice said, "Yes."

"Can you describe the study mantelpiece?"

She showed a faint surprise. She said,

"Of course. It's one of those heavy black marble affairs."

"Any ornaments?"

"A clock, and four gilt figures—"

"Four gilt figures?"

"Yes—The Seasons."

"Miss Cray, can you tell us whether they were there on Wednesday night?"

The question took her back. She saw the study in a bright small picture—James with the light shining down upon him, his eyes watchful, teasing her—the littered ash of the letters she had written to him—his mother looking down on them, a handsome young matron in white satin with her ostrich-feather fan—the graceful golden figures posed on the black marble slab. She said,

"Yes, they were there."

"You are quite sure they were there when you left at a quarter past nine?"

"Quite sure."

There was a pause. He had to make headway against his crowding thoughts. How ghastly pale she was. She looked at him as if she had never seen him before. How else should she look? He was neither friend nor lover. He wasn't even a man, he was a police officer. That horrible moment was the first in which he consciously used the word love in his thoughts of Rietta Cray. He said,

"Can you tell us anything about these figures?"

She seemed to come back from a long way off. Something, some shadow, darkened her eyes. He thought she was remembering, and felt a sharp inexplicable pang. She said,

"Yes—they're Florentine—sixteenth century, I think."

"Then they are valuable."

"Very." Then, after a slight pause, "Why do you ask?"

"Because they have disappeared."

Rietta said, "Oh!" A little colour came into her face.

"Mr. Holderness is taking an inventory, and they are missing. Anything you can tell us will be a help in tracing them."

Her manner changed. It became controlled. She said in a hesitating voice,

"I suppose you know that they are gold?"

"Gold!" Drake looked up sharply, repeating the last word. March said, "Are you sure?"

"Oh, yes, quite sure. Mrs. Lessiter told me. They were left to her by an uncle who was a collector. They are museum pieces, very valuable indeed."

"And she had them out on the mantelpiece like that?"

"Oh, yes. She said nobody would know."

The Superintendent came in rather sharply,

"They're not even mentioned in the insurance."

Rietta turned her Pallas Athene look upon him.

"Mrs. Lessiter didn't believe in insurances. She said you paid away a lot of money and got nothing for it, and if you had anything valuable it was just drawing attention to it. She kept on her husband's insurance on the house and furniture, but she didn't bother about any of her own things. She had some valuable miniatures and other things. She said if you just left them lying about, everyone got used to them, but the more fuss you made, and the more you locked things up, the more likely they were to be stolen."

March was frowning.

"Would the Mayhews know about these figures, that they were gold?"

"I should think so. They are old servants."

"Was the son brought up here?"

"Yes—he went to Lenton Grammar School. He was rather a clever boy."

"Would he have known about the figures?"

"How can I tell?" Her look changed to one of distress. It went from one man to the other. "Why do you ask that?"

Randal March said,

"Cyril Mayhew was down here on Wednesday night, and the figures are gone."

Chapter Twenty-nine

IT WAS JUST before half past three that Mrs. Crook ushered the Chief Constable into Mrs. Voycey's drawing-room. Miss Silver rose to meet him with a good deal of pleasure. She could not even now look at the tall, personable man without recalling the frail, determined little boy who, after resisting all previous efforts at discipline, had by her own peculiar mixture of tact and firmness been guided into the paths of health and knowledge. She had never permitted herself to have favourites. It was perhaps on this account that, whilst referring to his sisters as "dear Isabel" and "dear Margaret," she had never been known to accord their brother any such prefix. Not even to herself would she admit that the conflict between them, and its happy termination, had given him a particular place in her affections.

"My dear Randal—how extremely kind!"

He had his customary smile for her, but it was a fleeting one. The ritual of their meeting proceeded.

"Your dear mother is well? I had a letter from her only last week. She is a most faithful correspondent. I think you will find this a comfortable chair."

The smile showed again for a moment.

"If you have heard from my mother you have had all our news. Margaret is well, Isabel is well, Margaret's last long-legged brat is shooting up. And now let us put the family on the shelf. I want to talk to you. Have you—perhaps I oughtn't to ask it, but I do—have you had any communication from Rietta Cray?"

Miss Silver's hands paused on the thin strip of knitting which represented, embryonically, the back of little Josephine's woolly jacket. She gave her faint dry cough and said,

"Why do you ask?"

"Because I very much want to know. She rang me up and asked me about you. I hoped you would have heard from her."

The busy needles moved again. She said,

"I have."

"You have seen her?"

"Yes, Randal."

"What do you make of it all?"

She lifted her eyes and looked at him steadily.

"What do you make of it yourself?"

He got up out of his chair and stood half turned away from her, looking down into the fire.

"She is quite incapable—" He had neither voice nor words to complete the sentence.

Miss Silver said, "Quite so. But there might be a strong case against her. She is aware of that herself."

He said, "Damnable—" and again had no more words.

Miss Silver failed to reprove him for the one which he had used. She continued to knit. After a little while she said,

"There is something which I think you ought to know—in your private capacity."

He pushed a log with his foot.

"I haven't got a private capacity. I'm a policeman."

She coughed.

"You are Chief Constable. You would not, I imagine, find it necessary to impart everything you knew to a subordinate."

He had a wry smile for that.

"Jesuitry!" Then, before she could summon up the look with which she had been used to quell him in the schoolroom, he went on in a voice quite broken away from its habitual control. "I'd better make a clean breast of it. You always do know everything whether one tells you or not, so its just as well to make a virtue of necessity. Rietta is completely incapable of harming anyone, but she is also completely incapable of defending herself at the expense of someone she loves."

Miss Silver answered this very directly. She did, in fact, justify his assertion that she always knew everything by answering what he had merely implied.

"You are afraid that Mr. Carr Robertson is the guilty person, and that Miss Cray will screen him at the risk of incurring suspicion."

He drove hard at the fire with his foot. A torrent of sparks rushed up. He said,

"Yes."

Miss Silver's needles clicked.

"I think I can relieve your mind. I was, in fact, about to do so. I have had no opportunity of questioning Mr. Carr, but one thing you may rely upon—Miss Cray has a very strong reason for being sure that he is innocent."

"What reason?"

"A most convincing one. In fact, one may say, the only one which could carry complete conviction. He thinks she did it."

Startled into turning quite round, Randal March said, *"What!"*

Miss Silver reflected that the scholastic profession was a discouraging one. How many times had she corrected such an interjection in the schoolroom, offering instead the politer "What did you say?" She continued without comment.

"Mr. Carr was at first quite sure that Miss Cray had done it. He did, in fact, come into her presence with the words, 'Why did you do it?' Even after he had heard all that she had to say, Miss Cray is of the opinion that he is still in doubt. This is naturally very painful to her, but it does relieve her mind with regard to his having any connection with the crime."

Resting both hands on the mantlepiece and staring down into the fire, March said,

"Then it was Carr who brought the raincoat back from Melling House."

She said very composedly, "You will not expect me to answer that."

"You needn't—it answers itself. He was with Elizabeth Moore until about ten minutes to ten. He took Melling House on his way home and brought the raincoat away. That means he either killed James Lessiter or found him dead."

Miss Silver coughed.

"I do not believe that he killed him. Miss Cray is very sure that he did not. She had to labour hard to shake his belief that she herself had done so."

He went on looking down into the fire.

"What is your own feeling? Do you believe he didn't do it?"

"Miss Cray is positive upon that point."

He said, "Oh, well—" Then he straightened up and went over to where he had left a small attaché case. He opened it, took out a sheaf of papers, and brought them to her.

"You had better read the statements and see what you make of them."

"Thank you, Randal."

He went back to his chair and watched her while she read. Her small, neat features remained expressionless. She made no remark, and never once looked up. When she had finished March said,

"There's a later development—you'd better hear that too. Mayhew's son is known to have been down here on the night of the murder. He is an unsatisfactory lad and has been in trouble with the police. He arrived by the six-thirty train and borrowed a bicycle in Lenton—which explains why Mrs. Mayhew went home early. Her husband had forbidden him the house. We have no absolute proof that he was at Melling House, but there isn't any reasonable doubt about it. Mrs. Mayhew denies the whole thing, and says she hasn't seen him for six months. It is quite certain that she is lying. And four sixteenth-century figures representing the Seasons which stood on the study mantel-piece are missing. Rietta says they were there when she left at a quarter past nine. She also says they were made of solid gold."

"My dear Randal!"

He nodded.

"A nice bright red herring, isn't it? Or is it?"

"It is extremely interesting. What is your view?"

He frowned.

"I don't know. Drake, who has been running the case against Rietta and Carr very hard, shows his versatility by producing a theory that Cyril had been put up to steal these valuable antiques, was caught out, and had recourse to the poker. I can't make that square with the facts. The figures were on the mantelpiece, and Lessiter was sitting at his writing-table when he was hit over the head. He had his back to the fireplace, and the blow was struck from behind. You can't square that with Cyril Mayhew being caught in the act of stealing four gold figures. But there is another possibility. You've got a plan of the room there—look at it. The door at which Mrs. Mayhew listened is in line with the fireplace. That is to say, it would be behind Lessiter's back as he sat at the table. Cyril could have opened that door, as his mother did, without being heard. He may not even have had to open it —she may have left it ajar. He could have come in in his stocking feet, reached the poker, and hit Lessiter over the head with it, all without being seen or heard."

"Extremely shocking."

He frowned more deeply still.

"It could have been done. The trouble is that I can't persuade myself that it *was* done."

Miss Silver gave a thoughtful cough.

"It is certainly difficult to see why the young man should go out of his way to do murder. He had only to wait for Mr. Lessiter to retire, when he could have removed the figures without this quite unnecessary bloodshed."

"You've hit the nail on the head—you always do! I can think of a dozen reasons for the theft, but not one for the murder. However badly I want a ram in the thicket, I can't persuade myself that Cyril Mayhew is going to fill the bill. He may or may not have come down to steal the figures. He may or may not have found Lessiter dead. He may or may not have then yielded to the sudden bright idea that all that gold might just as well be in his pocket."

Miss Silver coughed.

"What I cannot understand, Randal, is why such valuable ornaments should have been left out upon the study mantelpiece in what was practically an unused house. Mrs. Lessiter has been dead for two years. Mr. Lessiter had not been near the place for over twenty."

"Yes, it's a bit casual, but Mrs. Lessiter was like that." He told her what Rietta had said about the insurance, and then continued, "I asked Mrs. Mayhew just now, and she says the figures were put away at the back of one of the pantry cupboards after Mrs. Lessiter died, but she got them out again before Lessiter came down because they belonged to the study mantelpiece and she thought he would miss them."

Miss Silver said, "I see—" She knitted briskly. "Randal, what was Mr. Lessiter doing when he was killed? Was he writing?"

He gave her a curious look.

"Not so far as we can ascertain. He had obviously been clearing up—the fireplace was chocked with burnt stuff. On the writing-table itself there was only one paper—the old will leaving everything to Rietta. It had been scorched down one side and is rather badly stained. All the pens and pencils were in the pen-rack. All the writing-table drawers were shut."

"Then what was he doing at the writing-table?"

"I don't know."

She looked at him in her most serious manner.

"I think it may be very important to find out."

"You think—"

"I think there is a suggestion that some paper is missing. If so, it must be of vital importance. It may have been abstracted by the murderer. It certainly cannot have disappeared by itself. It is also quite certain that a man does not sit at his writing-table without any occupation. He must either be writing, reading, or sorting papers. The only paper before him was this short will. But both Mrs. Mayhew and Miss Cray make some slight reference to another paper. Miss Cray mentioned it to me."

"What paper?"

"The memorandum referred to by Mrs. Mayhew in reporting what she had overheard of the interview between Mr. Lessiter and Miss Cray. She reports him as saying that he had come across her letters when he was looking for a memorandum his mother had left for him."

"There is nothing to show that he had it out on the table."

"Not in Mrs. Mayhew's statement. But in conversation with me Miss Cray did refer to it. I asked her if she knew what was in it, and she replied that she believed it to contain information as to certain dispositions Mrs. Lessiter had made."

"Did she say that this paper was on the table during her interview with Lessiter?"

She weighed this thoughtfully.

"Not in so many words. I certainly received that impression."

"It may be important—" he paused, and added, "very important. Will you call her up and ask her whether the memorandum was actually there, in sight?"

"Yes, I can do that. The telephone is in the dining-room. You had better come with me."

Rietta Cray answered the call in her deep voice. No one would have guessed with what shrinking she had lifted the receiver. Miss Silver's voice brought relief.

"I hope I have not disturbed you. In describing your interview of the other night you mentioned a certain memorandum. Did you actually see this paper?"

The scene came back. James, with his smiling malice and his talk of her letters—"love's young dream.". . . And then, "The memorandum my mother left me . . . some people would be glad if they could be certain it was in ashes like your letters. . . ." Catherine's voice on the telephone—"He's found that damned memorandum."

The reassurance was all gone. She felt the buffeting of opposing loyalties—Catherine—Carr. It was characteristic of Rietta Cray that she did not think of herself. She tried to steady her thoughts, to determine just how much she could safely say.

Miss Silver repeated her question.

"Did you see this paper?"

She said, "Yes."

"Can you describe it?"

No harm in answering that.

"There were several sheets of foolscap. They had been folded up to go in an envelope, and taken out again. The envelope was lying there, and the foolscap half unfolded. I recognized the writing."

Miss Silver said, "Thank you," and hung up. She turned to face Randal March.

"You heard?"

He said, "Yes."

Chapter Thirty

MRS. CROOK BROUGHT in tea, and reported afterwards to her friend Mrs. Grover that the Chief Constable was ever such a nicelooking gentleman and ever so polite, "but no appetite for his tea, and the scones were lovely though I say it myself." In these circumstances the meal was not prolonged. When March refused a third cup of tea, Miss Silver coughed in a deprecating manner and said,

"I should like to ask you to do me a favour, Randal."

He smiled.

"What is it—the half of my kingdom?"

"I hope I should never ask you for what you would find it impossible to give."

"You alarm me! Let me know the worst!"

She gave him her own charming smile.

"It is really a very simple matter. I would very much like to see the study at Melling House."

"Well, it will make talk, you know."

"My dear Randal, do you imagine that people are not talking now?"

"Not for a moment. But I am not anxious that they should talk about a triangle consisting of you and me and Rietta Cray."

"It is quite impossible to stop people gossiping—especially in a village."

"What do you hope to effect? Drake is highly efficient. Everything will have been gone over with a microscope."

"I have no doubt of it."

Under her mildly obstinate gaze he gave way.

"Very well. You're taking an unfair advantage of me, you know. I am too anxious about this case to be sure of what I ought to do."

"My dear Randal—"

He pushed back his chair and got up.

"We had better make the best of a bad job," he said.

Mayhew, answering the door a little later, peered out. It was a dark afternoon, and the light on in the hall. He ought to be able to see who it was in the car, but he couldn't. He blinked up at the Chief Constable and wondered what had brought him back again. Dreadful times when you had to brace yourself up every time the front door bell rang.

He said, "Yes, sir?" in an enquiring tone, and went on bracing himself.

It appeared that no blow was about to fall. March was saying,

"I'm sorry to trouble you again. I just want to go through to the study. Nothing's been done to the room yet, I suppose?"

"No, sir. Superintendent Drake told me they'd finished and we could get on with it, but I thought I'd leave it till the morning."

"Oh, well, I shan't be long. I've a lady with me. She may find it cold waiting in the car. I'll just ask her if she would prefer to come in."

With this discreet piece of camouflage, March ran down the steps again. His voice came back to Mayhew at the door.

"It's cold for you here. Perhaps you would rather come in. I won't be any longer than I can help."

Miss Silver emerged. Mayhew knew her at once—the little governessy person who was staying with Mrs. Voycey. Mrs. Crook had a tale of her being some kind of a detective. Maybe she had a fancy to see the room where a murder had been done. Maybe not. It wasn't his business. He'd enough on his mind without troubling about other people's affairs. Anyway she was coming in with the Chief Constable.

He showed them to the study, switched on the lights, and went over to draw the curtains. Then he went across the hall, and through the baize door to the housekeeper's room where his wife sat dabbing her eyes and staring at the unwashed tea-things.

Randal March gave him time to get away before he said,

"Well, here you are. What do you make of it? The stain on the writing-table shows you where he fell forward. It won't come out. The grate was choked with burnt paper. Drake had it removed and gone through, but there was nothing left. If your memorandum went that way it's gone for good."

Miss Silver shook her head.

"I do not imagine that the murderer would have risked waiting to burn it here. The ash came from Miss Cray's letters."

His face was quite impassive.

"You are probably right. There was a full set of her prints on the mantelshelf—none anywhere else. If Carr was here, he did not leave any. Mrs. Mayhew's prints are on the outer knob of the door into the hall. That's where she stood and listened. The handle of the poker had been wiped clean, and so had the outer handle and edge of the glass door to the garden. The inner handle had Lessiter's prints."

"Yes—he opened the door to Miss Cray."

"I forgot to say that a stained half-burnt handkerchief was found on the top of the ash in the fireplace. It is Lessiter's own, and is presumably the one he lent Miss Cray when he noticed the scratch on her wrist. That is about all I can tell you."

She went over to the window and parted the curtains.

"Miss Cray found this door shut when she arrived. She knocked, and Mr. Lessiter let her in. She went away in a hurry, and may have left it ajar. I shall be glad if you will help me with a little experiment. I am going outside. When I have shut the door, will you go over to the other side of the writing-table and say anything you like in your natural voice?"

"All right. . . . Be careful—there are two steps."

When the door had closed behind her he crossed the room and stood before the empty hearth.

"Is this what you want? Can you hear me at all? One feels a good deal of a fool, saying something just for the sake of saying it."

The door opened and the curtains were divided. The pansies on Miss Silver's hat appeared.

"No more than on many social occasions, my dear Randal. I could hear you perfectly."

"Then come in out of the cold, my dear Miss Silver." He said the last words with a disarming smile.

She shook her head.

"Not just yet."

She disappeared again. A cold draught blew in. Coming out upon the steps, he found her standing on the path below, in the act of producing a torch from her capacious handbag.

"What are you looking at?"

She said, "This."

After the brightly lighted room the dusk baffled him. She switched on the torch and directed its disc of light upon a small patch of earth at the extreme edge of the lower step. He said,

"What of it?"

"It has dropped from someone's shoe."

"The men have been up and down."

Miss Silver coughed.

"It is soft black earth mixed with white particles. I think you will find them to be lime. The gardener who works at Cecilia Voycey's has been spreading lime upon the roots of her lilac bushes this week. Lilacs apparently require a great deal of lime. I am not a gardener, but that is what Cecilia tells me."

"Yes."

"The path leading to these steps is of flagged stone, but here, where the shrubbery ends by the window, there are lilac bushes. Let us see if their roots have been dressed with lime."

He came down to where she stood and parted the bushes. The torch sent a most efficient beam into the opening, picking out every small twig and passing to and fro across the earth below. It had been newly dug. Everywhere on the soft turned surface the light picked up those white particles. It picked up more than that—footprints deeply sunk in the soil.

March exclaimed, reached back with his left hand, and took the torch. It was plain enough that someone had stood among the lilacs. The deepest prints were farthest in. Someone had stood there. Four prints in all—one going in, one coming out, and the two deep ones nearest to the wall. They were the prints of a woman's shoe.

Randal March stood back and switched off the torch. His mind was dark. He had nothing to say.

Miss Silver coughed.

"You are troubling yourself unnecessarily. Miss Cray has a well shaped foot at least two sizes larger than the one which made those prints. She is a tall woman."

The darkness passed. He said,

"I'm a fool. As you probably guess, I'm—vulnerable."

She said, "Yes," very kindly. And then, "This is important evidence, Randal. It means that a woman who was not Miss Cray stood here among the bushes and afterwards ascended the steps. This would seem to indicate that she had suddenly to find some place of concealment. Let us say that she had come up here to see Mr. Lessiter, that she heard someone else approaching, that she stepped back amongst the bushes. It may have been Miss Cray who disturbed her. The thought then suggests itself that she may have mounted the steps and listened at the door. She could, in that case, have overheard the greater part of Miss Cray's interview with Mr. Lessiter.

We must not assume that she had any motive for wishing him dead. But if—I say *if*—she had such a motive, how suggestive that conversation would be. It would inform her that Mr. Carr Robertson had just identified Mr. Lessiter as the seducer of his wife, and that he had rushed out of the house in a state so alarming to Miss Cray as to bring her up to Melling House to warn Mr. Lessiter. She would also learn of the existence of the will benefiting Miss Cray. If you desired to commit murder, could you hope for a situation better calculated to enable you to do so with impunity?"

He laughed a little unsteadily.

"I suppose not. And now, I suppose, you are going to give me a description of the hypothetical murderess."

She said very composedly,

"Not at present. I think I had better leave you now. You will wish to communicate with the Superintendent and have casts made of these footprints. It is fortunate that no rain has fallen since Wednesday, but it is never safe to trust to a continuance of fine weather. I think it possible that a very careful search would disclose particles of lime on the upper step, and on the study carpet if this person did indeed enter the room. Have you a torch—or shall I leave you mine?"

"I have one in the car."

"Then I will leave you. The air is quite pleasant now. I shall enjoy the walk."

Randal March went back into the study and rang up Lenton police station.

Chapter Thirty-one

JONATHAN MOORE SET down his cup, said, "No, thank you, my dear," in rather an absent voice, and continued to gaze vaguely at his niece Elizabeth and at the gloomy young man to whom she had, rather precipitately he considered, reengaged herself. The radiant air of a betrothal was entirely absent. He might be out of touch with the world—it pleased him to think so, because there was a good deal about this post-war world that he disliked—but it was borne in upon him that Carr Robertson was being talked about, and that Elizabeth had been precipitate. The quality of the look with which he now

regarded Carr began to resemble that with which he was wont
to consider some object of doubtful authenticity. True, he had
known Carr for a long time, but look at the pedigree he had got
with that buhl writing-table! Fifty years in the one family, and
a receipted bill from the old marquis with the guarantee of
another hundred years before that. Yet at some time in that
hundred and fifty years a fake had been substituted. There are
times in a man's life when he may turn to fakery. Conscience
slips, the pressure of events comes down hard upon a weak
spot, and the honest man turns rogue. Easier still to picture
the sudden splintering control, followed by a quick protective
build-up to hide the smash.

Elizabeth could read his thoughts so well that it was with a
good deal of relief that she saw him shake his head doubtfully,
get up, and go out of the room. As the sound of his feet
retreated, Carr said,

"Not much doubt about what Jonathan thinks."

She gave him a strange look. Her eyes were always bright.
They had now the added brilliance of unshed tears. She said,

"Oh, yes, there's plenty of doubt. If there wasn't—"

"I wouldn't be here?"

She nodded.

"Something like that. Officially forbidden the house, and I'd
be getting out at the back to meet you in a purlieu."

"Would you?"

Her voice had all the sweetness in the world as she said,

"Yes, my darling."

It brought him to his knees beside her chair. Without word
or kiss he pressed his head against her shoulder, holding her
close. They stayed like that for a long time.

When he raised his head it was to say,

"Holderness has changed his mind. He says I'll have to
make a statement at the inquest but I'd better not wait for it to
be dragged out of me. He thinks it will make a better
impression if I go to the police now."

"Are you going to?"

"I don't know. I wanted to talk to you about it. It seems to
me the moment I make that statement they're bound to arrest
me—or Rietta." His face went hard and bleak as he repeated
the last words—"*Or Rietta.*"

"Carr!"

"The man was dead by half past ten, a couple of hours after I
had threatened him. Sometime in those two hours I was there,

and Rietta was there. Sometime in those two hours he was killed. And I fetched away Rietta's raincoat soaked with blood. The fact that it wasn't really Rietta's coat but an old one of mine just helps to distribute the probable guilt—Rietta gets half a million, and I get my revenge. The scales are about equal there. I should think it's fifty-fifty as between murder for money and murder for revenge."

He was still kneeling beside her, but drawn back from touching her. She made no attempt to bridge the gap between them, only looked at him and said thoughtfully,

"You think Rietta did it—"

He drew back farther still, got up, and stood there with his hands clenched.

"I don't think anything—I can't. I can just see the facts—I can't deal with them at all. If you put those facts before a thousand people, at least nine hundred and ninety-nine of them are going to say that if Rietta didn't kill him, I did. We shan't have a thousand opinions to spread the chances, we shall have twelve. It's very long odds they'd make it unanimous."

Her soft wordless protest fired him.

"What's the use? It lies between the two of us. If I didn't do it, Rietta did. Well, I didn't—so what?"

"Carr, you don't really think—"

"I told you I couldn't, and I can't. When I try, it always comes out like that—Rietta or me—me or Rietta."

"And when you don't think, Carr?"

"I get quite long sane patches when I know she couldn't have done it."

"I'm glad you call them sane."

The dark look had come back. He said,

"But we're not sane any longer, my dear—we're in a nightmare. When you're in Rome you do as the Romans do—*à la guerre comme à la guerre,* and all the rest of the proverbs. What in the name of all that is damnable has sanity got to do with our nightmare?"

She got up and came to him.

"Well, I think it's what is going to pull us through."

"*Us?*"

"Yes, darling."

His hand closed so hard upon her arm that she found a bruise there afterwards.

"If I was sure about Rietta I'd make this damned statement and be done with it."

"I'm sure."

"Why?"

"Oh, because—" She broke off with something that was half a laugh, and half a sob. "Oh, Carr, please wake up! It must be a very bad dream in which you can think that Rietta could creep up behind someone and hit him over the head with a poker. You couldn't let it worry you for a moment if you weren't fast asleep. Wake up! It's just too silly for words."

Chapter Thirty-two

MISS SILVER WALKED the drive. The air really was quite pleasant. Cold of course, but she was warmly clad—her tippet so cosy, her coat of such good strong cloth. She felt a sober gratitude for these and all her other blessings. There had been a time when she had expected to serve all her life in other people's houses with no prospect but that of an indigent old age. Now, thanks under Providence to her change of profession, she was in an enviable position of independence. She had a comfortable flat, an attentive and devoted maid, and an insurance policy which would enable her to continue these comforts.

It was really dark under the trees—not quite dark enough to necessitate the use of that excellent torch, a present from a friend and devoted admirer, Sergeant Frank Abbott of Scotland Yard, recently promoted to the rank of Inspector. The shrubbery was somewhat overgrown. She considered the sad condition of neglect to which labour shortages and heavy taxation had reduced so many fine country places. During her lifetime the whole way of living had changed. The good things of life were being spread more evenly, but it was sad to watch the passing of so much that was beautiful.

Just before she came to the two tall pillars which marked the entrance she turned to the right, took the narrow path which led to the Gate House, and rang the bell. Catherine Welby, opening the door, permitted herself to look a little more surprised than she would have done if her visitor had been anyone but Mrs. Voycey's dowdy old school friend. She could not for the life of her think why Miss Silver should be paying her a visit—elderly ex-governesses were not in the least in her line. She prepared to be bored, and with not at all too good a grace.

As it turned out, boredom was not the sensation which this interview was to arouse. Miss Silver, passing before her into the sitting-room, regarded it with interest. Surroundings are often an index to character. She noticed the brocade curtains, the pastel colouring, the quality of the furniture, all good, some of it valuable. Over the mantelpiece a round Dutch mirror with a cut-glass border charmingly reflected the scene. It reflected Catherine in a blue dress which matched her eyes.

Miss Silver seated herself and said gravely,

"You are wondering what has brought me here, Mrs. Welby."

"Oh, no." Catherine's tone was light—the small change of social observance, so carelessly scattered as to come very near to rudeness.

Loosening the tippet at her neck, Miss Silver said,

"I think so."

Catherine said nothing. She too had seated herself. Her beautiful dark blue eyes held an enquiring expression, the arch of her eyebrows was a little raised. She really might just as well have said, "What the devil do you want?" and had done with it.

Miss Silver did not keep her waiting.

"I am here because Miss Rietta Cray has asked for my professional assistance."

"Has she?" The eyebrows rose a little higher.

"Yes, Mrs. Welby. You are an old friend of Miss Cray's."

"Oh, yes." Catherine leaned sideways, took a cigarette from a tortoiseshell case, and struck a match.

Miss Silver coughed after the manner of a teacher who calls the class to order.

"It will not have escaped you that Mr. Lessiter's death has placed Miss Cray in a somewhat serious position."

The tip of the cigarette glowed. Catherine blew out a cloud of smoke.

"I shouldn't think it had escaped anyone."

"You are perfectly correct. As an old friend of Miss Cray's, you will, of course, be willing to do all that is in your power to clear her."

"I'm afraid there's nothing I can do."

"I think there is. As you are no doubt aware, Miss Cray was called to the telephone at twenty past eight on Wednesday night. She talked to her caller for ten minutes, and almost immediately afterwards went up to Melling House, where she had an interview with Mr. Lessiter. You were the caller, were you not?"

Catherine drew at her cigarette. When she spoke her tone was openly rude.

"What put that into your head?"

"I think it would be very unwise of you to deny it. The girl at the exchange will no doubt remember the call. She is probably familiar with your voice and that of Miss Cray."

The blue haze between them thickened. Catherine said equably,

"If she says I called Rietta up, then I did. I very often do. I'm alone here—it passes the time. Anyhow I suppose you have asked Rietta. She would know."

Miss Silver was sitting upon the couch. There was a bright wood fire and the room was warm. She removed her yellow tippet and laid it beside her. In some purely feminine manner this small incident stirred Catherine's temper. In her own mind she stigmatized the tippet as a mangy cat and resented its contact with her sofa. That a woman who wore a thing like that should thrust herself into her house and cross-examine her about a private conversation was the ultimate limit.

Miss Silver's reply did nothing to allay her anger.

"Miss Cray is under suspicion. It would therefore be important to corroborate any account she might give."

"Very well—give me Rietta's account, and I'll give you my corroboration."

Since Miss Cray had resolutely refused to give any account of the conversation, this was unfortunately not practicable. Miss Silver coughed, and employed the old device of the red herring.

"In the statements which have been made there are references to a memorandum left by Mrs. Lessiter for the information of her son. I believe it was concerned with some disposition of her effects."

Catherine said, "I really don't know."

The haze hung between them, but something had happened. It would have been difficult to say just what it was —the tensing of a muscle, the momentary halting of a breath, the slightest involuntary movement of a finger. Miss Silver had always found it useful to give particular attention to the hands of anyone whose response to questioning inclined towards reticence.

The hand with which Catherine was holding her cigarette remained steady. If the fingers pressed a little more closely, it was a movement impossible to detect. But the little finger had jerked.

Miss Silver coughed.

"I believe that to have been the case. I should be very glad, Mrs. Welby, if you could bring yourself to be frank with me."

"Frank?" Catherine laughed. "I really don't know what you mean!"

"Then I will tell you. Mr. Lessiter had been absent for more than twenty years. He met Miss Cray here, in your house, and walked home with her. The subject of his conversation was the disposition of his mother's effects. On the evening of the murder you had a conversation with Miss Cray which lasted for ten minutes. Was that also a conversation with regard to the disposition of Mrs. Lessiter's property?"

Catherine laughed.

"Why don't you ask Rietta?"

"I am asking you. I believe that some dispute was going on between you and Mr. Lessiter. These things are in the air in a village. It is common knowledge that Mrs. Lessiter lent you the furniture of this house."

Catherine blew out a cloud of smoke.

"She gave me some furniture—yes. I don't know what business it is of yours."

"Miss Cray has engaged me to protect her interests. It is clear that there are two possible points of view involved. I have heard that the furniture was lent—you say that it was given. Mr. Lessiter talked to Miss Cray about the disposition of his mother's effects. On the night of the murder you called Miss Cray up to talk about a matter of business. Later that evening she had a sharp difference of opinion with Mr. Lessiter over a business matter which involved a friend. Can you be surprised that I put two and two together and arrive at the conclusion that Mr. Lessiter was taking the first point of view? He believed that the furniture had been lent. He endeavoured to obtain corroboration from Miss Cray. At some time during the hours immediately preceding his death he discovered a memorandum in his mother's writing. I think it is quite clear that this memorandum supported his view. I believe he rang you up and said so, and that you then rang Miss Cray. Later on, during her interview with Mr. Lessiter, Miss Cray recurred to the subject and endeavoured to change some course of action which he was contemplating. I think that what he intended must have been of a nature to cause her serious distress. She told me that their quarrel was about business, and that the business concerned a friend. You cannot be surprised if I conclude that you were the friend. The whole sequence of events is then explained."

Catherine Welby had not Rietta Cray's quick temper. She could take a wound as well as give one. But all through the interview anger had been rising in her, retarded by caution, checked once or twice by fear, but still rising. It went cold in her now. She felt as if she had just been neatly dissected, her thoughts, her motives, the movements of her mind laid bare. It was not alone the few formal sentences, it was the feeling that this old maid's small, shrewd eyes did really see what she was thinking. She even had the strangest feeling that it might be a relief to let go—to open her mind of her own free will, unpack her thoughts, and spread them out to be looked at, weighed, and judged. It was only for the shortest possible space of time. These moments come—and go. We take them, or we let them go.

Catherine Welby let her moment go. She had no idea that in letting go she had committed herself to an irremediable disaster. She was not hurried by anger. She took her time before she said,

"You've got it all very nicely settled, haven't you? I wouldn't dream of disturbing the picture." She got to her feet and dropped the stub of her cigarette into a jade ash-tray. "And now perhaps you'll go."

Miss Silver was very well qualified to deal with insolence. She regarded Catherine in a manner which relegated her to the nursery—a badly conducted nursery in which the child had not been taught her manners. Rising without hurry, she put on the elderly tippet and fastened up her coat. When she had reached the door she said soberly,

"If you should change your mind, you will know where to find me."

Chapter Thirty-three

As Miss Silver emerged between the pillars which marked the entrance to the drive of Melling House, a light was flashed in her face. It was a little startling, but since there was an immediate murmur of apology in a young man's voice, she concluded that the owner of what appeared to be a bicycle-lamp had merely been anxious to identify a friend. In words rather more familiar than she herself would have employed, it was a case of "boy meets girl." She crossed the road and found her way along the edge of the Green to the path which would take her back to Mrs. Voycey's.

When she first heard the footsteps behind her she gave them no attention. A nervous person would not adopt the detective profession. It did not occur to Miss Silver to be nervous. There was enough light for her to distinguish her path from the Green it traversed. She was not, therefore, using her torch. The footsteps continued behind her. Presently they drew nearer, and a voice said,

"I—I beg your pardon—"

It was the same voice which had apologized for flashing the bicycle-lamp in her face, a young voice and embarrassed.

Miss Silver stood still, allowed the footsteps to come up with her, and said,

"What is it?"

The bicycle-lamp must have been switched off, for all she could see was a tall black shadow. The voice said,

"I beg your pardon, but you are staying with Mrs. Voycey, aren't you? Your name is Miss Silver—"

"What can I do for you?"

"I really do beg your pardon—I hope I didn't startle you. I'm Allan Grover. My father and mother have the Grocery Stores—I think you've met them. I'm in Mr. Holderness's office in Lenton."

Miss Silver began to be very much interested. This was the young man Cecilia Voycey had talked about, the clever boy who had won scholarships. She remembered that there was something about an infatuation for Catherine Welby who was, as Cecilia had not failed to point out, more than old enough

142

to be his mother. Since this had never yet prevented a young man of twenty from falling in love with a pretty and experienced woman, Miss Silver had dismissed it as irrelevant. She began to wonder why he had been waiting outside Catherine's house. Was it just the familiar case of the moth and the candle, and if so, why was he now following herself? She said,

"Yes—Mrs. Voycey has spoken of you. What can I do for you, Mr. Grover?"

He was standing quite close to her now. His voice continued to show embarrassment.

"I wanted to see you—"

Miss Silver coughed in rather a surprised manner.

"To see me, Mr. Grover? You could not know that I should be at the Gate House."

"No—no—I didn't—I couldn't. I was going to see Mrs. Welby—but I had been wanting to talk to you—and when you came out it seemed like an opportunity—"

Even in his embarrassment she was struck with his manner of speech. There was no trace of the village accent. It is not every clever boy who is so adaptable. She said gravely,

"Why did you want to talk to me?"

He came to the point with a simple directness which pleased her.

"You are staying with Mrs. Voycey. Her housekeeper, Mrs. Crook, is a friend of my mother's. I have heard that you are a detective, and that you are advising Miss Cray."

"Yes, Mr. Grover? Shall we walk? It is chilly standing here, and we may be remarked."

They moved on together, Miss Silver setting a slower pace than she was used to. Allan Grover began to pour out what he had to say.

"I haven't known what to do. I thought of coming round to Mrs. Voycey's—but then she would be there, and Mrs. Crook would know. I wanted to catch you alone, but I didn't see how it was going to be done. Then when you came out of the Gate House I thought if I let the opportunity slip I'd never get another, so I followed you. It's about Cyril—Cyril Mayhew."

"Yes, Mr. Grover?"

"Miss Silver—this is just between you and me, isn't it? Because I'm not supposed to talk about office business, but I had to go up to Melling House with Mr. Holderness this morning—a matter of checking up on the inventory with the police to see if anything was missing. Well, right away we found that there were four gilt figures gone from the study mantelpiece."

"Yes—they represented the Four Seasons, did they not?"

"You know about them?"

"Oh, yes, Mr. Grover."

"Then you know they think Cyril took them."

"Do you know of any reason why he should have done so?"

"I'm quite sure that he didn't. That's what I wanted to tell you."

Miss Silver coughed.

"Do you know whether they had any special value?"

He hesitated, and then came out with,

"They're down in the inventory as 'Four gilt figures.'"

"Is that all you know about them?"

"No, it isn't. I used to go up to the house to play with Cyril. Mrs. Lessiter was fond of my mother. I've been in the study often and seen those figures. Cyril always said they were gold. We used to make up stories about them and say they were pirates' treasure."

It occurred to Miss Silver that he was not making things any better for Cyril Mayhew. She said in the tone of an earnest enquirer,

"And are they gold?"

Allan Grover laughed.

"Oh, no, of course not! That was just talk. They wouldn't have been left out like that if they had been gold."

"But they were, Mr. Grover."

"Who says so?"

"Miss Cray for one. I think the Mayhews are aware of the fact, and in all probability so is your friend Cyril."

He actually put his hand on her arm.

"Miss Silver, Cyril isn't mixed up in this—I swear he isn't. He may have been down here that night—they say he was —but as for taking those figures or laying a finger on Mr. Lessiter, I'll swear he didn't. That's what I wanted to see you about. I'll swear Cyril hadn't anything to do with it."

"What makes you so sure about that?"

His hand was still on her arm. Its pressure increased.

"Just knowing Cyril—that's all. If you knew him like I do you'd be just as sure as I am. I've thought it all out, if you'll just listen to me."

"I shall be very pleased to listen to you, Mr. Grover."

"Well then, it's this way. By all accounts Mr. Lessiter was in

his study all that Wednesday evening. They say Cyril came
down by the six-thirty and borrowed Ernie White's bike to
come out here. Mrs. Mayhew says he didn't come, but I
suppose that's what she's bound to say. Well then, suppose he
took those figures—when did he take them? If it was early on,
Mr. Lessiter was there, wasn't he? And if he was out of the
room for a minute he'd have been bound to notice they were
gone when he came back—gold things, showing up like that
against the black marble."

Miss Silver coughed and said,

"They were still there at a quarter past nine when Miss Cray
left."

"Well, there you are. They say Mr. Lessiter was killed some
time after nine o'clock. Cyril would never have dared take
those figures with him using the room. And this I can tell you,
and I'd swear to it, he'd never have taken them with Mr.
Lessiter lying there dead."

"Why do you say that, Mr. Grover?"

"Because I know Cyril. I don't say he mightn't take something that didn't belong to him—he—he'd got a weakness that
way—but he wouldn't do it if he thought it was running any
risk. And as for killing anyone or going into a room where
there was a man with his brains beaten out, I really do know
what I'm talking about, and I tell you he just couldn't do it at
all. I've seen him run out of the kitchen with his fingers in his
ears when his mother was going to kill a mouse. And when it
came to rabbiting, or ratting, or anything of that sort, he was
worse than a girl—a drop of blood, and he'd come over sick. I
tell you he couldn't have gone into that study with Mr.
Lessiter dead the way he was, any more than he could have
taken up the poker and killed him—and I can't put it stronger
than that. You see, Miss Silver, it isn't as if there could have
been anything like a struggle. Even a rabbit will bite if it's
cornered—any creature will. Cyril, he might have hit out with
one of those figures if he'd been caught taking them, but it
didn't happen like that. Whoever killed Mr. Lessiter, it was
someone he was comfortable and easy with. There he was,
sitting up to the writing-table and someone just behind him
over by the fire. You don't sit that way with anyone unless
you're easy with them. And whoever it was meant murder.
There wasn't any struggle. I don't see how there could even
have been a quarrel. You don't quarrel with someone like that,
sitting with your back to them, do you? But the one that was

behind him, he meant murder, and he picked up the poker
and let him have it. Well, I tell you Cyril couldn't have done
that. There are things people can do, and things they can't do.
I've known him all my life, and he couldn't squash a wasp, let
alone hit a man over the head with a poker. If you told me he'd
lifted some loose change or a shilling's worth of stamps, I'd
believe you, but murder, or going into a room with a
murdered man—well, it's just plain nonsense, he couldn't
have done it."

They had reached the edge of the Green. Miss Silver had
only to cross the road in order to see the welcoming glow from
the curtained windows of Mrs. Voycey's drawing-room. She
paused at the end of the path. Allan Grover's hand dropped
from her arm. After a moment's thoughtful silence she said,

"You have interested me extremely, Mr. Grover. There is a
good deal in what you say, and I will give it my most careful
attention. Goodnight."

Chapter Thirty-four

A GOOD DEAL later than this Randal March was taking his way
home. He was glad to be done with the day's business, and
very glad to be done with Superintendent Drake. Drake's
reactions to the footprints discovered by Miss Silver had been
quite extraordinarily irritating. He was mortified, he was
huffed, he took umbrage. He suggested that the footprints
might have been made at any time, and when March pointed
out that there had been heavy rain on Wednesday afternoon,
and that they must have been made since then, he took
umbrage all over again. There is, of course, nothing more
trying for a police officer than to have a well substantiated
theory undermined, or to see it tottering to its fall without
being able to give it a sustaining hand. With Rietta Cray and
Carr Robertson as suspects, Drake had been in a state of
blissful and offensive self-satisfaction. It was his first important
murder case. He saw promotion looming. The social position
of the suspects ministered agreeably to his class-
consciousness. When Mr. Holderness produced Cyril Mayhew as a possible alternative he wasn't pleased—nobody could
have expected him to be pleased—but he put up a very

creditable performance as a fair-minded officer anxious only to come at the truth.

And then completely unrelated footprints of an unknown woman. It was enough to put any man out of temper, let alone that he knew, and the Chief Constable knew, that he ought to have found them himself. It wouldn't have been so bad if they could have been made out to be Miss Cray's footprints, but they couldn't, and it wasn't any good trying. He didn't need the Chief Constable to point it out to him either. He remarked with some acerbity that if he'd got to choose between a crime without a clue at all, and one where they were buzzing round like so many bluebottles, he'd take the first and say thank you. It was one of the few times during their association that the Chief Constable felt inclined to agree with him.

Well, the business was over now. The footprints had been photographed by flashlight, cement had been poured into them to provide casts, and a tarpaulin spread to protect them from the weather. Randal March was taking his way home.

He came out on the far side of Melling and drove slowly along a dark, narrow lane. There was a hedgerow on either side, rather wild and unkempt, with the black mass of holly breaking it here and there. There was no one else abroad—no lights of any other car, no low-set gleam of a bicycle-lamp, no foot-passenger shrinking back against the hedge. The dark loneliness pleased him. He was more physically tired than he could remember to have been for years, and his mind was tired to death. To and fro in it for the last two days his thoughts had paced, struggled, and rebelled. Even as he strove to order them, to hold the balance between the prosecution and the defence, to do his job without fear or favour, he could not be sure that the scale did not tip.

He drove on down the bright path which his headlights made for him, and wished with all his heart that he could see his way as plainly.

Half a mile out of Melling what should be a prolongation of the lane becomes the footpath which descends from Rowberry Common, the lane itself taking an unexpected turn to the left. The beam of the headlights streaming on to the footpath just before the turn picked up the figure of a woman. For the moment of time before the car swung round she stood there dazzled by the glow, her head uncovered, her eyes wide, her face unnaturally white. It was startling in the extreme—like seeing a drowned face.

He took the car past the turn, drew up, got out, and walked back. She was moving, he heard a stone slip from her foot. A relief quite outside reason flooded over him. He would have confessed to no conscious fear, but the sound of that sliding pebble was an extraordinarily welcome thing. He said,

"Rietta! What are you doing here?" and saw her come towards him like a shadow.

She said, "I've been walking on Rowberry Common. I couldn't stay indoors."

"You shouldn't go up there in the dark. It's got a bad name."

She said with heart-breaking simplicity,

"No one would hurt me—I'm too unhappy."

"Does that protect one?"

"Yes. People can't reach you—you're all alone—"

"Rietta, don't talk like that!"

She said, "I'll go home now."

She took a step away from him, and something happened. He was a temperate man in mind and body. He had never before been so swept from his own control. He couldn't let her leave him. With a purely instinctive movement he reached out to stop her. His hands met the rough cloth of the coat she was wearing. He found that he was holding her.

"Rietta!"

She said, "Oh, let me go!"

"I can't. I love you. You do know that, don't you?"

"Oh, no!"

"What's the good of lies? We might as well speak the truth, if it's only for once. You do know I love you."

"No—"

"Stop lying, Rietta! If we can't do anything else for each other we can at least speak the truth. If you didn't know, why did you sit there this afternoon accusing me with your eyes? Every time I asked you a question you accused me—every time I sat by and let that damned fellow Drake cross-examine you, you accused me. If you didn't know that I loved you, there wasn't any reason for it. You knew."

"Yes—I knew. It doesn't matter, does it? It's like knowing something that died a long time ago—it's gone."

His hands closed hard upon her. She felt the strength in them.

"What are you talking about? Do you think I would let you go?"

She said on a curious sobbing breath,

"I've—gone—"

In a most horrid and disturbing manner there came back to him the feeling he had had when he saw her drowned in the glare of the headlights. His pleasant voice was harsh as he said,

"Don't say things like that—I won't have it! I'm asking you to marry me."

"Are you, Randal? And do we send an announcement to the papers? There would be some nice headlines, wouldn't there? Chief Constable weds chief suspect in Lessiter murder case! No, I suppose they couldn't say that before I was arrested. It would be contempt of court or something like that, wouldn't it? And once I was arrested I should be the accused. Randal, why should this have to happen to us? We could have been so happy."

A flood of grief broke in her. She didn't know it was going to happen. It had hurt her too much when she thought of what might have been. She had no more pride, no more control. She did not even think of being glad that it was dark. The tears ran down, and would have done if it had been broad day.

At first he didn't know. She stood there quietly under his hands. He had his own emotions to deal with, and found them hard to curb.

Then one of those hot tears splashed down upon his wrist. He took his hand from her arm and put it up to her face. The tears ran over it. He pulled her up close and kissed her, and she kissed him back, not quietly but with a despairing passion. It this was all they could ever have, let them take their fill of it.

They might have been alone in the universe, so close that breath and pulse were one. A single heart-beat shook them both. They did not know how long it was before she drew that deep shuddering breath, and said,

"We're mad."

Randal March said, "No—sane. Hold on to that—we'll stay sane together."

"Can we?"

He had come back to his centre of gravity. Thought steadied. He said,

"Yes."

There was another of those long breaths.

"I don't know—I feel as if I had gone away—too far."

"I'll bring you back."

"I don't think you can."

She drew away from him.

"Randal, will you tell me something—honestly?"

"I'll do my best."

"Your best won't do unless it's really honest. I've got to know. Are you—quite sure about me? I don't mean just now when we're here together like this, but have you always been quite sure—first thing in the morning, and when you wake up suddenly in the night, before you've had time to sort yourself out, and argue about it?"

"Yes, I've always been quite sure. It's not the sort of thing I've got to argue about—it's in my bones."

She came up close again and said,

"Carr isn't sure."

"Rietta!"

"It's not his fault. He wants to be sure—he wants it dreadfully."

"He's a young fool."

She shook her head.

"He tried—I've seen him try. Sometimes he pulls it off—for a little. And then it comes over him again—'Suppose she did it.' He doesn't say anything, but I know. If it was ever like that with you, I couldn't bear it."

"It won't ever be like that with me—I can promise you that."

She said again, "It isn't Carr's fault. I might be thinking the same sort of thing about him, only it's been so plain that he thought it was I who had killed James. He asked me why I'd done it. And he made me wash the raincoat. I'm afraid I did it very badly."

"You oughtn't to have done it at all."

She put up a hand and pushed back her hair—the familiar gesture which wrung his heart.

"I know. What I don't know is whether I wouldn't do it again. It was all so horrible, so sudden—and I was frightened for Carr, and he was frightened for me. Only I ought to have made a better job of it. It seemed the best thing to do at the time, but now of course it's going to make any jury believe I did it."

He said with a rough edge on his voice,

"Don't talk about juries—it won't come to that. Somebody killed Lessiter, and we're going to find out who it was. If you get worried, go and see Miss Silver. You'll find her very bracing."

She said, "I like her. I don't quite know why she impresses

one, but she does. It's a sort of mixture of being back at school again and finding yourself wandering about in the fairy story where you meet an old woman and she gives you a hazel nut with the cloak of darkness packed inside it."

He laughed out loud.

"I wonder what Miss Silver would say if you told her that! She might just smile indulgently, or you might get a reproof for talking in what she would describe as an exaggerated manner. She's rather a wonder, you know. I've heard that impudent chap Frank Abbott call her Maudie the Mascot. Not to her face, but he always says that if she comes in on a case, the police come out of it in a blaze of glory."

"Is it true?"

"Just about. She has the most extraordinary flair. No, it's something more than that. She knows people. All the things they hide behind—appearance, manner, the show we all put up to prevent other people knowing too much about us—she sees right through them, and judges you on what's left. I can still remember the awful feeling we used to get when we were children and we'd been up to something she didn't approve of. Even Isabel, who was a fairly hardy liar, used to give up and burst into tears."

"I can't imagine Isabel bursting into tears."

"No—she was tough, wasn't she? But I've seen her do it. As for me, I always felt it wasn't even worth trying to hold out on Miss Silver, so I didn't try. I don't mind confessing that she still has very much the same effect on me."

Rietta laughed a little unsteadily.

"Yes, she's like that. It came over me when I was talking to her that if I'd had anything to hide, she'd have found it out. As it was, I told her things I didn't mean to." She stepped back. "Randal, I must go. They'll think something has happened to me."

Chapter Thirty-five

FRIDAY SLIPPED AWAY into the past. Before it was quite gone Randal March received a telephone call. He had the lover's thought that it might be Rietta, and knew this at once for the folly that it was. Miss Silver's schoolroom French came to him along the wire.

"I am sorry to disturb you, but if you could make it convenient to call here tomorrow as early as possible, I should be glad. I have had two conversations which I should like to pass on to you."

That was all, without either greeting or farewell.

He whistled softly as he hung up the receiver. He knew his Miss Silver. When she dispensed with observance it meant quite serious business. He made a mental note to be with her by half past nine. If Melling had to see the Chief Constable's car turn in at Mrs. Voycey's gate, he supposed Miss Silver would have reckoned on that and considered that the game was worth the candle. He finished what writing he had to do and took his way to bed, and to the dreamless sleep which was his fortunate portion.

There were others who were not so fortunate.

Rietta Cray, lying sleepless in the dark, saw painted upon it the cold decay of hope. The glow that had been in her died, slowly but without respite. The bleak voice of common sense set out in chill, convincing terms just how much she would damage Randal's career if she were to marry him. There are possible things and impossible things. If the impossible seems possible and you grasp at it, you are left with only your own folly to mock you. For an hour she had believed that happiness was possible. Now she watched it withdraw.

Carr Robertson slept, and dreamed a frightful dream. He stood in a dark place with a dead man at his feet. The cold hand touched him. He woke sweating.

Up at Melling House Mrs. Mayhew called out in her sleep. She had cried until she could cry no more, and then passed into a dream in which a child wailed. The child was Cyril. He was cold, he was hungry, he was hurt, and she could not go to him. She called out in her sleep with such a lamentable voice that Mayhew sat up and lit the candle. She cried out again, and turned and went back into her dream. He sat up in bed with the flame of the candle blowing and thought how cold it was, and wondered what was going to happen to them all.

Catherine Welby was awake. Like Mayhew she was sitting up in bed, but unlike Mayhew she had taken precautions against feeling cold. A small electric fire was turned on, the window was shut, and she wore a becoming quilted jacket of the same pale blue as the eiderdown. Without any make-up her skin was pale. Her fair hair was hidden by a lace cap. She had three pillows behind her, and she sat up straight against them and read—line after line, page after page, chapter after chapter. Her will drove her, but if she had been asked what she read she might have been put to it to find an answer.

The longest night comes to an end, just as the last night comes, whether we know it is the end or not. For one of these people it was the last night.

When the dull, reluctant day returned, each one of them got up and went about his business.

Catherine Welby dressed to catch the nine-forty bus into Lenton. She made herself some coffee and a couple of slices of toast. She was no longer pale, because she had taken steps to avoid anything so unbecoming. She looked very much as she always did, except that she was wearing a hat—grey, to match her suit, with a jay's feather stuck in the band.

She came out of the front door, locking it behind her, and saw Mrs. Fallow come down the drive, hurrying and all agog with news. Catherine said good-morning, and it all came pouring out.

"It's my morning for Miss Cray, and I expect you'll wonder what I'm doing, but I said to Miss Rietta how I couldn't get that poor soul Mrs. Mayhew off my mind. It's terrible the way she's been carrying on. Mr. Mayhew can't get her to eat a thing. She just sits and drinks a cup of tea and cries down into it all the time. So I said to Miss Rietta, 'I've got a hen laying, and I've brought two of the eggs along, so what about slipping up to the house and seeing she gets one whipped up in her tea?' And Miss Rietta she says, 'All right,' and off I went."

Catherine glanced at her wrist-watch. The bus stop was just beyond the gate. She had five minutes. She said,

"I should think you would have gone up the back way."

Her voice was quite smooth and even. All the same she

didn't think Mrs. Fallow had come out of her way to tell her whether Mrs. Mayhew had taken a beaten-up egg in her tea.

Mrs. Fallow's thin, dark face twitched with impatience. She wanted to get on with her story, not be kept pottering about.

"So I did," she said. "And when I got up there, well, it was as much as I could do to remember what I'd come for. Such a to-do! It seems the Chief Constable came back in the afternoon, and the lady with him that's visiting Mrs. Voycey, and they go into the study. And a piece after that Inspector Drake comes along, and the photographer chap and two more, and there's photographs taken and plaster casts. But that Miss Silver, she'd gone by then. She'd be in the way, and I expect the Chief Constable packed her off."

Catherine was drawing on her gloves, smoothing them carefully over the fingers.

"And what were they photographing and taking casts of?"

Mrs. Fallow came up close and said in a flesh-creeping tone, "Footprints."

"Footprints?" said Catherine. She stepped back.

Mrs. Fallow followed her.

"Footprints," she said. "Right there by the study window under the lilac bushes. Seems someone must have been standing there Wednesday night about the time Mr. Lessiter was killed. And they've got everything photographed and measured, so they'll be able to tell who it was. And thank heaven they can't put it on Miss Rietta, for they say the footprints was small, and that's something no one couldn't say about her. Nice shaped feet she's got, but small they're not, and you can't get from it. So that's one for Miss Rietta, and one for Cyril Mayhew too. We all know he's a bit of a weed, but fours in lady's shoes he doesn't take and never could. And I needn't really have bothered about the eggs. Mrs. Mayhew's like a different creature—that cheered up you wouldn't know her, and had a kipper for breakfast and three pieces of toast and marmalade. So I thought I'd come along this way and give you the news if you were anywhere about. Only I mustn't stop —Miss Rietta's counting on me."

They walked out between the pillars. Catherine got into the bus.

Chapter Thirty-six

BUT OF COURSE, my dear, you must see him in the drawing-room. Bessie shall light the fire before breakfast."

"It is very good of you, Cecilia."

It really was, because Cecilia Voycey was dying of curiosity, and finding it very hard to bear in mind that you didn't—you simply didn't—ask questions about other people's private affairs. Moral maxims are notoriously hard to live up to. The effort brought quite a deep flush to her face. But when the Chief Constable's car drew up she merely repeated for the third time that she wouldn't dream of intruding, and fell back upon the dining-room, where she recalled that Maud had always been provokingly discreet even at school.

In the drawing-room Miss Silver recounted her interview with Catherine Welby and the confidences of Allan Grover. March didn't exactly pooh-pooh the latter, but he permitted himself to observe that what the solicitor's clerk said was not evidence. With which Miss Silver agreed, adding with a mild cough that she had been impressed by his sincerity, and that she did not wish to expose herself to the reproach of having withheld information from the police.

The Chief Constable was in notably better spirits than he had been the day before. He laughed and said,

"A thing you would never do!"

If his tone was light, hers in return was serious.

"Very seldom, and only for very good reasons, Randal. And now there is something I would like to suggest to you. It may have been done already, but if not—"

"What is it?"

"It is the matter of the telephone calls on Wednesday night."

"Calls?"

"Yes. We know that Mrs. Welby had a ten minutes' call to Miss Cray between eight-twenty and eight-thirty—"

"It was Catherine Welby who called up?"

"Yes. Miss Cray refuses to say what they were talking about. When I suggested that it was a matter of business she said, 'You might call it that,' and when I asked her if it was

155

connected with Mr. Lessiter she just said, 'Oh!' in an extremely startled manner. Mrs. Welby was angry and, I think, shaken when I referred to the call. When I spoke of the missing memorandum she had, I am convinced, a moment of acute fear. Putting all the small things together which I have observed or gathered from local talk, I feel quite sure that Mrs. Welby found herself placed in a very awkward position by Mr. Lessiter's return. Mrs. Lessiter furnished the Gate House for her. More things have been added from time to time, some of them of considerable value. Mrs. Welby has given everyone to understand that these things were gifts. Then Mr. Lessiter returns. It would not be unnatural that he should ask for some proof that his mother had given Mrs. Welby so many valuable presents. There is evidence that he was searching the house for a paper which I believe to have been the memorandum mentioned in his conversation with Miss Cray. Mrs. Fallow who works at Melling House told Mrs. Voycey's housekeeper that he was 'pretty well turning the house upside down' for a paper Mrs. Lessiter had left for him. We know that paper was found, because Miss Cray saw it on his table. But it cannot be found now. I do not think you can escape the inference that this memorandum would implicate someone who took steps to remove it. I do not go so far as to assert that this person was the murderer, but it certainly presents itself as a possibility. In my opinion the memorandum implicated Mrs. Welby. I think it contained proof that the contents of the Gate House were not given, but merely lent. If, as I am convinced, she had sold some of them—"

"My dear Miss Silver!"

She inclined her head.

"I am convinced of it. Her income is extremely small, her clothes are extremely expensive. She is, and has been, very much alarmed. She did not anticipate Mr. Lessiter's return."

"With all respect for your convictions—"

She gave him her charming smile.

"You may consider if you like that I am putting a hypothetical case, but it is what I believe to have happened. Mr. Lessiter finds the memorandum at, let us say, somewhere between half past seven and eight o'clock on Wednesday evening. He rings Mrs. Welby up, and makes her realize that she has put herself on the wrong side of the law. When he has rung off she calls Miss Cray. I can deduce those two telephone conversations. We know that one of them did in fact occur.

What we need is evidence that the other also did take place, and evidence as to what was said on both occasions. Has the girl on duty at the telephone exchange been approached?"

"I should think not—Drake would have mentioned it. There has been nothing until now to suggest that the call Rietta Cray received on Wednesday night had anything to do with the murder."

"Then, Randal, will you see that the girl is questioned, and at once. We should know what telephone calls were sent out from Melling House that evening, and whether she overheard what was said. And whether she overheard any part of the conversation between Mrs. Welby and Miss Cray."

"They are not supposed to listen."

Miss Silver coughed.

"We all do a great many things which we are not supposed to do. There has been some local interest about Mr. Lessiter's affairs. I hope we may discover that Gladys Luker was sufficiently curious to listen in."

"You know who was on duty at the exchange?"

"Oh, yes—she is Mrs. Grover's niece. A very nice girl. She has not repeated anything, but Mrs. Voycey's housekeeper, who is friendly with her aunt, seems to think that Gladys has something on her mind."

He laughed.

"I'll have her questioned, but don't be disappointed if we find the blight is due to the boy friend having missed a date. Well, I must be off. By the way, Drake is fed to the teeth about your footprints. You are always adding to the debt of gratitude I owe you."

"My dear Randal!"

"My dear Miss Silver, you have no idea how I dislike that worthy and efficient man, and I can't say so to anyone but you. Zeal, zeal—all zeal! You may be interested to know, on his authority, that the lady of the footprints takes a small four."

"I take a small four myself, Randal."

He could not restrain an exclamation.

Miss Silver coughed.

"And so does Mrs. Welby," she said.

Chapter Thirty-seven

CATHERINE WELBY GOT off the bus in the Market Square at Lenton and took the narrow cut called Friar's Row. The Friary has been gone for so long that only the name survives, but there are some old houses lurking behind modern shop windows in Main Street. In one of these Mr. Holderness had his offices. The bookseller's shop on the ground floor had changed hands more than once, but the firm of Stanway, Stanway, Fulpurse and Holderness had occupied the upper storeys for a hundred and fifty years. There was only one Stanway now, an invalid whose appearances at the office had become few and far between. A nephew of the name would in due course be admitted to the firm. He was at the moment completing his military service. Dark portraits of ancestral Stanways showed them shrewd-eyed, hard-mouthed, and eminently respectable. The type had not changed with the years. There had only been one Fulpurse, dead in 1846 when the first Holderness appears—his mother Amelia Fulpurse, his father connected in the female line with the Stanways. Altogether one of those old-established family concerns which are still to be found in country towns.

Catherine went up two steps to the open doorway beside the bookseller's entrance. A flagged passage led to the gloomy stair, and the stair to the first floor and the room where Mr. Holderness kept his state. On the door next to his the name of the last Stanway lingered, only to be discerned on some unusually bright day.

Catherine Welby hesitated for a moment, then passed this empty room, devoted now to deed-boxes and dust, and opened the door of the room beyond. The tapping of a typewriter ceased, a girl looked up, and down again. Allan Grover rose to meet her.

He was to remember it all afterwards so many times. This room had a single window on to Friar's Row. In any except the brightest weather the electric light was on all day. It was on now. It dazzled on the gold of her hair, on the small diamond brooch at her throat. It emphasized the deep blue of her eyes. She brought with her the very breath of beauty, the very pulse of romance. At twenty-one these are easily evoked. Youth is its own enchantment. He heard her say, "Good-morning," and stammered over his reply.

Miss Janet Loddon, who had returned to her typing, gave him a quick glance of contempt and set the ensuing wrong letter down to his account. She was a year older than he was, and had been despising men a good deal for the last week or two owing to an obstinate quarrel with a boy friend whose stubbornness in refusing to eat humble pie was giving her a good deal of trouble. It restored her self-respect to observe Mr. Grover's change of colour and the hesitation in his speech, but she felt no warmth towards Mrs. Welby, whom she set down as old enough to know better. She heard Allan go out of the room, she heard him return. Then they both went out together. He was taking her along to Mr. Holderness's room, and being long enough over it.

To Allan there was a flash of light when Catherine came in, an interval of darkness during which he went along to Mr. Holderness's room and came back again, and another terribly brief flash during which he walked beside her to the door at the end of the passage, threw it open, announced, "Mrs. Welby, sir," and withdrew. He went back to his table and the contempt of Miss Loddon. She could hear a rustling of papers, the scratching of a pen. Then suddenly his chair was pushed back, he got up, and made for the door. He said,

"If I'm wanted, I'll be in Mr. Stanway's room. Mr. Holderness wants to look at the Jardine papers."

Miss Loddon remarking that she supposed everyone would be able to get along without him for ten minutes or so, he went out and shut the door rather more sharply than Mr. Holderness would have approved.

Catherine Welby sat where James Lessiter had sat during his last interview with his solicitor. The windows looked upon Main Street. Being closed, the hum of the traffic was pleasantly subdued. The light striking over her left shoulder fell upon one of the Stanway portraits—William, first of the name, dark against the panelling. Beyond the fact that it was a portrait there was very little to be seen. The past engulfed it. There was a flavour of respectability, and a great deal of gloom.

Mr. Holderness appeared in vigorous contrast, his colour high, his grey hair thick and handsome, his dark brows arching over fine dark eyes. Having known Catherine from a child, he

addressed her by her name. The echoes of his resonant voice
saying, "My dear Catherine!" followed Allan Grover down the
passage.

The interview lasted for about twenty minutes. Catherine,
not unusually given to confidence, had now no impulse to
withhold it. Under Mr. Holderness's startled gaze she imparted details of a predicament which were certainly calculated to occasion his grave concern.

"You see, I have sold some of the things."

"My dear Catherine!"

"One has to have money. Besides, why shouldn't I? Aunt
Mildred gave them to me."

Mr. Holderness looked shocked.

"Just what have you sold?"

"Oh, odds and ends—there was a Cosway miniature—"

He made a horrified gesture.

"So easily traced!"

"I tell you Aunt Mildred gave it to me. Why shouldn't I sell
it? I would rather have kept it of course, because it was quite
charming. Romney period, you know—curls and floating
scarf, like the pictures of Lady Hamilton. Her name was Jane
Lilly, and she was a sort of ancestress. But I had to have the
money—things are such a shocking price." This refrain recurred. "I must have a decent amount of money—you do
understand that, don't you?"

Mr. Holderness's complexion had taken on a considerably
deeper shade. He said with less than his usual suavity,

"You must cut your coat according to your cloth."

Catherine had a rueful smile for that.

"My trouble is that I do like the most expensive cloth."

He told her bluntly that she had got herself into a very
dangerous position.

"You were foolish enough to sell things that didn't belong to
you, and James Lessiter did more than suspect you. He sat in
that chair where you are sitting now and told me he was
convinced that you had been defrauding the estate."

Catherine continued to smile.

"He always had a very vindictive nature. Rietta was well out
of marrying him. I told her so at the time."

Mr. Holderness made the sound which is usually written
"Tush!"

"He told me he was prepared to prosecute."

"He told me that too." She paused, and added, "So naturally I went up to see him."

"You went up to see him?"

"On that Wednesday night. But Rietta was there, so I came away."

"My dear Catherine!"

"But I went back—later."

"What are you saying?"

"Just what you said to me—that I am in a very serious position. Or I should be if it was all going to come out."

"There is really no reason why it should come out. You can hold your tongue, can't you?"

"Oh, yes—I have—I do. And I shall go on—unless I simply can't help myself."

"I don't follow you."

"Well, there's a tiresome meddling old maid of a governess who has got herself mixed up in the affair. She's staying with Mrs. Voycey."

"My dear Catherine, how does she come into it?"

"Rietta has dragged her in. It seems she fancies herself as a detective."

Mr. Holderness leaned back in his chair with an air of relief.

"I should think the police would make short work of her. They don't take kindly to interference."

"She used to be Randal March's governess," said Catherine. "Rietta says he thinks the world of her. Anyhow she came to see me yesterday afternoon, and I can tell you this, she's got the whole thing pretty well pieced together."

"What do you mean, Catherine?"

"I don't think Rietta had talked—she wouldn't. But this Miss Silver knew or guessed about the things from Melling House, and about James cutting up rough. She guessed I'd rung Rietta up about them on Wednesday night, and if that Luker girl at the exchange was listening in, I shall be in the soup. Of course I was a fool to talk about it on the telephone, but James had just rung me, so if anyone was listening they'd heard everything that mattered already, and I was feeling desperate. I told Rietta I was."

"Then you had certainly better hope that the young woman at the exchange was not listening."

Catherine waved this away.

"Oh, I don't suppose she was—she can't do it all the time. It's Miss Silver who worries me. She knows about that damned memorandum—don't ask me how. If she goes on the way she's begun, there's going to be a day of judgment all round. I just wonder whether I hadn't better make a statement to the police and have done with it."

Mr. Holderness looked scandalized.

"It would be most uncalled for, and—" he paused— "extremely dangerous. Prudence, my dear Catherine—"

Ten minutes later Catherine Welby got up to go. She turned at the open door and said in her clear voice,

"All right, I won't do anything rash, I promise you."

Allan Grover, coming out of Mr. Stanway's room next door, saw that she was smiling. He heard what she had said, but he did not hear whether Mr. Holderness made any reply. He took a step towards her, and they walked together to the head of the stairs. She brought a scent of violets with her. His heart was beating hard. He couldn't think of anything to say, but if he didn't say something she would go. What can you say when your heart is full of forbidden things? He changed colour as he thought of them, and hastened into common place.

"Are you taking the bus out to Melling?"

"Well, yes."

"You're not staying in Lenton for lunch? You couldn't— I mean you wouldn't—have lunch with me, would you?"

He didn't know how he got it out. The colour burnt his face. But she wasn't angry, she was smiling.

"That's terribly sweet of you, Allan, but I must get home."

"I—I'd do anything for you, Mrs. Welby."

"Would you? I wonder. No, I really believe you would. You're a dear boy. Come round and see me some time like you used to."

"Oh, Mrs. Welby—may I?"

She nodded, smiling, met his eyes, and let the smile slide into a laugh.

"You mustn't be foolish, you know."

"Is it foolish to—to love you?"

"Very." She was still laughing. "But rather sweet. There!"

She leaned forward, kissing him lightly on the cheek, and ran down the stairs with a backward wave of her hand.

Chapter Thirty-eight

SATURDAY SLIPPED AWAY. Catherine Welby bought some face-cream, a box of powder, and a new lipstick, after which she took the next bus back to Melling. Saturday being a half day at the office, Allan Grover snatched a hasty lunch and went to watch a football match. Returning home in time for a six o'clock tea, he had a wash and brush up and went out again, announcing that he thought he would look in at The Feathers for a game of darts. He was home by half past ten and in bed a few minutes later, but sleep remained obstinately aloof.

Mrs. Grover, in the next room, decided for at least the hundredth time that she really must do something to stop that bed of his from creaking so. Every time he turned over it made a noise like a door with a rusty hinge, and why a healthy boy should turn and twist like that was beyond her. But there, boys and girls were all the same—a trouble over their teething, and a trouble over their schooling, and a trouble over their lovering. The way Allan was going on he'd got something on his mind, and she didn't have to think twice to know what it was. Pity he couldn't have just gone on quiet with Gladys Luker that was a real nice girl and thought the world of him. But there—a man wouldn't be a man if he didn't make a fool of himself some time in his life, and better first than last. He was young, and he'd get over it and be married and settled one day, and Doris too. And then there'd be the same trouble all over again with their children—you couldn't get from it. She pulled the bedclothes well up over her ears and went to sleep.

Sunday morning came in bright and clear. Mrs. Fallow, professionally off duty, took time from her own domestic affairs to run up to Melling House just to keep in touch. If, for instance, Cyril had been arrested, it would be a severe affront to hear the news from anyone but Mrs. Mayhew herself. Passing the Gate House at half past nine, she thought Mrs. Welby was lying late—no smoke from the chimney and the milk not taken in. She remarked to Mrs. Mayhew that she only wished she had the time to lie in bed of a morning.

A cup of tea having been proffered and accepted, twenty minutes slipped away. After which Mrs. Fallow buttoned up

her coat and said she didn't know what she was thinking about,
sitting like this with everything waiting at home and the
Sunday dinner to cook. She made off down the drive at a quick
trot. Slackening her pace when she came to the Gate House,
she was astonished and a little shocked to see the milk bottle
still on the step and no trace of smoke coming from the
chimney. A good lay-in on a Sunday was one thing, but best
part of ten o'clock was what you might call overdoing it. She
went out between the pillars, and something nagged at her to
go back again. All the years she'd known Mrs. Welby she
hadn't ever known her to be late in the morning. If it was some
she could name, it wouldn't be anything to think twice about,
but Mrs. Welby was one of the early ones—always had been
so long as she'd known her.

She went along the flagged path to the little porch and stood
looking at the milk bottle. It ought to have been taken in best
part of two hours ago. She didn't like it. On the other hand,
Mrs. Welby wasn't one that would care about your poking
your nose into her business. If she hadn't been one of the most
inquisitive women on earth Mrs. Fallow would have turned
round and gone away.

She couldn't bring herself to do it. She went round the
corner of the house and saw all the curtains closely drawn and
the windows shut. It was downright unnatural. Always slept
with her windows open Mrs. Welby did, the one to the side of
the house and the one to the front, and if she was up and about
she'd be airing the room. Talking about it afterwards, she said
she got a cold creep all down her back, and what came into her
mind was it looked for all the world as if there was someone
dead in the house.

She walked all the way round. There wasn't a window open
or a curtain pulled aside. She came back to the porch and
pressed her finger on the electric bell. No one answered, no
one came.

Mrs. Fallow found herself getting out her handkerchief and
wiping her hands. It was a bright, cold morning, but they were
clammy with sweat. The silence in the house seemed to be
seeping out of it like—she didn't know what it was like, but it
frightened her. She rang again and again, and when that failed
she beat upon the door loud enough, in her own words, to
wake the dead. Nobody waked, nobody came. She picked up
her feet and ran for the White Cottage.

She looked scared to death when Rietta Cray opened the

door, and next minute she was crying, and saying she thought
something had happened to Mrs. Welby and what did they
ought to do about it. It was Rietta who suggested the
telephone, but when there was still no reply they all went
round to the Gate House, she, and Carr, and Fancy, and Mrs.
Fallow.

It was Fancy who tried the door and found that it wasn't
locked. The key was on the inner side, but it wasn't locked.
They went through into the living-room, and found the light
turned on in the reading-lamp and the curtains closed. The
light showed the gold waves of Catherine's hair against one of
her pastel cushions. She lay on the sofa in her blue house-
gown and looked as if she was asleep. But she was dead.

Chapter Thirty-nine

THE CHIEF CONSTABLE'S car drew up at Mrs. Voycey's front
door. He rang the bell, asked for Miss Silver, and was shown
into the drawing-room where she and Mrs. Voycey were
sitting by the fire. Cecilia Voycey displayed a commendable
degree of tact. She shook hands, she beamed a welcome, and
removed herself and her novel to the dining-room. When the
door was closed upon her Randal March turned to Miss Silver
and said,

"Well, I suppose you have heard the news."

She had her knitting in her lap. The two fronts and the back
of little Josephine's jacket having been completed and sewn
together, she was engaged upon the left sleeve, for which four
needles were in use. They clicked briskly as she replied,

"Oh, yes. It is extremely shocking."

He dropped into the chair which Mrs. Voycey had vacated.

"You were, of course, perfectly right. I don't know how you
do it. I must confess I was sceptical, but—we got a statement
from the Luker girl. She did listen in on Wednesday night,
and this is what she says." He took out some folded sheets of
typescript, straightened them, and began to read aloud:

"'I was on duty from Wednesday evening at seven o'clock.
Things were quiet. There weren't many calls. At a quarter to
eight Mr. Lessiter rang through from Melling House to know
if I could help him with Mr. Holderness's private address. I

looked it up and put him through. I wouldn't have listened, only I was worrying about something and I thought maybe it would stop me thinking about it. But I'd another call to see to, so all I heard was Mr. Lessiter saying, "Good-evening, Mr. Holderness. I've found my mother's memorandum." The call was quite a short one, and I didn't listen any more. A little after eight Mr. Lessiter called again. He gave Mrs. Welby's number, and I put him on. There has been a lot of talk about Mr. Lessiter in Melling. I don't listen as a rule, but I thought I would, just to see what he sounded like talking to someone like Mrs. Welby—'"

He looked up from the paper and said,

"We didn't get all this straight off, you know. She was a good deal upset. There seemed to be something behind this listening in—some animus against Mrs. Welby. Do you know of anything that would account for it?"

Miss Silver was knitting composedly. She said,

"Oh, yes. Gladys Luker used to be very friendly with Mrs. Grover's son at the Grocery Stores, the young man I told you of in Mr. Holderness's office. He has been rather advertizing a foolish infatuation for Mrs. Welby."

He broke into a half laugh.

"How in the world do you discover these things?"

She gave her faint dry cough.

"My friend's housekeeper is Gladys Luker's aunt. Pray continue."

"Yes—we now approach the meat. . . . Where was I? . . . Oh, here—'I thought I would, just to see what he sounded like talking to someone like Mrs. Welby. He began just the same as he did to Mr. Holderness—"Well, Catherine, I've found the memorandum. I thought you'd be pleased to know. You are, aren't you?" I wondered what it was all about, because it sounded as if he was saying something nasty. Mrs. Welby didn't sound at all pleased. She said, "What do you mean?" And he said, "You know very well what I mean. It's all down in black and white. My mother never gave you any of those things. She lent them, and they are my property. If you have disposed of any of them, I shall prosecute." Mrs. Welby said, "You wouldn't do that!" and he said, "I don't advise you to count on it, my dear Catherine. I've an old score to settle, and I always settle my scores. I've just been ringing old Holderness up—" I didn't hear any more than that, because another call came through. At twenty past eight Mrs. Welby rang Miss

Cray. I can't remember everything she said, but it was all telling Miss Cray about Mr. Lessiter finding this memorandum, and his saying the furniture and things she had were only lent to her. She wanted Miss Cray to tell Mr. Lessiter that his mother's memory was bad and she didn't know what she was doing, and Miss Cray wouldn't. Mrs. Welby went on at her, but she wouldn't. Mrs. Welby got very worked up, and right at the end she said, "Well, if anything happens, it'll be your fault. I'm desperate." And she rang off.'"

He laid the paper down.

"It's just what you thought, isn't it? And if you'll let me say so, I don't think even you have ever done a better bit of work —bricks without straw, and good solid bricks at that. I think it's quite clear now what happened. Catherine Welby's bluff was called. She was faced with prosecution. Lessiter was a vindictive devil and he had it in for her. When she found she couldn't get Rietta to say what she wanted she went up to Melling House to make a personal appeal. But when she got there Lessiter wasn't alone. Rietta had taken the short cut and got in first. She may have passed Catherine, or I suppose Catherine may have passed her and waited to see who it was behind her. That would account for the footprints under the lilacs. We have found the shoes which made them. There's a little of the black earth and a grain or two of lime between the heel and the upper."

Miss Silver nodded. She was knitting busily.

"Pray go on."

"Well, there it is. She must have waited for Rietta to go. Then she went in herself, tried to soften him, but failed. He would be sitting at the table with the memorandum in front of him. It would be easy enough for her to pick up the raincoat and put it on—he wouldn't notice or care. It wouldn't occur to him to be afraid of anything she might do. He was pretty full of himself, and he'd got her under his thumb. She had just told Rietta she was desperate. She could have gone behind him to the fire and picked up the poker. Well, there you are."

Miss Silver said nothing at all for quite a little while. Her needles clicked. When she did speak it was to say,

"You consider that she has committed suicide."

"I shouldn't think that there was any doubt about it. There will have to be a post-mortem of course, but there's no reason to doubt that her death was due to an overdose of sleeping tablets. There was an empty bottle on the table by her side

—one of those new preparations which everyone seems to fly to the minute they have anything the matter with them nowadays."

"How had they been taken?"

"Oh, in coffee. The tray was there on the table—coffee-pot, milk-jug, the cup with the dregs still in it."

"It would take a good deal of coffee to dissolve enough tablets to kill a healthy young woman. What size was the cup?"

"An old one—quite a fair size. Why?"

"I was wondering if the tablets had been dissolved in the cup, or in the pot, or whether they might have been separately dissolved in water and added to the coffee either in the pot or in the cup, in which case I should not expect any sediment to be found."

He looked a little surprised.

"There was no sediment from the powdered tablets. But I'm afraid I don't quite—"

She gave him a brief smile.

"It does not matter, Randal. Have you anything more to tell me?"

"Not about Catherine Welby. But we have had a report on Cyril Mayhew, and there, I must admit, you score again."

She coughed in a protesting manner.

"My dear Randal, I merely repeated his friend Allan Grover's opinion, with the comment that it appeared to be reasonable and sincere."

"Well, the boy seems to have turned up at his lodgings in pretty bad shape. He said he missed the last train and had to thumb a lift. He's been in bed with a temperature ever since. The gold figures are certainly not in his room, and he doesn't seem to have any opportunity of disposing of them. The only time he could have done it would be between leaving Melling and arriving at his lodgings, and that's out, because we've traced the man who gave him the lift—a doctor called out of town to a consultation. He says the boy seemed ill when he picked him up in Lenton, so he went a mile out of his road and took him all the way home."

Miss Silver knitted briskly. The sleeve of little Josephine's jacket lengthened.

"What does Cyril Mayhew say himself?"

"Oh, he admits going down to see his mother, and admits that it was because he wanted money, but he says his mother gave it to him. When he was pressed he broke down and said it was his father's money and his father didn't know. Well, that's a family matter—unless Mayhew makes a charge, which he won't. But it accounts for Mrs. Mayhew getting so hot and bothered. I suspect she has been strictly forbidden to go on providing the prodigal with pocket-money, and she's been doing it behind Mayhew's back."

Miss Silver's needles clicked.

"You did not find the gold figures at the Gate House?"

"No, we didn't."

She said in a thoughtful tone,

"They must be somewhere."

He laughed.

"Too true! But we haven't found them yet."

She continued in the same manner.

"A woman in Mrs. Welby's position would find it extremely difficult to dispose of that kind of stolen property."

He made a gesture of protest.

"She disposed of other things."

"They were not known to be stolen. I do not suppose for a moment that she regarded them as stolen. She had probably quite persuaded herself that Mrs. Lessiter had given them to her, and she had no reason to suppose that her actions would ever be called in question. There is a vast difference between that and the disposal of these four gold figures, taken at the time of a murder and in the very presence of the murdered man."

"She may have hidden them somewhere."

Miss Silver coughed.

"Why should she take them at all? For a woman of her type to kill by violence she must have been very highly wrought. Mr. Lessiter was threatening her with prosecution. If she was so beside herself with fear as to have recourse to an unnatural degree of violence, would she choose that moment for a theft which must involve her in a fresh series of risks and would, if traced, convict her of the murder? That is one thing I find difficult to believe. But there is another. Miss Cray left Mr. Lessiter at a quarter past nine. We know that Mrs. Welby stood behind the lilacs, and we have drawn the deduction that she was waiting for Miss Cray to go. We know that she ascended the step, and it is fair to conclude that she listened at the door. Miss Cray broke off her interview in anger, and she admits that the anger was on behalf of a friend. Can you doubt that the friend was Mrs. Welby, and that Miss Cray's generous anger arose from his obstinate determination to prosecute?"

"Yes, I admit all that."

"Then, Randal, can you explain why Mrs. Welby should have allowed more than half an hour to go by before entering the study?"

"Where do you get your half hour?"

She said very composedly,

"From Mrs. Mayhew's statements. You will remember that she opened the study door at a quarter to ten and saw Miss Cray's raincoat hanging over a chair. She described the cuff as being stained with blood. When she was later pressed on this point, it appeared that the stain was no more than could be accounted for by the scratch on Miss Cray's wrist. But when Mr. Carr Robertson brought the raincoat home more than an hour later the sleeve was quite soaked with blood. If this soaking occurred whilst the coat was being worn by Mrs. Welby, then it happened after Mrs. Mayhew opened the door at a quarter to ten. From what Miss Cray has told me, I believe that it must have happened considerably later than that. Miss Cray says the blood was still quite wet. Blood dries quickly, and she says it was very hot in the study. If Mrs. Welby stained that coat in the act of murdering Mr. Lessiter, then she must have deferred her interview with him for something between half an hour and an hour and a quarter. Why should she have done so?"

"I don't know."

"Nor do I, Randal."

He said in an exasperated voice,

"My dear Miss Silver, what are you trying to prove? The case is solved, the murderer has committed suicide—two and two have made four. What more do you want?"

She coughed in a deprecating manner.

"You say that two and two have made four. I regret to say that at the moment they appear to me to be making five."

Chapter Forty

MISS SILVER KNOCKED at the kitchen door and went in. She found Mrs. Crook sitting in front of the fire listening to the B.B.C. light programme.

"Pray do not disturb yourself. I will not detain you for more than a moment."

Mrs. Crook reached out sideways and reduced the volume of an accordion band.

"Thank you, Mrs. Crook. It is wonderful how faithfully your set reproduces the tone—but just a little difficult when one is talking. I only came in to ask whether you would by any chance be going out this evening."

"Well, I thought I might look in on Mrs. Grover."

Miss Silver coughed.

"I wondered if you would be doing that, and whether you would mind taking a note for me to her son."

"He'll be in a dreadful way," said Mrs. Crook.

"I am afraid so."

"Thought the world of Mrs. Welby. I don't want to say anything about them that are gone, but she shouldn't have encouraged him the way she did—a boy like that! Where was her pride?"

"I expect she just looked upon him as a boy, Mrs. Crook."

Bessie Crook bridled.

"Well, he's got his feelings, hasn't he? She might have thought of that. And so has my niece Gladys. Mrs. Welby didn't think about her, did she? Come between two loving hearts, that's what she did. Gladys and Allan, they'd been going together ever since they were in their cradles, as you might say. Living or dead, you can't get from it—it's not what a lady ought to do."

This was a very long speech for Mrs. Crook. Her colour had deepened. She looked accusingly at Miss Silver.

"Let young people alone is what I say. But she couldn't. Only yesterday morning she was off into Lenton and in Mr. Holderness's office. Gladys had the morning off, and they went in on the same bus, so she thinks to herself, 'I'll see where she goes.' And she hasn't got to see far—straight

171

through Friar's Cut and into Mr. Holderness's office! And nothing'll make Gladys believe she didn't go there after Allan. Quite downhearted she was when I saw her for a minute outside the Stores."

Miss Silver's note was a very short one. It ran:

Dear Mr. Grover,
    I should very much like to see you if you can make it convenient.

Yours sincerely,
MAUD SILVER.

Having dispatched it by the hand of Mrs. Crook, she decided that she would not accompany Cecilia Voycey to evening service. She was therefore alone in the house when in response to a hesitating knock upon the front door she went to open it and saw the same tall, dark figure which had accompanied her across the Green.

She took him into the comfortable warmth of the drawing-room, and was able for the first time to receive an impression of him beyond that conveyed by his voice and his height. He was a goodlooking boy, even with his eyes red and swollen from weeping. He had a certain charm of youth, sincerity, and ardour. He took the chair she indicated, stared at her in a grief-stricken way, and said,

"I was coming to see you."

"Yes, Mr. Grover?"

He said, "Yes. And then your note came. I'd been trying to make up my mind, because I can see it may ruin me. But I don't care for that any more, only it will be hard on my people."

"Yes?"

He sat forward with his hands hanging down between his knees. Sometimes he looked at her, and sometimes he stared upon the ground. His hands hung down.

"You can't always hold your tongue because it will get you into trouble—"

Miss Silver was knitting quietly. She said,

"Not always."

"I've been going over it in my mind all day, backwards and forwards, ever since I heard about her. It wasn't fair to tell my father and mother, because you see, it may ruin me, and it would be like asking them to have a hand in it. And they'd think about it afterwards—it wouldn't be fair. Then I thought about you. You let me talk to you about Cyril. I thought you'd understand—there's something about you."

As he said this he looked up suddenly.

"You don't think I'm rude, do you? I don't mean to be."

She gave him the smile which had won so many confidences.

"I am quite sure about that. You can tell me anything you like. I am sure it is best to tell the truth. Concealments are of no real benefit to anyone. They breed more crimes."

He looked startled, and said,

"*More?*" And then, "There's been enough, hasn't there?"

"Yes, Allan."

The silence gathered, until he broke it with a sigh so deep that it was almost a sob.

"I'd no business to love her, but I did! I can't let them say things about her and hold my tongue—can I?" Then, without waiting for an answer, "She came to the office on Saturday morning—that's yesterday. It seems much longer ago than that. I was in the room where I work. She opened the door and came in. I took her along to Mr. Holderness's room. Then I went back, but I couldn't settle down. You see, there had been a lot of talk—talk about Mr. Lessiter coming back—talk about whether he would make it up again with Miss Cray—talk about whether he would let Mrs. Welby stay on at the Gate House, and whether he would let her keep the things Mrs. Lessiter had given her. I was worried for her in case she was turned out, or Mr. Lessiter wouldn't let her keep the things. I didn't know how things were, and I couldn't sleep thinking about it. I couldn't go and see her, because there had been talk —everyone talks in a village—and she'd told me to keep away. It was driving me silly." He looked up, and down again, and drew one of those sobbing breaths. "When she came into the office I knew what she had come for—to talk to Mr. Holderness and get his advice. I was desperate to know how things were, and—well, I listened." He threw up his head with a jerk and met Miss Silver's calm, compassionate gaze. His face worked as he said with a mixture of pride and defiance, "I'd no right to—I'd no business—I know that. I just didn't seem able to help myself."

Miss Silver coughed.

"It was, of course, reprehensible, but I can understand your

feelings. You say you listened. May I enquire how you
contrived to do so?"

Her tone was kind and perfectly matter of fact. It steadied
him. He said in a much quieter voice,

"We're very short-handed. Mr. Jackson, the head clerk, has
been laid up. Mr. Stanway, the other partner, is an invalid. He
doesn't come down to the office more than once in a blue
moon, but he's got his room there next to Mr. Holderness.
When I joined the firm there was a clerk there called Hood.
He told me, making a joke of it, that Mr. Stanway kept a
brandy-bottle behind one of the panels in his room. I don't
know how he found out about it, but he took me in and showed
me one day when we thought there wasn't anyone about. It
was a regular secret cupboard opening with a spring. There's a
bit of carving you move and the door comes open. Well, he
showed it to me, and there was the brandy-bottle like he said.
And whilst we were standing looking at it we got an awful start,
because there was Mr. Holderness saying something as plain
as if he was in the room. Just for a minute we thought he was,
and we got the wind up properly. I can't remember what he
said. It was just something like 'Now where on earth did I put
those papers?'—talking to himself, you know. Hood looked at
me and put up his hand and shut the panel ever so gently, and
we got out of the room as quick as we could. We hadn't any
business to be there, and we wouldn't have been there, only
we thought Mr. Holderness had gone out."

Miss Silver laid the sleeve of little Josephine's jacket out flat
upon her knee and measured it with her hand. It was still a
couple of inches short of the right length. She said,

"You opened the cupboard in Mr. Stanway's room yesterday
and listened to what Mrs. Welby was saying to Mr. Holderness?"

"Yes, I did. I made an excuse to the girl who works in the
same room with me. There were some papers Mr. Holderness
had asked for, and I said I was going to look for them. I hadn't
ever opened the cupboard since Hood showed it to me, but I
remembered how. It opened quite easily, and it didn't make
any noise—I expect Mr. Stanway kept the spring well oiled.
Everything was just the same, only the cupboard was empty,
the brandy-bottle was gone. And I could see why you could
hear what was going on in the next room. The panel had
warped and there was a crack all down one side, and there was
a knot-hole too. I looked through it, and I could see Mrs.

Welby sitting there. When I found I could see her I wasn't thinking about listening any more—I just wanted to look at her. And then I couldn't help listening, because Mr. Holderness said in the most—well, the most brutal way, 'You've got yourself into a very dangerous position.' "

Miss Silver said, "Oh!" and he caught her up.

"I've got to tell you this, but I can't if you're going to think anything wrong about Mrs. Welby. Mrs. Lessiter gave her the things, and of course she thought they were hers to do what she liked with, and then Mr. Lessiter came along and he threatened—Miss Silver, he threatened to prosecute."

"Yes—I was aware of that."

He stared at her, his lip twitching.

"How anyone could be such—such a devil!"

"Pray go on, Allan."

"They talked about it, and she said Mrs. Lessiter had given her the things. No, I think that was later—or before—I don't know which—" He dropped his head into his hands and kept it there, fingers pressing in upon the temples. "She said he had told her he was going to prosecute, and she went to see him."

"On the night of the murder?"

"Yes. But Miss Cray was there, so she came away."

"She went back later."

"You know that?"

"Yes."

"How?"

"I do know it."

"Yes, she went back. She told Mr. Holderness. She said she was in a very serious position, and he said why should it come out—she could hold her tongue. You know, when I was going over it afterwards, that's when I began really to think. Up till then I was just frightened—terrified for her—but when he said that, I could see her. She wasn't frightened, she was enjoying herself. I know how she looks when she's pleased about something, and she was pleased. She didn't exactly laugh, but there was that kind of sound in her voice. He said, 'You can hold your tongue, can't you?' and she said, 'Oh, yes—I have —I do. And I shall go on—unless I simply can't help myself.' " He lifted his head again. "That's what got me. He was the one who was in a state—she wasn't. I shifted so that I could see him, and he looked dreadful. I thought to myself, 'He's got the wind up,' and I couldn't make out why. Then they began to talk about you."

Miss Silver's needles clicked. She said,

"Dear me!"

"Mrs. Welby was afraid you were finding out about things. There was something about a memorandum. She called it 'that damned memorandum,' and she said you knew about it. And then she said, 'I wonder if I hadn't better make a statement to the police and have done with it,' and Mr. Holderness said it would be extremely dangerous." His tone became suddenly harder, older. "That made me think some more. I didn't like the way he said it. It sounded—it seemed ridiculous at the time—but I couldn't help thinking it sounded as if he was threatening her."

Miss Silver coughed.

"You interest me extremely."

Allan Grover went on as if she had not spoken.

"It was when he said 'dangerous.' I was watching him through the knot-hole. He looked at her. It scared me, but she wasn't scared. I moved so that I could see her, and she was laughing. And she said, 'Dangerous? For whom?' That's where I got the feeling that I didn't really know what they were talking about. It didn't seem as if it could mean what it seemed to be meaning, because the next thing she said was, 'If I make that statement I shall have to say what I saw when I came back.' Mr. Holderness said her words over again, 'When you came back—' and she said, 'I told you Rietta was with him the first time I went, and I told you I came back. I waited whilst she talked to him. It was highly entertaining. He told her he had found the old will he had made in her favour when they were engaged, and, do you know, she tried to get him to burn it! I always knew Rietta was a fool, but I didn't think anyone could be quite such a fool as that. He told her he'd rather she had the money than anyone else. He said he had found the will when he was looking for the "memorandum." From what he said, it was there on the table.' And she said, '*It was, wasn't it?*'" He made an abrupt movement. "When she said that, I didn't seem to take it in. I don't know if you can understand. I've got a very good memory—I could tell you everything they said and not miss a word."

Miss Silver inclined her head. She had that kind of memory herself.

He went on.

"I can remember it all, but when I was listening to it it didn't seem to mean anything. Mrs. Welby went on talking. She said

Miss Cray quarrelled with Mr. Lessiter. It wasn't about the will, it was about Mrs. Welby. Miss Cray wanted him to stop going on about the things his mother had given her, and he wouldn't. He said he was going to prosecute." Allan's voice took on a tone of horror. "And then Miss Cray lost her temper and came out in a hurry. Mrs. Welby had only just time to get out of the way."

Miss Silver's needles clicked.

"Yes—I was sure that was how it happened. What did Mrs. Welby do after that? The interval has puzzled me. Did she go in then and see Mr. Lessiter?"

He shook his head.

"No, she didn't think it was any use—not on the top of that quarrel. She went home and made herself some coffee. She told Mr. Holderness she sat there smoking one cigarette after another and thinking what she could do, and in the end she came round to where she had begun—she must go back and have it out with Mr. Lessiter. By the time she'd made up her mind it was ten o'clock. When she got as far as that, telling Mr. Holderness, he said, 'That was a pity, Catherine.' He hadn't spoken all the time she was telling him until he said it was a pity. I didn't know what he meant then, but I do now." A quick shudder went over him. He stared piteously at Miss Silver. "I think that's when he made up his mind to kill her."

Miss Silver rested her hands on the small pale blue jacket and said,

"Yes, I suppose so."

"She couldn't see it, you know. I don't think it ever occurred to her for one single moment that it would be dangerous to threaten him."

Miss Silver coughed.

"Did she threaten him?"

"I don't think she meant it that way, but that is how he would take it. You see, when she went back to Melling House he was there in the study talking to Mr. Lessiter. There was something in that memorandum about him—money Mrs. Lessiter had handed over to him to invest. And he'd kept it, and Mr. Lessiter was going to prosecute. That's why he killed him."

"Mrs. Welby was actually a witness of the murder?"

"No, no, no—you mustn't think that! She left them quarrelling, and she came away. It wouldn't have been any good her seeing Mr. Lessiter on the top of a scene like that. She had got back to the Gate House, when she heard him coming down the drive. She stood behind a bush and watched him go."

"A very shocking affair."

"He had his car parked about a hundred yards along on the grass. I saw it."

"You saw it?"

He nodded.

"I'm a fool. I used to go round and see her in the evenings. Then she said I mustn't come any more—people were talking. But I couldn't seem to get out of the way. I used to go round there and walk up and down, and watch to see her light go out, and then go home. I was there on Wednesday—that's how I saw the car."

"And you did not inform the police?"

His voice became suddenly natural and boyish.

"Miss Silver, I give you my word it never crossed my mind that Mr. Holderness being there had anything to do with the murder—how could it? I thought he was out there seeing Mrs. Welby. It made me feel downright sick—an old man like that! I didn't sleep all night. I could have killed him—but I never thought he had anything to do with Mr. Lessiter's death—not till I was in Mr. Stanway's room listening, and heard what Mrs. Welby had to say."

Miss Silver had resumed her knitting. She said,

"I see. Will you go on?"

The energy went out of him. He said,

"There isn't much more. By the time she had finished it was all as clear as daylight. That's to say, it's as clear as daylight now, looking back at it, but while they were talking it didn't seem as if I could take it in—it didn't seem possible. She never said right out, 'I know you killed Mr. Lessiter and took the memorandum, and if I tell the police, you'll be hanged for it.' It was all what a serious position she was in, and she would hold her tongue if she could, but of course if they tried to put it on her, she would have to say what she knew. And then a piece about how awful it was for her having so little money, and how grateful she would be if he could help her out. Of course she didn't realize—she couldn't have realized—how that sounded to him. He was old enough to be her father, and all she would think about was that she was in a tight place and he could help her out. But going over it in my mind—and I haven't been able to help going over it all day—I can see that what he thought was—was—" The breath caught in his throat.

He stared miserably down at the pattern of Mrs. Voycey's carpet.

Miss Silver coughed discreetly.

"That she was blackmailing him. It would certainly appear to him in that light."

Without looking at her Allan stammered out,

"She wouldn't—Mrs. Welby wouldn't!"

Little Josephine's jacket swung round with something of a swish. There was no doubt at all in Miss Silver's mind that Catherine Welby had embarked upon a deliberate attempt at blackmailing, and that this attempt had brought her to her death. Very dangerous—very dangerous indeed, and in a murder case extremely likely to prove fatal. She did not, however, make this comment aloud, but continued to knit until the silence was broken by a choking sob.

"What I can't get over is that I might have saved her. I told you I didn't take it all in at the time. When she came out of Mr. Holderness's room she was extra sweet to me. It—it put everything else out of my head. The office shut at one, and I went off with some chaps to a football match. I didn't get home till late, and after I'd had my tea I went out again. I told my mother I was going to get a game of darts at The Feathers, but when it came to the point I couldn't face it. I went and walked up and down by the Gate House and watched her light. Round about half past nine I saw the car drive up again and park on the verge. There's a tree hangs down over the wall. I stood back under it and watched him go past. He went between the pillars and up to her door and in. I nearly went mad thinking of them there together." He looked up, his face twitching. "Do you know, I went up to the door and put my finger on the bell but I couldn't ring it. I went away again—but if I'd gone in—it would have saved her."

Miss Silver looked at him very kindly.

"That is more than anyone can say. You cannot know it. Do not torment yourself by thinking of what might have been. I do not see how you could have interrupted an interview between Mrs. Welby and her solicitor. Can you tell me how long he stayed?"

"It seemed like hours, but it wasn't more than twenty minutes. He came out, and got into his car and drove off."

Miss Silver coughed.

"You say 'he,' and 'his car,' but could you swear to this 'he' being Mr. Holderness, or could you swear to the car?"

He gave a jerky nod.

"Both. I saw him by the hall light when he let himself out, and I saw the number of the car, last night, and on the Wednesday night. When he had gone I went on walking up and down for a bit. Then there were some people coming along, and I cleared out and went home." He dropped his head in his hands and groaned. "If I'd stayed—if I'd only stayed—I'd have known there was something wrong when her light didn't go out."

Chapter Forty-one

AT HALF PAST nine o'clock on Monday morning Mr. Holderness gathered his letters together and rose from the breakfast table. A childless widower of many years standing, his house had been kept ever since his wife's death by an unmarried sister, a faded invalidish person with an expression of chronic discontent. As her brother picked up the *Times* and put it under his arm, she looked up with a puckered brow.

"Are you going already?"

"It is half past nine."

"Did you have your second cup of tea?"

He laughed.

"You poured it out yourself."

Miss Holderness clasped her head.

"Did I? I'm sure I hardly know what I'm doing. I didn't sleep a wink. I can't think how I came to run out of my tablets—I thought the box was half full."

"You probably had a glorious burst and took them all the night before."

Miss Holderness looked shocked.

"Oh, no—it would have been *dangerous*."

"Well, my dear, danger is the spice of life."

He had reached the door, when she asked him if he would be in for lunch. He said, "No," and went away out of the room, and out of her life.

He did not very often drive to the office. His house was the one in which he had been born, and his father and his grandfather before him. Standing at what had been the edge of the town when it was built, there was still a garden behind it, but the open spaces beyond were now all quite built over. Since the distance to the office was under half a mile, he was used to making the journey on foot.

This day did not differ from any of the other days, running into uncounted numbers, on which he had shut the door briskly behind him, stood for a moment to savour the air, and then come down the two shallow steps on to the pavement and, turning to the right, set off in the direction of Main Street, his hat a little on the side of his head and a small leather case in his hand. At a quarter to ten he would be at the near end of Main Street, and by the time the clock of St. Mary's was striking the hour he would be at his table looking through the morning's mail.

This Monday morning was no different from all the other Mondays. A dozen people could remember afterwards that they had seen him and bidden him good-morning. Each of them severally made the same comment in varying tones of wonder—"He looked just as usual"—"He didn't look no different"—"You wouldn't have thought there was anything wrong."

Mr. Holderness wouldn't have thought it himself. It was a fine September morning. He felt alert and vigorous, and very much on the top of the world. His forebears came from the North of England. If it had been their fortune to be born as much farther north as the Highland line, his state of mind might have been described as "fey." He had been in very great danger, he had taken a very great risk. Risk is the spice of life. He had pulled success out of failure, security out of danger, and he had done it by the cleverness of his brain, by the swiftness of his thought and the strength of his right hand. Not so bad for a man of sixty-five. Younger men than he might have gone under. He had saved himself, and he had saved the firm. The world was a good enough place.

He called Allan Grover in and asked him for the Jardine papers. When he had brought them and gone away again, Mr. Holderness looked after him, frowning. The boy looked like nothing on earth—eyes bunged up, hand shaking. His frown deepened. He hoped to goodness Grover hadn't been drinking. Wouldn't do if he was going to start that sort of thing —wouldn't do at all. Always seemed a particularly steady young fellow, but you never could tell.

He was bending his mind to the Jardine case, when he heard the footsteps on the stair—heavy steps of more than one

person, coming up the stairs and along the passage to his
room. He looked up, and that is how they saw him as they
came in, the Chief Constable and Inspector Drake. Behind
them Constable Whitcombe closed the door and stayed outside.

The door was shut. They stood just inside it looking at him,
seeing the upright figure in its well cut suit, the thick grey
hair, the dark eyebrows arching over fine dark eyes, the florid
colour. Except for the modern dress he might have been his
own great-grandfather. The thought went through Randal
March's mind—eighteenth century, that's what he is. "That
they should take, who have the power, and they should keep
who can." He couldn't remember where the lines came from,
but they fitted.

The shadowy Stanway above the hearth gloomed on the
room. There was just a moment's silence. A great deal can
happen in a moment. The whole towering structure built up in
pride, self-will, and arrogance can come to a crashing fall—a
crashing and irrevocable fall.

Randal March came forward and said gravely,

"We have come on a painful errand, Mr. Holderness—"

He showed nothing, except that his colour had deepened.
He said, "Indeed?" and he said it without a tremor.

Inspector Drake came up to the table and stood there. He
brought out a notebook and read from it.

"Is the number of your car XXM. 312?"

"Certainly."

"We have information that it was parked on the grass verge
outside the drive of Melling House between ten and ten-
twenty p.m. on the night of Wednesday last, and again for
about twenty minutes between nine-thirty and ten o'clock on
Saturday night."

Mr. Holderness remained in his upright position, one hand
on the table edge, the other holding the paper which he had
been perusing.

"May I ask who has given you this information?"

"Someone who knows the car. It will be sworn to."

There was a faint crackling sound from the paper in Mr.
Holderness's hand. His fingers had closed upon it. The sound
must have attracted his attention, for his eyes turned that way.
His grip relaxed. He smoothed the paper out and laid it down.
When this had been done he said,

"My clerk Allan Grover in fact—he lives in Melling. Well,

gentlemen, I called upon Mrs. Welby on both those evenings. It is not a criminal offence to call upon a pretty woman. One may not be anxious to advertize the fact, especially to a tattling village, but I am quite willing to admit that I paid those two calls. What of it?"

Drake said sharply, "You were in the neighbourhood of Melling House between ten and ten-thirty on the Wednesday night."

Mr. Holderness smiled.

"I was calling on Mrs. Welby."

"At that hour?"

The smile was maintained.

"My dear Inspector—"

"You say that you were with Mrs. Welby?"

"She will, I am sure, confirm it."

There was a brief electric silence. Drake looked at the Chief Constable.

March said, "Do you not know that Mrs. Welby is dead?"

The hand which had held the paper was lifted with a jerk. It fell again upon his knee. The florid colour had ebbed perceptibly. He said,

"No—no—how shocking!"

"You did not know?"

"No, no—how could I?"

"You were with her on Saturday night. She was found dead on Sunday morning."

"How?"

"An overdose of sleeping tablets."

Mr. Holderness leaned back in his chair. He said under his breath,

"It's a great shock—I've known her since she was a child—" And then, "Just give me a minute."

When it was gone by, he had composed himself. He said soberly,

"I see that I must tell you what I hoped not to have to tell. Mrs. Welby was not exactly a client, but she was a very old friend who sometimes asked my advice. She came here on Saturday morning and told me that she was in a very serious position. I must tell you that she had been living in the Gate House practically rent-free for some years. Mrs. Lessiter had furnished it for her, and, rightly or wrongly, Mrs. Welby assumed that all these furnishings were gifts. She even went so far as to sell some of them. When Mr. Lessiter came home he at once took the matter up—he came to see me about it. He suspected that some of the things had been sold, amongst them a Cosway miniature of considerable value, and he was in an extremely vindictive frame of mind. I did my best to mollify him, but he persisted in his determination to prosecute if he could lay his hands on sufficient evidence. On the Wednesday evening he rang me up to say that he had found a memorandum left for him by his mother which made it perfectly clear that the contents of the Gate House were lent to Mrs. Welby, and not given. He reiterated his intention to prosecute. Guessing that Mrs. Welby would have had a similar communication, and knowing how distressed she would be, I got out my car and went over to see her." He paused.

When neither Drake nor the Chief Constable made any comment, he lifted his hand in the same gesture as before, let it fall upon his knee, and went on speaking.

"I found her in a state of extreme distress. She told me she had been up to Melling House to try and see James Lessiter, but finding that Miss Cray was with him, she had come away again. She wanted me to go up and see him, but I told her that I did not consider it would be at all a prudent course—it would be very much better to allow him to sleep on the matter. I told her that he would be sure to come and speak to me about it, and that I would then suggest to him the harm that would be done to his own reputation if he were to proceed to extremities. I assured her that it was most unlikely that he meant to do so. She said something about making another attempt to see him herself, but I begged her not to think of it. When I left her I believed that she had given up the idea." He paused, looked across at the Chief Constable, and said, "Do you not wish to take any of this down? I see that the Inspector is not doing so."

March said gravely, "A statement can be taken later if you wish it. You will realize, of course, that it may be used in evidence."

"Naturally. Well, I will continue. On Thursday morning I heard of James Lessiter's death. I was very much shocked. The police asked my assistance with a view to ascertaining whether there was anything missing from the house, and I accompanied the clerk who checked over the inventory. Carr Robertson consulted me with regard to his position, and I thought it right to pass on his information that Cyril Mayhew had been seen in Lenton on the night of the murder. I advised young Robertson to make a full statement to the police. On Saturday morning Mrs. Welby came to see me. I do not feel at liberty to disclose all she said, but in the circumstances I do feel bound to tell you that she intimated that she did go back to Melling House after I left her on Wednesday night. Her state of mind filled me with alarm. I begged her to go home and rest, and I would come and see her in the evening. My position was a painful one—I had known her since she was a child. I wanted time to think things over. In the end she went away."

Inspector Drake cleared his throat.

"You reached Melling at about half past nine?"

"It would be somewhere about that time. I didn't look at my watch."

"How did you find Mrs. Welby?"

"Much quieter. She had a tray with some coffee beside her. She offered me a cup, but I refused. I said it would keep me awake. She smiled and said it didn't have that effect on her."

"How many cups were there on the tray?"

"Only one. She was going to get another, when I stopped her."

"Mr. Holderness, why was there only one cup if she was expecting you?"

"I had not said what time I would come."

"Was the coffee made when you got there?"

"Yes—her cup was half empty."

"Doesn't that seem strange to you, her not waiting for you if she knew you were coming?"

Mr. Holderness brought his hands together and looked down at the joined fingertips. He said in the easy tone he would have used to a client,

"No, I don't think so. She knew I didn't take coffee. She always offered it to me, but it was just a polite form—she knew I didn't take it. I didn't stay very long, you know. Her manner reassured me, and she said she would take a sedative and get a good night's rest."

"She was in the habit of taking sedatives?"

Mr. Holderness met the look of sharp enquiry with a faint melancholy smile.

"I have no idea. If I had thought at the time that she meant anything more than perhaps a couple of aspirins, I would not have left her."

"You did not see any box or bottle of sleeping tablets?"

"Oh, no."

There was a pause. Then Randal March said,

"Mr. Holderness—your conversation with Mrs. Welby on Saturday morning was overheard."

As he said the words which he had come there to say he was conscious of a certain sinking feeling. They had not behind them that firmness of conviction which a case of this kind demanded. A fretted feeling that for once in his life he had allowed himself to be rushed lurked in the uneasy recesses of his mind. What had seemed not only possible but final last night was no longer so. In this office, devoted for a hundred and fifty years to the service of the law—under the authoritative gaze of the latest of a line of respectable solicitors, it was extremely difficult to resist the horrid supposition that Allan Grover in a fit of jealousy might quite easily have been telling the tale. That the boy had been infatuated with Catherine Welby and bitterly jealous of his employer, and that he was now nearly beside himself with grief, were self-evident facts. They were, indeed, the very basis of his story. In the momentary silence which followed March's statement these facts offered very little encouragement.

As the moment passed, Mr. Holderness's colour was seen to deepen alarmingly. He said in an incredulous voice,

"My conversation with Mrs. Welby was overheard?"

"Yes."

"May I ask how, and by whom?"

Receiving no answer, he leaned forward and said in a voice vibrant with anger,

"No doubt the person who obliged you with the number of my car! An eavesdropping clerk with his ear to the keyhole—a young man who had made himself such a nuisance to Mrs. Welby that she had had to ask him to discontinue his visits! She spoke of the matter to me, and in her kindness begged me to take no notice of it. She had been good to the young man, lending him books and helping him to improve himself, and now as soon as she is dead this is the return he makes—to throw mud upon her name!"

Randal March said, "In his account of the conversation he stated that he heard Mrs. Welby tell you that she returned to Melling House just after ten o'clock on Wednesday night. She did not go in, because you were there. According to Allan Grover's statement she said that you were engaged in a violent quarrel with James Lessiter, that he was accusing you of

having misappropriated money entrusted to you by his
mother, and that he was declaring his intention of taking
proceedings against you. Grover states that, according to what
he heard Mrs. Welby say, she then gave up any idea of seeing
Lessiter herself and returned to the Gate House."

Mr. Holderness regarded him with a majestic air.

"An eavesdropper's account of an interview between his
employer and a client—a morbid lovesick puppy's account of
his own jealous imaginings! My dear Mr. March, you must be
perfectly aware that this sort of stuff isn't evidence. No court
of law would admit it."

March said quietly, "I am telling you what he has said. His
evidence as to your car would be admitted."

"I have admitted it myself, and accounted for it in a
perfectly reasonable manner."

"Allan Grover will swear that he saw you come down the
drive on Wednesday night—and not from the Gate House."

"I have no doubt that he will be prepared to back his jealous
fancies, but I think I could make very short work of them." He
paused, levelled a brilliant indignant glance first at March and
then at Drake, and said, "And now are you going to arrest
me?"

His tone demanded and challenged. It had all the effect of a
blunt "If this is bluff, I call it." It increased the Chief
Constable's sense of being on ground by no means secure
against a most disastrous collapse, whilst at the same time
stimulating his determination to maintain that ground. There
was hardly any pause before he replied,

"I am afraid we shall be obliged to make a search of the
premises."

Mr. Holderness laughed scornfully.

"It would take you some time to go through all our
deed-boxes. Perhaps if you were to give me some idea of what
you expect to find in them—"

"I think, Mr. Holderness, we should like to begin with your
safe."

Still with that angry, dominating look, he threw himself
back in his chair.

"And if I refuse?"

"Inspector Drake has a search-warrant."

The deep colour of fury rose to the very roots of the thick
grey hair, the dark eyes glared, the left hand lying on his knee
jerked into a clench, the right hand tightened upon the arm of

the chair until every knuckle showed as white as bone. To the two men who were watching him it seemed as if at any moment all this intense rage and protest must break into a violence of invective, yet moment by moment fell into the silence and he made no sound. Then very slowly the purple colour ebbed away. The eyelids dropped over the glaring eyes. When they rose again the paroxysm was over. He was left very much his usual self—a little paler, a little sterner, a little more dignified. He said,

"Very well. I have, of course, no objection to offer. I do not know what you expect to find. I should have thought my years of practice in this town and the record of my firm might have protected me from what I can only describe as an outrage. I have nothing to conceal, and I can only hope that you will have as little to regret."

He pushed back his chair, rose to his feet, and crossed to the left-hand side of the hearth, where he stood in a very composed manner whilst he pulled a steel chain out of his pocket and selected one of the keys depending from it.

The panelling about the hearth was enriched with a double row of heavily carved rosettes rising from the floor to a level with the mantelshelf, after which they turned inwards to frame the Stanway portrait. Mr. Holderness took hold of two of these rosettes and twisted them. There was a click, and a section of the panelling started opening like a door until it disclosed the steel front of a modern safe. Nothing could have been more ordinary than the manner in which he unlocked the steel door, set it wide, and withdrew the key.

He said, "There you are, gentlemen," and went back as far as his chair, where he stood to watch them, one hand in his pocket, the other still holding the bunch of keys.

The safe was fairly full. There were packets of docketed papers. Drake lifted them out, only to find more of the same behind. These too were taken out. Three old-fashioned leather cases followed. They contained an amethyst necklace, set after the Victorian manner in heavy gold, with two matching bracelets. As Drake opened the cases, Mr. Holderness remarked in a sardonic manner,

"I do not really know that these will help you—or Mr. Allan Grover. They were my mother's. Since my sister does not care to wear them, I keep them here, and sometimes please myself with looking at them. They are not of any great value."

At the back of the safe two cardboard shoe-boxes stood one

upon the other. As Drake reached for them, Mr. Holderness's hand came out of his pocket. He walked round to the other side of the chair and sat down. Drake lifted the first box clear and raised the lid. March saw a crumpled mass of tissue paper, Drake's hand with the reddish hairs on the back taking it away, and under the paper a gold foot gleaming, the long line of bare shining limbs—a golden rose-crowned Summer, ten inches high.

Drake said, "There's another, sir," but before the paper had fallen from the companion Spring, Mr. Holderness groaned and slumped sideways in his chair.

Chapter Forty-two

MISS SILVER WAS alone in Mrs. Voycey's drawing-room. It being Monday, Cecilia had gone forth with a shopping-basket to the Stores, from which she would presently return replenished with groceries and gossip. Miss Silver, for this time, had excused herself.

"I should, perhaps, write a letter or two, so I feel that I would on the whole prefer to stay at home this morning, if you will not think me rude, my dear Cecilia."

Mrs. Voycey did not think it at all rude. Stimulating as she found dear Maud's company, it would have made it difficult for her to have a heart-to-heart talk with Mrs. Grover, and a heart-to-heart talk she meant to have. On Bessie Crook's authority Maud Silver had sent for Allan Grover yesterday evening, and when she, Bessie, had returned after a good hour in Mrs. Grover's parlour, not only was Allan still there, but the Chief Constable's car at the door, and he and Inspector Drake in the drawing-room for the best part of three-quarters of an hour. And when Mrs. Voycey got home from the evening service all dear Maud could say was, "My dear Cecilia, I would tell you if I could, but at present it is all very confidential."

Cecilia Voycey had always been told that discretion was a virtue. She would not for the world have denied or questioned it. All the same there are virtues which are very well in the abstract, but which, encountered in the flesh, can be a source of extreme irritation. Maud was perfectly right of course, but

Cecilia felt the need of an uninhibited gossip with Mrs. Grover.

Miss Silver sat in the drawing-room and knitted. She was well away with the second sleeve of little Josephine's jacket, and hoped to finish it before lunch. She would then crochet an ornamental edging all round and furnish it with bows of washing ribbon, after which she could start upon the knickers. The day being chilly, a small fire of logs burned on the hearth, which was set with bright rose-coloured tiles. They did not quite strike the same key as the damask curtains, which in their turn just failed to hit it off with the paeonies, roses and other floral adornments which bloomed so brightly on every chair and sofa. Miss Silver, who liked colour and liked it in profusion, considered the whole effect very tasteful, very bright. She had inhabited some drab schoolrooms in her time.

She knitted, but her thoughts were far away. She did not exactly expect a visit, but she thought it possible that she might receive a telephone call.

When Randal March came into the room she rose to meet him and gave him her hand. He clasped it strongly, held it for a little longer than usual, and said in a tone of extreme gravity,

"Well, you were right."

As he released her and moved over to the fire, she said,

"Did you arrest him?"

"No. He had cyanide on him. He is dead."

"How extremely shocking!"

"It will save a lot of scandal, but of course—it shouldn't have happened."

She seated herself. He dropped into the chair on the other side of the hearth and went on speaking.

"You know, he put up such a good case that I began to think I was heading for a crash. Even if Allan Grover's evidence had been admitted it could have been torn to shreds. Nobody loves the eavesdropper—and a clerk eavesdropping on his employer!" He made a gesture. "If it hadn't been for your backing, I would never have taken it as far as I did this morning, and right in the middle I got one of the worst hollow sinkings I can remember. The fellow was so respectable, so imposing, so virtuously indignant—it just didn't seem possible."

"What happened, Randal?"

"We had a search-warrant. He opened his safe and stood back to watch us whilst we turned it out. At some point in the

proceedings he must have walked round his chair and sat down
with his back to us. He had the poison on him, and he must
have taken it when Drake fetched out the two shoe-boxes
which were right at the back of the safe. Remember the gold
Florentine figures—the four Seasons? There were two of them
in each box. We had just got Summer out, when he groaned
and fell over."

Miss Silver repeated a previous comment.

"Very shocking indeed."

March said grimly, "I shall probably be criticized for having
allowed it to happen."

"You can hardly be said to have allowed it."

"No, but I was off my guard. The fact is, my mind was a
good deal taken up with the idea that we had bitten off more
than we could chew."

"My dear Randal!"

"Sorry—it slipped out. Anyhow that's what I was feeling
like. And then Drake was opening one of those shoe-boxes,
and I saw a golden foot sticking out. Holderness must have
seen it too, and once anyone had seen it the game was up. I
ought to have gone over to him at once, but I took just that first
moment to feel relieved and to see the figure come out of the
box, and by that time the mischief was done. Now why in
heaven's name did he take those figures to start with, or having
taken them, why did he keep them?"

Miss Silver gave a gentle cough.

"I imagine that there may have been two reasons. The loss
of the figures would suggest a burglary. And without doubt
Mr. Holderness would be aware that they were extremely
valuable. He may have thought that he would be able to
dispose of them abroad by some roundabout method—there
are ways in which these things can be done. As far as keeping
them in his safe is concerned, where else would you expect
him to keep them? The possibility of suspicion falling on him
would not, I think, have entered his mind. He could lock the
figures away and feel quite secure. And so he would have been
if it had not been for Allan Grover and your search-warrant."

He smiled at her.

"You are too modest. The proper ending to that sentence is
—'if it hadn't been for Miss Maud Silver.' And as to its being
my search-warrant, I can tell you there was a time when I
came very near to disowning it. I had some embittered
thoughts about my own weakness in having given way to your

very considerable pressure. May I ask you now what you did expect us to find?"

"Just what you did find, Randal."

"The figures?"

"If Mr. Holderness was the murderer, I had no doubt that they would be there. And after hearing Allan Grover's story I had no doubt that Mr. Holderness was the murderer."

"Then it comes back to 'if it hadn't been for Miss Maud Silver.' "

She was knitting industriously. Over the clicking needles she shook her head.

"Oh, no—I can claim no credit. I merely noticed one or two points, and having met Allan Grover, I thought it might be helpful if I could have a talk with him."

Randal March continued to smile at her with a good deal of affection. He leaned forward now and said,

"Ah—those points. Are you going to tell me what they were? I should very much like to know."

"Certainly, if you wish it. As you are aware, I came to the case with a perfectly open mind. I knew none of the people, I had no preconceived ideas, and I was therefore very much on the alert for the impressions which I was bound to receive. To begin with Miss Cray. I found it quite impossible to believe that she had any guilty knowledge. I found her open, candid, honest, and extremely scrupulous about involving anyone else. It was quite out of the question that she should have taken those Florentine figures or committed a murderous attack upon Mr. Lessiter."

The warm colour came up into Randal March's face. He nodded and said,

"Go on."

Miss Silver measured the pale blue cuff which she was knitting. It wanted half an inch of the right length. She pulled a fresh strand of wool from the ball and continued.

"With regard to her nephew Mr. Carr Robertson, my impressions came to me almost entirely through other people. He was in no mood to allow me to question him, and I did not expect him to do so. But when Miss Cray with obvious sincerity declared that he had at first been quite certain that it was she who had killed Mr. Lessiter, and that even now he was not quite sure that she had not done so, I was inclined to accept her statement, and to consider that the murderer must be looked for elsewhere. The third suspect, Cyril Mayhew, I dismissed after hearing what Allan Grover had to say. Everything else apart, if he had wished to steal, there must have been many things which might have been taken and either not missed for months or never missed at all. The extreme improbability of his removing these noticeable ornaments from the room most constantly occupied by Mr. Lessiter, and the certainty that such a theft would immediately be discovered, occurred to me with considerable force. The more I thought about it, the more it seemed clear that the figures had been stolen, not only by someone who knew their value, but by someone who intended that value to suggest a motive for Mr. Lessiter's murder which would disguise the real motive."

March said, "That might have involved Carr Robertson."

Miss Silver shook her head.

"Superficially, yes—but actually, no. Consider the evidence. He has suddenly discovered that it is James Lessiter who has seduced and deserted his wife—he rushes out of the house. But he does not go up to Melling House—he walks over to Lenton and spends quite a long time with Miss Elizabeth Moore. They were at one time engaged, they had been separated, they now become reconciled. It is just possible that a man in those circumstances might commit a murder, but I think it extremely improbable, and I certainly do not think that if he had done so he would have brought that bloodstained raincoat home and introduced it to Miss Cray with the accusing remark, 'Why did you do it?'"

"He did that—"

"Yes, Randal. It convinced Miss Cray of his innocence, and it convinced me. Though I had not seen much of him, I had received a very definite impression of his character. He might have been worked up to the point of violence, but he was incapable of duplicity or theft. And if he had killed Mr. Lessiter, it was inconceivable that he should have tried to shift the blame on to Miss Cray."

"Yes, that's true enough. And where did you go from there?"

She coughed gently.

"I considered Mrs. Welby, but I could not arrive at any conclusion. Both from my own observation and from what I had heard about her I judged her to be of a cold and self-centred disposition. I was sure that she was untruthful, and I suspected that she was dishonest."

He raised his eyebrows.

"How devastating! All that, but not murder?"

She shook her head reprovingly.

"I could not believe that she could have brought herself to hit a man over the head with a poker. If she had been going to murder anyone she would, I am sure, have employed poison. A woman of her fastidious refinement would have to be carried quite outside herself with passion before she could kill a man in so brutal a manner. And Mrs. Welby was, I am convinced, incapable of being carried out of herself by passion. All the same, I was sure she knew something that she was keeping back, which was of course the case."

Leaning back in his chair, March looked at her with a half-quizzical admiration.

"And now we come to Mr. Holderness. You know, I really would like to know how you got there."

"In the simplest manner in the world." She paused to measure the pale blue cuff, and finding it long enough, began to cast off. "The whole thing really turns on those gold figures. They were not taken by accident, but for a definite purpose. I believed that purpose to be twofold. The value of the figures entered into it, and the question of making the whole affair appear to be the result of a burglary. I had to consider who would have the necessary special knowledge about the figures. I had already discarded Miss Cray, Mr. Carr Robertson, and Mrs. Welby. The latter might have taken them so far as any moral scruples were concerned, but she was already under suspicion owing to her previous misappropriations, and I was sure she was much too clear-headed to have added to her danger by so compromising a theft."

"Did you never consider the Mayhews? They could hardly have helped knowing all about the figures."

"I think they probably took them for granted. When a thing has always been there, you do not think about it. I was naturally struck by Mrs. Mayhew's extreme distress and prostration, but this was explained by her anxiety on account of her son. As soon as this was relieved, she made a remarkable recovery. As regards Mr. Mayhew, I found that he enjoyed the respect of eveyone in Melling. I think in a village it would be very difficult for him to bear the kind of character he bears without deserving it. Also, on comparison of the time of his arrival by bus from Lenton with the time of Mr. Carr Robertson's visit, it did not seem possible that he could have committed the murder. Mr. Robertson must have reached Melling House about ten-thirty. Mr. Lessiter was dead and the raincoat heavily stained. Mr. Mayhew, I believe, came out from Lenton on the last bus, which does not arrive until eleven. I had, therefore, to consider who else would be likely to know about the figures. It was at this point that the name of Mr. Holderness presented itself."

"But my dear Miss Silver—"

She gave him a look faintly tinged with reproof.

"I did not say that I suspected him. His name presented itself as that of a person who must surely have known the value of the figures."

"They were entered in the inventory and for probate merely as four gilt figures."

She coughed.

"I found that a suspicious circumstance. It was common knowledge that Mrs. Lessiter was on very confidential terms with her solicitor, and according to Miss Cray she was both proud of the figures, which were a legacy from her side of the family, and fond of talking about them to her intimates. I thought it impossible that Mr. Holderness should not have known their history."

March said drily, "He evidently did."

"I was sure of it. The next thing that attracted my attention was Mr. Holderness's advice to Mr. Carr Robertson, who had consulted him professionally. He advised him to make a full statement to the police."

"Very correct."

With some half dozen stitches left on her last needle, Miss Silver paused in her task of casting off.

"My dear Randal, it is no part of a solicitor's duty to advise a course which must lead to the immediate arrest of his client, at so early a stage and with an inquest pending. The reason why Mr. Carr Robertson was not arrested was, I imagine, the emergence at that time of a new suspect in Cyril Mayhew. But my attention had been once more directed to Mr. Holderness. I found myself wondering why he should have given his client such dangerous advice."

"You are very acute."

"We now come to the matter of the telephone conversations as reported by Gladys Luker. I was extremely anxious for this information. Miss Cray was protecting Mrs. Welby and would give me no help, but I had rather more than a suspicion that Gladys would be able to do so. Her aunt is a friend of Mrs. Voycey's housekeeper, and I had learned from Mrs. Crook that the girl seemed to have something on her mind. When you let me see a copy of her statement I was struck by the recurrence of Mr. Holderness's name. Consider those two calls and their implications. Mr. Lessiter has been looking for a memorandum left by his mother. He has, by all accounts, turned the house upside down to find it. When he finds it, what is the first thing he does? He asks Gladys Luker for Mr. Holderness's private number. She only catches the first words he says, but they are quite illuminating. He says, "Good-evening, Mr. Holderness. I've found my mother's memorandum.' A little later, when he is ringing up Mrs. Welby, he says the same thing, 'Well, Catherine, I've found the memorandum.' After which he goes on to tax her with misappropriation of his property, and after stating his intention to prosecute he says, 'I've an old score to settle, and I always settle my scores. I've just been ringing old Holderness up.' Randal, those words made me think very seriously indeed. They would pass as an indication that he had consulted his solicitor about Mrs. Welby's fault, but I rather doubted if he would have rung Mr. Holderness up at that hour, and at his private address, if he had not had some more particular reason. In the light of those two telephone conversations, both beginning in the same way, and the remark about paying off old scores—not *an* old score, you will observe—I began to consider whether the memorandum referred to might not contain something which would embarrass Mr. Holderness as well as Mrs. Welby. Mrs. Lessiter's circumstances would have made a fraudulent manipulation of funds comparatively easy. She was not businesslike. She trusted her solicitor, and treated him as an intimate friend. Her son had been absent for so many years that no one expected him to return, or to take any great interest in his mother's dispositions."

She cast off the last stitch, pulled the wool through the loop, drew it tight, and transfixed the pale blue ball with the needles she had been using.

"Well, Randal, there you have what was in my mind. When it came to Mrs. Welby's death, I found myself unable to believe that she had committed suicide. I felt sure that she had not murdered James Lessiter, but I also felt sure that she knew a good deal about the crime. Those footprints under the lilacs were hers. I paid her a visit after their discovery, and she was very much alarmed. My impression with regard to Mr. Holderness's connection with the affair was naturally deepened when, after her death, I found Mrs. Welby had hastened in to Lenton by an early bus on Saturday morning and gone straight to his office."

"And how in the world did you know that?"

She answered very composedly,

"Gladys Luker was off duty and went out on the same bus. She had been made very unhappy by Allan Grover's infatuation for Mrs. Welby, and she followed her to see whether it was her intention to visit the office in which he was employed."

He made a mock gesture of despair.

"How can a poor policeman compete? You can take the village lid off and see how the wheels are going round. Gladys and Allan are people to you. You know their relations to the ninth or tenth degree, where I don't even know that they exist."

She gave him a deprecating smile.

"You are falling into Frank Abbott's trick of exaggeration. I am only trying to convey to you how very small and slight were my grounds for suspicion when I decided to ask Allan Grover if he would come and see me. I could not have anticipated what he had to disclose, but it was village talk that he haunted the neighbourhood of the Gate House, and I thought it just possible that he might have seen or heard something of interest either on the Wednesday or the Saturday night."

She folded little Josephine's jacket neatly and put it away in her knitting-bag.

"Well, Randal, I do not think there is anything more that I can tell you. As soon as I heard what Allan had to say I rang you up. I suppose there can be no doubt that Mr. Holderness went to the Gate House on Saturday night with every intention of silencing the woman who had it in her power to implicate him in James Lessiter's murder. She had already shown him plainly that she intended to make a profit out of what she knew. I am constantly amazed at the criminal folly of the amateur blackmailer. It does not seem to occur to them that the course on which they have embarked is not only unprincipled but extremely dangerous, and that where the crime in question is murder their attempt is only too likely to lead to a second fatality. I do not suppose that Mrs. Welby gave a thought to the danger she was inviting. Mr. Holderness was evidently in the habit of visiting her. When he arrived on

Saturday evening she received him as usual. She made coffee—"

March interrupted her.

"The fact that there was only the one cup on the tray is accounted for. His explanation is that he never took coffee, though she always offered it. He said it kept him awake, and added that it did not have the same effect on her. In the circumstances I found that rather grim."

Miss Silver inclined her head.

"I think he would have brought the sleeping tablets with him, probably already dissolved. He could easily distract her attention for long enough to give him the opportunity of introducing the mixture into the coffee. We know from Allan Grover that he did not stay for more than twenty minutes. She had drunk the coffee, and was probably already beginning to feel drowsy. He had doubtless made himself very charming, and had promised everything she asked. There was nothing to wait for. He left her and drove home."

"Yes—it would have been like that." He got to his feet. "There will be quite a lot of ends to tidy up. Drake will be in his element."

He took both her hands and held them for a moment.

"I am going to Rietta. Don't tell anyone yet, but I'm going to be the happiest man in the world."

Chapter Forty-three

AFTER ALL, IT was not until a good deal later that Randal March rang the bell at the White Cottage. When he looked at his watch, on Mrs. Voycey's front doorstep, and found that it was past half past twelve he decided to run out to Lenton and lunch there before trying to see Rietta, who would at this moment be engaged in the homely task of getting the midday meal. He considered that he would certainly be in the way, and that no reasonable chance of seeing her alone would occur until after two.

At a quarter to he had his finger on the bell. Coming to the door, Rietta Cray stood for a moment looking at him. They looked at one another. Then he put his arm round her, took her through to the living-room, and shut the door. They had a great deal to say. Time slipped by whilst it was said. They talked quietly, gravely, soberly, but behind everything, and constantly gaining in strength, there was a deep sense of having come home.

After a little silence Rietta said,

"I don't think we ought to be engaged."

Randal laughed.

"I would rather be married."

"I didn't mean that."

"What did you mean?"

"I don't think we ought to be engaged until all this horrid business is over."

He took her hand and held it.

"My dear, there'll be the inquest, and, I suppose, three funerals, and then as far as we are concerned there will be no more to say. I agree that we should wait until all that sort of thing is over, if that is what you mean. If, on the other hand, you are suggesting that we should put off our marriage until Melling has stopped talking about the affair, I am not taking any."

"People will talk."

"They always have—they do—they always will. It amuses them quite a lot, and it doesn't really hurt us at all. I shall write to my mother tonight, and you can tell Carr. The village can wait for a week. By the way, I've told Miss Silver. She is the soul of discretion. But of course she knew already—I gave myself away half a dozen times."

She said, "So did I," and they fell into a brief companionable silence, hands linked, thoughts ranging. His went back to their meeting at the edge of the Common, her face, caught by the headlights, a blanched mask of tragedy. Now, in the daylight, what a change. Her eyes had their calm beauty again. There was bloom, softness, colour. As he watched, it brightened. She said,

"About the Mayhews—"

He burst out laughing.

"How in the world did you get to the Mayhews?"

She looked surprised.

"I was thinking about them. I went up to see Mrs. Mayhew this morning."

"Why?"

"Mrs. Fallow said she wanted to see me."

"And why did she want to see you?"

"Well you know, Randal, it really is extraordinary how things get round in a village. She wanted to see me because she thought perhaps you could do something about Cyril."

"Do you mind saying that again, darling?"

Her lips trembled into a smile.

"I know it sounds funny, but that's what she said."

"She wanted to see you because she thought I could do something about Cyril? It doesn't look to me as if we should have to do very much about giving out our engagement!"

They were both laughing. Rietta said,

"Things do get round."

"They do! Well—what am I supposed to do about Cyril?"

She was serious again.

"Well, it's this way. He did come down on Wednesday, and he came because he was desperate for money. And she took some of her husband's savings and let Cyril have them—she didn't tell me how much. But the point is this. The wretched boy was in trouble a year ago and was put on probation. He got into bad company, and now one of his old associates is blackmailing him on account of something which didn't come out at the time."

"We can soon put a stop to that."

"What can you do?"

"Get on to the Probation Officer—he'll see the boy. And you'd better tell Mrs. Mayhew to write and tell him to make a clean breast of everything. He'll be all right if he does that."

After a little she said,

"Randal, about that money of James's—I'd like to tell you what he said about it."

"What did he say?"

"He showed me the will, like I said in my statement. I said it was nonsense and put it on the fire, but he picked it off. He said if he was making another will, he would probably do the same thing all over again, and that he would rather I had the money than anyone else. And then he asked me what I would do with it, and at first I said I wouldn't discuss it, but when he said, 'Well, just as a hypothetical case—' I told him."

"And what did you tell him?"

"Oh, just an old sort of dream of mine. No, dream isn't right, because it was a sort of plan, only I hadn't any money to do it with, and of course the place didn't belong to me."

He was watching her with delight.

"Darling, do I know what you are talking about?"

"Yes—Melling House. It did seem such a pity it should stand empty when there were all those rooms, and people all over the country with nowhere to go—particularly elderly people. After having a home of their own and being the head of a family, it's so really horrid for them to have to go and live with a daughter-in-law on sufferance. It's hard on the daughter-in-law too. In fact it's wrong all round. So I told James I would turn the house into little flats—one room—two rooms—and the big groundfloor rooms a dining-hall and for recreation. He seemed quite interested. I hadn't liked him so much since I was twenty-one. And then when I thought he was all softened I began to ask him not to harry Catherine the way he was doing, and he was so abominable about her that I lost my temper. I told him just what I thought of him and walked out—and that's how I came to forget that wretched raincoat."

There was a pause. Then he said,

"You mean to take the money then?"

She looked surprised.

"Oh, yes. He wanted me to have it—he really did, you know. And there are no near relations. In fact I don't really know that there are any relations. Catherine and I were both distantly connected—and Catherine's gone. I should like Melling House to be some good to somebody, and I think it would be nice for the Mayhews."

This was in such a practical voice that it made him laugh.

"That settles it, of course!"

"Well, they would hate to move, and they would fit in. It's nice when things fit in all round." Then, a little more hesitatingly, "You won't mind, will you? My taking the money, I mean."

It occurred to him that it was typical of Rietta to be afraid that he might not like her to be enriched. He found himself answering honestly,

"A little."

"Please don't. You needn't. He wasn't in love with me, or I with him. I think he just thought I'd use it—" she paused for a word, and then said, "sensibly."

At this moment the door opened and Fancy Bell ran in, checked with graceful abruptness about a yard from the threshold, and said, "Oh, I beg your pardon!"

Rietta said, "Don't go away. You know Mr. March—"

"But I didn't know he was here, though I did wonder when

you didn't hear the telephone, because you generally do, and —I'm so sorry, Mr. March—how do you do?"

Randal shook hands with her. She wore her scarlet suit and looked quite distractingly pretty. Her eyes shone, and her colour came and went. She turned back to Rietta, a little breathless.

"So I thought I had better answer it—and it was Carr. And Mr. March being here, I expect you know it's all out about Mr. Holderness being the one that murdered everyone, and his committing suicide and all. I thought I'd be the first to tell you, but Mr. March being here—"

Rietta said, "Yes, he told me."

After a momentary disappointment Fancy brightened.

"And Carr's bringing Elizabeth Moore over to tea, and they're giving out they're engaged. He says I'm to call her Elizabeth. He sounded ever so pleased. It's nice, isn't it, and makes a sort of change after these murders. I mean, they're all very well in the newspapers, but when it comes to having them right where you live, and the police in the house—" A wave of perfectly lovely colour swept up to the roots of her hair. "Oh, Mr. March, I didn't mean to be rude!"

He laughed.

"Don't worry—I'm off duty."

"I only meant—Miss Cray, I only meant—well, an engagement does make a nice change, doesn't it?"

Rietta said quite simply and earnestly,

"Yes, it does."

ABOUT THE AUTHOR

PATRICIA WENTWORTH began her career writing historical novels. She wrote her first mystery, *The Astonishing Adventure of Jane Smith*, in 1923. Miss Maud Silver, elderly spinster-detective, was introduced in 1928 in *Grey Mask*, and her immediate popularity was so great that she became a regular in Wentworth mysteries. At the time of her death in 1961, Miss Wentworth had been writing for fifty years, producing over seventy-five novels, including, *The Fingerprint*, *The Ivory Dagger*, *The Listening Eye*, *Poison in the Pen*, *She Came Back*, and *Through the Wall*.

Murder Most British

With these new mystery titles, Bantam takes you to the scene of the crime. These masters of mystery follow in the tradition of the Great British crime writers. You'll meet all these talented sleuths as they get to the bottom of even the most baffling crimes.

Elizabeth Daly

☐ 24883	THE BOOK OF THE LION	$2.95
☐ 24610	HOUSE WITHOUT THE DOOR	$2.95
☐ 24267	SOMEWHERE IN THE HOUSE	$2.95
☐ 24605	NOTHING CAN RESCUE ME	$2.95
☐ 24616	AND DANGEROUS TO KNOW	$2.95
☐ 25129	UNEXPECTED NIGHT	$2.95

Margery Allingham

☐ 25102	TETHER'S END	$2.95
☐ 25214	BLACK PLUMES	$2.95
☐ 24548	PEARLS BEFORE SWINE	$2.95
☐ 24814	THE TIGER IN THE SMOKE	$2.95
☐ 24190	FLOWERS FOR THE JUDGE	$2.95
☐ 24852	DANCERS IN THE MOURNING	$2.95
☐ 25411	DEADLY DUO	$2.95
☐ 25412	FASHION IN SHROUDS	$2.95

Dorothy Simpson

☐ 25192	SIX FEET UNDER	$2.95
☐ 25292	CLOSE HER EYES	$2.95
☐ 25065	PUPPET FOR A CORPSE	$2.95

Prices and availability subject to change without notice.

Buy them at your local bookstore or use this handy coupon for ordering:

Bantam Books, Inc., Dept. BD2, 414 East Golf Road, Des Plaines, Ill. 60016

Please send me the books I have checked above. I am enclosing $_____ (please add $1.50 to cover postage and handling). Send check or money order —no cash or C.O.D.'s please.

Mr/Mrs/Miss _____

Address_____

City_____ State/Zip_____

BD2—1/86

Please allow four to six weeks for delivery. This offer expires 7/86.
